THE
METROPOLITANS

THE METROPOLITANS

CAROL GOODMAN

VIKING

VIKING

An imprint of Penguin Random House LLC

375 Hudson Street

New York, New York 10014

First published in the United States of America by Viking,
an imprint of Penguin Random House LLC, 2017

LIBRARY OF CONGRESS CATALOGING-IN-PUBLICATION DATA IS AVAILABLE.

ISBN 9781101997666

1   3   5   7   9   10   8   6   4   2

Printed in U.S.A.

Set in Excelsior

Book design by Nancy Brennan

To my mother, Margaret Agnes Catherine McGuckin Goodman,

ring-a-levio champion of Bay Ridge and champion mother.

For all the stories.

1923–2016

CONTENTS

BEWICK'S *BIRDS*

THE PICKUP WENT smoothly. He was sure no one had followed him to the bookstore on Fourth Avenue. The shop was deserted; the old bearded proprietor barely looked up from his Yiddish newspaper at the jingle of the bell over the door. The younger man wished, though, that the shop would get rid of the bell. Every time he heard it, he thought of alarms going off and sirens blaring.

The folded paper was between pages 166 and 167 in Bewick's *History of British Birds*. He used to worry that someone would purchase the book, but in the half dozen times he'd been inside the store, he'd never seen another customer, let alone one who would venture beyond the lone circle of lamplight at the cash register into the dim and murky stacks in the rear section. In fact, he'd noticed last time that the only interruption in the strip of dust along the metal shelf was in front of Bewick's. He'd used his own handkerchief (carefully laundered and ironed by his sister Sophie) to wipe down the shelf, lest anyone who had followed him discover which book he had pulled out.

But no one had followed him. He was sure of that. The bit of shadow he'd glimpsed on the corner of Tenth Street and Fourth Avenue had been only a scrap of newspaper blown by the wind. When he turned to look, there was only the steam rising from the grate in the street. On cold days, the steam looked like ghosts rising from the pavement. Only a few weeks ago one of those ghosts had resolved into a man in a nondescript beige trench coat and a gray fedora pulled low over his face. The man who had changed his life, and he didn't even know his real name. He called himself Mr. January.

The young man slipped the folded page into his right coat pocket and the twenty-dollar bill into the other and left the store. Fourth Avenue was deserted this early on a Sunday morning. He turned right and walked south to where the avenue merged with the Bowery. Here under the shadow of the Third Avenue El there were people— gaunt men huddled over fires burning in trash cans, passing around tin cans of coffee and the dregs of something that smelled like rubbing alcohol. One lurched into his path, holding out a trembling hand for a dime, but when the bum looked up and met his eyes, he started and shambled away as if something he'd seen there had scared him. Instinctively the young man clutched his chest where the book Mr. January had given him was tucked into a special pocket he had sewn into the lining. He felt its solid rectangular shape through the thread-bare lining and his thin shirt and felt warmed by it. *He could have been one of these hopeless men if Mr. January hadn't picked him out and given him a mission.* All he had to do was give Mr. January a little information—and learn the book by heart.

In case you ever have to get rid of it, Mr. January had explained. *Whatever you do, you must not let the book fall into the wrong hands.*

He crossed Houston, walked west to Mulberry Street, and turned south. Better to lose himself on the smaller streets. Not that he was being followed—

If you're being followed, Mr. January had told him, *you must destroy the book. That's why it's vital you memorize it. You must never let the book fall into the wrong hands.*

At first he had wondered what all the fuss was about an old book. He understood why he had to be careful about the messages he received. He always burned those once he had committed them to memory. But the book—couldn't they use another if this one was lost?

But no, Mr. January had explained, this one was special. There were only five like it in all the world and three of those copies were with his companions. The fourth, Mr. January was placing in his hands, and the fifth—

The fifth had been lost many years ago. He shouldn't worry about the fifth. Make sure no one got his copy.

He didn't need to be told twice. Once he began using the book, he had grown attached to it. He slept with it under his pillow at night. He would sooner die than let it fall into enemy hands.

He wound a serpentine path through the streets between Houston and Canal before coming to the café. Mr. January had told him he should vary the location where he read the messages, choosing large, anonymous places such as libraries, churches, or men's rooms in train stations, but in this one thing, he followed his own wishes. The café was very quiet on a Sunday morning, most of its usual patrons at church. There were only the ancient waiter wiping down the marble counter, the baker in the back preparing the bread and pastries for the old Italian grandmothers who would come after Mass at the Church of the Most Precious Blood, and one white-haired old man in a rusty black suit sipping espresso.

He always chose the same table, in the back by the window, so he could watch the street and the door. If he hadn't been able to get that table—or if there had been anyone sitting close to it—he would have gone on to the Tompkins Square library, where there was a desk hidden in the stacks that was private, or to Precious Blood after Mass, where he could sit in a darkened pew. But there was only an old man reading one of the Italian newspapers that were kept on wooden racks by the door. He helped himself to a copy of *Corriere della Sera* and nodded to the waiter behind the marble bar, indicating he would have his usual. He sat down at the little marble table and, after checking the street, took out the book.

The leather felt warm and slightly spongy—damp, even. Had he allowed it to get wet? The idea made his heart race. But when he laid his hand on the cover, he felt calmer. No, the book always felt like this. It must be a feature of the leather it was bound with—whatever kind that was. Deerskin, perhaps. It was so old that the gold stamp on the cover was almost too faded to make out, but he knew what it represented because the same image appeared on the first page of the book, which he turned to now—a quartered shield that contained a sword, a cup, a crown, and an ocean wave.

After the waiter had brought him his espresso and *cornetto* and gone back behind the bar he took out the folded page. He unfolded it carefully and laid it flat on the table. It was the longest message he had received yet. The page was crammed tight with minuscule handwriting, all of it encoded, divided into five sections, the first section headed by a picture of the quartered shield, and the other sections each headed by one of the symbols inside the shield and a number. He knew that each symbol corresponded to a section of the book and he'd have to use that part of the book to decode that part of the message. His fingers itching at the thought, he took out the good fountain pen his father had given him when he graduated from university. This must be *it*: he'd proved himself to his masters and now he was being entrusted with a special mission. He could hardly wait to wrest the message—his *mission!*—from the pages. But he knew it was more important now than ever to remain calm and be careful. He looked at the first symbol: a shield. He knew that each section of the book was marked by a symbol on the shield. Only on the last page of the book—the epilogue—did the shield appear again. He knew the epilogue by heart! To test his memory, he closed his eyes and recited the words to himself.

At long last Arthur returned to Camelot with his companions, and they resumed their lives there, never telling anyone of the strange adventure they had shared in the Hewan Wood and the Maiden Castle or the grave portents told to them by the Lady of the Lake. They kept their secret through the terrible years that followed—through war, betrayal, exile, and death—for they knew that in the end, whatever they lost would be restored to them when they were reunited on the Isle of Avalon, and whenever great evil arose in the world, four brave knights would arise in their names to vanquish it.

That last bit always gave him courage. Wasn't he like a knight of times gone by on a sacred quest?

Reassured, he opened his eyes . . . and caught the old man looking at him. His heart thudded. The man didn't look away—surely a spy *would*—but only lifted his demitasse and said, "A fellow lover of the muse! *Bellissimo!*"

He tried to smile back, but it may have come out as a snarl, because the old man lowered his head and returned to his newspaper.

Perhaps it really was foolish to read the note in public, but it was one of his few pleasures. To sip a cup of espresso with the book in front of him. He took a sip of the strong coffee now to steady himself and turned the pages to the last passage of the book and confirmed that he had the lines right.

At long last Arthur returned to Camelot . . .

Yes, he had the lines memorized exactly. He could dispose of the book if need be. But for now he wrote out the line on the top of the paper as Mr. January had taught him to, and followed the instructions for the key as he had been taught. As he began decoding the message, he thought how fanciful these men were—to use an old book as a codebook, to use symbols from a sentimental romance as keys! *It's because we're knights, acting in a valiant cause, on a quest to save the kingdom. . . .* He paused, pen in hand, and looked at the enciphered message. He had only decoded the first word but suddenly, looking at the rest of it, he *understood* it. Not only could he *read* the message, he could actually *hear* the words as if they had been spoken, and not in just one voice but a whole *chorus* of voices. As if all the characters in the book were speaking to him. He scanned the rest of the page and it all became clear to him! It must be a sign that he was truly worthy of the mission he'd been given. And what a mission it was! He got up, sliding the paper into the book. This was it! After weeks of training, he had proved his mettle and he would be entrusted with a crucial mission.

He paid with the crisp twenty-dollar bill he'd taken from Bewick's *Birds* that morning and left a generous tip. The rest he would give to Sophie to buy groceries and pay the rent. Was there enough for her if he should not survive the mission? He counted up the money in his head as he walked blindly through the now-busy streets, the voices buzzing in his head like a swarm of bees as he made his way through Chinatown, past City Hall, and west toward Little Syria, where the cafés sold Turkish coffee and sticky sweet pastries. He stopped at one and bought some sugared almonds for Sophie. *You must make sure there's enough money*, one voice whispered. *If there isn't, you might have to ask Mr. January to wait*, another voice cautioned.

Coward! yet another voice hissed. He was looking for an excuse not to perform his duty. If he put them off now, the call might not come again. He must heed the call—as a knight heeds the call of his lady when she bids him to ride out and slay the monster that threatens her castle. That was why they had given him the book. It wasn't just a key to the coded message—which lay within the pages of the book; he must remember to burn it—the book was meant to inspire him. It told the story of a brave king, his lady, and his companions who went on an adventure to save the kingdom from evil. They were asked to make a great sacrifice and in return were promised that their legacy would live on and that whenever evil arose, four would rise in their names to take their places. . . .

But you are only one, all the voices whispered together. Could he complete the mission on his own?

He touched the book for reassurance and felt it beat as if it were alive. But of course it was his own heart racing, galloping like a startled rabbit. Icy sweat was streaming down his face. The voices in his head had grown silent, but he knew they were still there. *Waiting.* He stopped and fished his handkerchief out to wipe his damp brow—and saw the old man from the café drawing the collar of his coat up and hurrying down another street.

He stood, clutching his handkerchief in his hand, his heart squeezed tight as a fist under the book. It felt as if the book had gotten heavier and was weighing on his heart, crushing it—

He *was* being followed. The old man from the café was following him. He was after the book!

He must not let him get it. He turned around—and around again—spinning in a circle like a child's top. *Idiot! Think!* He had to find a fire to burn the note and the book. One of the trash cans the tramps stood around—he'd find one of those—

He started down the street, not sure where he was. He'd wandered blindly for so long, he'd lost his way. He smelled saltwater and—something burning. He went toward the burning smell. *Find a fire!* There ahead of him was a park—bare trees, a band shell, children running over brown grass, a stone building with rounded towers—a castle! *Like the one in the book.* Surely that was a sign he'd come to the right place. In front of the castle was a cart selling roasted sweet potatoes and chestnuts. That's what he had smelled. Could he use the chestnut vendor's brazier to burn the book? No, the fire wasn't big enough. If the old man saw him dump the book in it, he'd get it out before it burned all the way. He looked behind him to see if the old man was behind him, but he didn't see him in the crowd.

There were lots of people now. Sunday holidaymakers streaming into the park, heading for the ferry, walking along the river—

The river. That's what he'd smelled before. He heard it now too, slapping against the piers in time to the beating of his heart. He went toward it, drawn to the clean salt smell that reminded him of when he and Sophie would take the ferry out to see the Statue of Liberty, and Sophie would say that the lady was like a queen in a fairy tale. . . . There she was now! The lady in her copper robes and crown. She was like the lady in the book—*like a fairy tale!*

Sophie's voice was so clear in his head that he thought she was there beside him. He almost felt her hand in his. He spun around to find her—

Dead leaves, scraps of paper, smoke from the chestnut vendor all swirled together like a carousel. In the center was the old man from the café. Yes, he was following him. He was here for the book. He was walking toward him now. He couldn't let him get it. He must toss it in the water, let the river carry it away. He put his hand under his coat to take the book out of its pocket in the lining, but it felt like he was ripping out his own heart. *How can you live without your heart?* one voice asked, and another close behind it crooned, *This is your mission! Take the book down to the bottom of the harbor!*

He heard the old man shout as he swung his leg over the seawall, but it was faint beneath the slap of the waves and the cry of the seagulls that seemed to be echoing the voices from the book. They were calling him to perform one last quest. Only as the cold water rushed up to greet him did he hear another small voice in his ear asking him, *Why, Nino? Why are you leaving me here alone?* Sophie! What had he been thinking? She would be all alone—she didn't even know where the money was hidden. He tried then to stroke with his arms, to pull himself to the surface, but the book had its steel claws in his heart and was pulling him down into the darkness.

1

OUT FROM UNDERFOOT

EVERY SUNDAY, MADGE McGrory had two main jobs: Stay Out from Underfoot and Cause No Trouble. These were the conditions her aunt Jean had made when she took Madge in after her mother had died. Cause No Trouble meant making herself breakfast (cold cereal because Aunt Jean, who worked late-night shifts at a diner, couldn't stand the smell of cooking) and getting herself off to school in the morning. Madge didn't mind this. She used to get up early to help her mother with the twins and to walk Frankie to school. As Roosevelt had said, everyone had to pitch in to end the Great Depression, old and young alike. The WPA had given her dad a job when he needed it, so Madge didn't mind doing her part. *My little organizer*, her mother would call her as she rallied her brothers to order. *Bossy*, the nuns called her. It was easier now that she only had herself to worry about, although she did miss the smell of her mother's oatmeal cooking on the cast iron stove, and Frankie's company.

Stay Out from Underfoot meant sleeping on the pull-down Murphy bed and keeping her clothes stored in the kitchen pantry and her boots in the stove (Aunt Jean meant it about no cooking) and clearing out on Sundays when Aunt Jean had her boyfriend, Tony, over. Tony worked the morning shift at his family's bakery on Carmine Street, so the only time he and Aunt Jean could find together was on Sunday. Madge understood, didn't she? Madge didn't exactly, but it seemed little enough to do for Aunt Jean, who had taken her in and kept her off the streets and out of someplace like St. Vincent's Home for Boys, where Frankie and the twins had gone when their father had Gone to Pieces.

When she woke up on this Sunday and saw that a wedge of sunlight had reached the radiator, Madge knew she'd better get up before Tony arrived, but she squeezed her eyes shut and tried to get back to the dream she'd been having. In her dream, her mother had been leaning over the fire escape calling her home for dinner. The delicious smell of her mother's Irish stew had been wafting out of the tenement window, and Madge, in the middle of a game of ring-a-levio, had stopped the game by calling *Olly olly oxen free!*, releasing all her teammates from "jail" (Mrs. Murphy's front stoop). As she'd turned to run for home, a plume of steam had come up out of the sewer grate and blocked her way. Somehow she had known with the certainty of dream knowledge that she mustn't step into that pillar of steam. That it was as "off block" as the boundaries of ring-a-levio. That it was as bad as stepping on a crack and breaking your mother's back. And sure enough, a man had stepped out of it—

Madge opened her eyes to the hiss of steam coming from the radiator. It was usually a comforting noise, but now it reminded her of the man emerging from the steam on the street, and she didn't want to remember him. She got up and made her bed (although why it mattered when it was going to be folded up against the wall, Madge couldn't have told you, only that her mother had always told her to make her bed every morning and so she did) and folded it back into its cupboard and latched it shut, reflecting as she did that if she could have folded *herself* back into the Murphy bed, she would have been well and truly out from underfoot.

Instead she made a plan for the day. She didn't have her brothers to organize, but she could still take control of her own time. Morning in the library, lunch in the park, afternoon—well, she'd think of something. After all, she was in *Manhattan*. Back when she lived in Brooklyn, she and Frankie used to stand on the roof of their building and pretend the skyline of Manhattan was a magical kingdom. *"We'll go live there someday,"* Madge had promised Frankie.

She opened the icebox and took out a paper sack of the uneaten sandwich halves Aunt Jean always brought back from the diner. It made Madge feel a little funny, eating the leftovers of strangers. *Why horseradish on pastrami?* she would wonder. *Who orders corned beef without mustard? Why would anyone ever eat liverwurst?* But if she didn't have to buy her own lunch, she might be able to afford a movie. *Suspicion* was playing at Radio City Music Hall. She'd seen it, but Joan Fontaine was her favorite actress, so she wouldn't mind seeing it again.

She checked before leaving the apartment that it was all tidy. Bed up, pajamas folded in the pantry, cereal crumbs swept away. Everything in its place. Except her. She really didn't know where she belonged anymore.

After the library, she walked to Central Park and sat on her favorite bench on Bethesda Terrace near the angel fountain. It was her favorite place to sit because it reminded her of her mother. She had once taken Madge and her brothers on a picnic here, and while the boys were running around playing knights and dragons, she had told Madge the story of the angel. *"When she touches the water, she blesses it, and the next person who steps into the pool is healed of any sickness or infirmity. Don't you think that would be a wonderful gift to have—to heal the sick?"*

Madge had thought at the time that she might choose being able to run faster than a speeding bullet like Superman or being able to turn into a grown-up by shouting *SHAZAM!* like Captain Marvel, but when her mother had fallen in the kitchen a year later and she couldn't do anything to help her, all Madge had wanted was the power to make her get up again.

Now she liked sitting beneath the fountain, looking up at the angel's face, because she could hear her mother's voice and that made her feel safe. Some parts of the park were dangerous. They'd cleared the Hooverville up in the reservoir a while ago, but there were still tramps living in the Ramble, the wooded patch between the Terrace and the Great Lawn. Madge had seen them—hard men she didn't like to look at because she was half afraid she would see her father peering out of those bleary eyes one day.

She had taken two books out of the library, but instead she read the one her mother had given to Frankie for Christmas last year: *The Boy's King Arthur*. Because it embarrassed her to read a children's book that said it was for boys, she'd taken the dust jacket off and made a new one of brown butcher's paper. When she read the story of how the sorcerer Merlin hid the baby Arthur and how Arthur proved himself the rightful king by pulling a sword from a stone, she imagined she was reading aloud to Frankie. *See*, she would tell him, *Arthur had to stay with Sir Ector until it was safe for him to reveal his identity, just like you and the twins have to stay at St. Vincent's for now and I have to stay at Aunt Jean's. But someday we'll all be together again, as soon as I'm old enough to get a job and make a home of our own.*

Since Madge was only thirteen, that would be a few years, but when she read about King Arthur and Guinevere and Lancelot and all the difficult quests the knights had to perform, she believed it would someday be possible.

When her stomach began to rumble, she put down her book and took out her sandwiches. There was a half cheese with pickle on a roll and a half roast beef with lettuce on rye. As she looked up from the sandwich sack, she noticed that there was a boy hiding behind the bench across from her. He had dark hair, and eyes the color of burnished copper. His skin was a lighter copper except where it was smudged with dirt on his sharp cheekbones. He was so still, Madge might have mistaken him for one of the park's statues, but then he blinked, and Madge knew he must be one of the tramps who lived in the park. Only he didn't look much older than her, and he didn't look hard like the other tramps. He looked . . . *hungry.*

Madge chewed her cheese and pickle half sandwich and pretended she didn't see the boy. She wasn't sure why. The old Madge would've yelled, "Whatcha staring at, Mister?" But she wasn't that Madge anymore. Every day she lived at her aunt Jean's, fitting herself into the narrow space allotted her, she felt as if a little bit of that old Madge was vanishing. The boy clearly didn't want to be seen, and Madge understood that. When she had finished the half sandwich, she crumpled the waxed paper into a ball and got up, leaving the half roast beef sandwich on the bench. It occurred to her that this was the second time this half sandwich had been left behind, which somehow made her feel sad. She walked slowly past the boy, studiously pretending not to see him, tossed the ball of waxed paper over her shoulder into a garbage can, and continued past the boathouse and the Ramble. That was where the boy with copper eyes probably lived.

Madge shivered and walked faster toward the Seventy-Ninth Street exit. The day had grown cold, and it was only a quarter past one, which meant she had four more hours to kill before she could go back to Aunt Jean's. She thought about the boy and wondered if he was cold. He'd had on only a thin denim jacket over his clothes. Where did he sleep at night? And what did he eat when no one left him half sandwiches? Then she thought about how if Aunt Jean hadn't taken her in, *she* might be sleeping in the park and eating twice-cast-off sandwiches. And if St. Vincent's hadn't taken in Frankie and the twins, they might have that same starved look as the boy.

It was one thing to read about knights questing through dark forests, and quite another to think of sleeping in the woods of Central Park at night.

She needed to get out of the cold. She had enough money to see *Suspicion*, but suddenly it seemed like a better idea to save her money just in case Aunt Jean ever got tired of her being underfoot. Ahead of her rose the white granite mass of the Metropolitan Museum of Art.

It looked like the white castle of Camelot on the cover of *The Boy's King Arthur*. One of her teachers had told her that the museum was free. She'd spend the rest of her afternoon there.

As she crossed Eightieth Street, a plume of steam rose from a manhole and wafted in front of her. Like any New Yorker, Madge knew there were pipes running below the city streets channeling steam to heat the buildings in winter, cool them in summer, and supply power to the city's tall skyscrapers. But because of her dream last night, she suddenly felt afraid. She dodged around the steam—and ran into a man in a beige trench coat with a gray fedora pulled down low over his eyes. Madge couldn't see his eyes, but she *felt* them, and they made her feel like she had just plunged into the frigid East River.

"Watch where you're going, Mister!" she cried, pulling the collar of her own thin wool coat up around her neck.

The man in the trench coat didn't apologize. Madge walked on as fast as she could, not looking back, a cold wind reaching down inside of her collar like icy fingers trying to yank her backward.

2

THE STONE GIANT

JOE HADN'T MEANT to follow the girl with the fiery hair and sky-colored eyes into the great white building. He'd only wanted to give her back the book she'd left on the park bench. It seemed the least he could do after she left the sandwich for him. It was the first meal he'd had in days, and the first act of kindness he'd met since he'd come to the city.

But she'd walked so fast, he hadn't been able to catch up with her, and then she'd gone up the steps of the building as if she owned it. It must be wonderful to feel as if you belonged. Joe hadn't felt like that . . . well, not since he'd left the Akwesasne reserve where his family lived, and that had been a long time ago.

He stood on the white steps and looked up at the row of white columns in front of the doors. They reminded him of the Mush Hole, the school where he'd been taken when he was five, which made him want to turn around and run the other way. The girl probably didn't care about the book she'd left behind any more than the sandwich, which she'd probably left for the pigeons, not him. He was about to turn away when he saw a policeman standing at the foot of the stairs, looking at him. Joe did what he always did. He ran.

The first time he'd run away, it had taken three days before they found him. He'd almost frozen to death, but he'd done what his *Tóta*, his grandmother, had told him the bears did in the winter: he found a cave with warm dry leaves and burrowed into them. He'd chewed leaves and drunk melted snow. His plan had been to work his way back to Akwesasne, but when he ventured out to the road on the third day, the first car that passed him had belonged to the principal. He took Joe back and gave him thirty lashes with a hickory switch for running. When Joe told him he wanted to go home, they beat him for using Mohawk.

Speak English, the teachers told him. But the words felt like lumps in his mouth, choking him. Like the mush they fed them morning, noon, and night. That was why they called the school the Mush Hole, but the name also described how the words felt in his mouth.

Now he ran through the great bronze and glass doors and into a vast hall lined with columns on three sides. A woman with a pinched face, who reminded him of one of the teachers at the Mush Hole, stared at him with eyes magnified by thick, round glasses. He looked around and saw the girl disappearing between two white columns and took off after her.

On the other side of the columns, Joe came to a room filled with hundreds of pictures painted on the walls. Some were of animals he recognized—snakes, owls, a sharp-nosed dog, a long-faced cat. Others he'd seen in books—great lions, fat hippos, an alligator. But in between were signs he didn't know: something that looked like a twisted rope, an eye, a squiggle. The signs looked like what English letters had looked like to him when he'd first started learning the language.

The second time he'd run away, he'd made it back to Akwesasne, but when he'd opened his mouth to tell his mother he was back, all that came out was a croak. As if he'd been turned into a crow. His mother had wept to see him, but his father looked away from him and told him that he had to go back. Billie had told him that he just had to tough it out until he was sixteen. Then he could come work on the steel towers in the great city at the mouth of the Hudson River. *Skywalkers* they called the men who built the towers that were taller than the oldest trees. Before he left, his *Tóta* had whispered his Mohawk name in his ear so that he would never forget who he was. But then the teachers' straps had beaten the words out of him and Joe had forgotten everything, even his own name.

There were paintings of men amongst the animals

and signs here—lean, muscular men, naked but for loin-cloths, working in fields, hunting with bows and arrows, herding cows, carrying limp geese—all painted the color of red clay. Joe put his own hand up next to one of the paintings, but his skin was paler.

The sound of angry voices nudged him forward into the next room, but the voices were coming from above his head. He looked up and saw that a balcony ran along the second story of the room. A man was pacing back and forth, shouting at a dark-haired girl who trailed behind him like a duckling swimming behind its mother. Joe couldn't understand the words the man shouted, but he felt the anger behind them.

That had been what he'd understood first at the school—the anger. The teachers were angry if he spoke his own language, if he cried to go home, if he took his shoes off, if he ate with his hands. For a while he thought English was a language only spoken in shouts and hisses. He preferred looking at the letters on the pages of the books the teachers gave them. *They* never shouted or hit.

The angry man wasn't speaking English. That had been a surprise about the city; the streets were full of strange languages. The woman at the boardinghouse where Joe had gone to find Billie had first spoken in a language that sounded like gargling, as if her words were stuck way back in her throat and she had to hawk them out before the English would come.

"They cleared outta here a month ago," she spit at

Joe. "The whole tribe of them—left owing rent. Last time I let to dirty Indians."

It wasn't like Billie not to honor a debt, but then Joe had done a lot of things since leaving the Mush Hole that he'd never thought he'd do. Like eating food out of a garbage can and stealing clothes from a clothesline. But he'd had to get rid of his uniform. The police were looking for an Indian boy running away from the Mush Hole. He couldn't be that boy.

The problem was, he wasn't sure who he was anymore. How could he be the boy he was before the Mush Hole when he couldn't even remember his own language? When he couldn't even remember the name his *Tóta* had given him?

"Otousan!"

The word, sharp and mournful as a loon's cry at dusk, pierced through Joe's fog. He looked up and met the girl's dark eyes. Was the man hurting her? But the man was striding away across the balcony. The girl followed him—and Joe kept pace with them on the lower floor, through a room with a statue of a cat-faced woman and one of a dog-faced man, and then into a room with a long coffin shaped like a man. Joe nearly skidded to a halt at this sight, but then the girl let out another wounded cry, and Joe followed below her, as if tracking a high-flying bird. He went through a wide doorway into a high-vaulted hall full of slanting light coming down from arched windows, flashing on silver-plated figures like lightning. Sky Girl was standing at the back of the hall, but she wasn't alone. She was talking to a boy who had red hair too—her brother, maybe, or a friend from school. How could he give back the book with the other boy there? They would think he stole it. They would call the police and then they would find out what he had done.

The third time he'd run away was after he struck the principal. Joe had been walking past his office when he heard the swish of the switch and heard a sharp cry he recognized as his sister Jeanette's voice, and before he knew what he was doing, he'd wrenched open the door and snatched the switch out of the principal's hand, and he was hitting him across the face with it, unable to stop, a roaring in his head like a train bearing down on them both. The principal stumbled under his blows and fell to the floor, where he hit his head against the iron railing in front of the fireplace. Only Jeanette's voice had brought him to his senses. "Run!" she'd told him. And he had, even though it had meant leaving her behind. No matter how far he ran, he couldn't get rid of the smell of blood.

He smelled it now. The smell before a thunderstorm, a crackle in the air that made the hairs on the back of his neck lift. He turned away from Sky Girl and the boy, and saw a man walking through the room with the big coffin. He was wearing a tan coat, the collar turned up high, and a gray hat pulled down low so you couldn't see his eyes. Joe froze. Last night he had dreamed of Stone Giants. His *Tóta* had told him about a race of fearsome monsters that hunted the people of the Six Nations to feast on their bones and flesh. No arrow could pierce their stone skin. No matter where the people hid, the Stone Giants' eyes could see into the darkest places. That's what it felt like when the Stone Giant in his dream had looked at him—like he saw into Joe's darkest places and wouldn't mind snacking on his bones—and the Stone Giant had worn the face of the man in the gray fedora.

The sound of Sky Girl's voice came from behind him, and the man lifted his head as if he were sniffing the air for prey. Joe wanted to run but he couldn't go if this *thing* was looking for Sky Girl. That would be like leaving Jeanette all over again. So he did the thing he was second best at after running. He stepped into a shadowy side gallery and hid.

3

GONE TO PIECES

MADGE FELT BETTER as soon as she was inside the museum. She tilted her head back and looked up at the high domed ceiling. "Swank!" she said out loud.

"I'm not sure that is the accolade Mr. Hunt had in mind for his classical Beaux-Arts design."

Madge turned toward the woman standing behind the information desk. She was tall and so thin she wouldn't have had any trouble folding herself up in the Murphy bed. She looked like she'd been pressed and folded already, except when she turned to the side and revealed a bulge beneath her skirt that looked like it was made by some kind of bulky undergarment. *Sheesh, someone should tell the old dame to get a better girdle at Gimbels!* It wasn't like the woman didn't have *any* style sense. She had on smart alligator shoes and an enormous pin on her lapel of a winged lizard which, Madge figured, must have cost a mint, even if it was ugly as sin. She might have been good-looking, too, if she'd ever smiled and those round glasses didn't make her eyes bulge out like a dead carp's.

"Who's Boze Art?" Madge asked.

"Not *who*, *what*. Beaux-Arts is the style in which the museum was built," the woman drawled. Whatever press Dead Carp slept in had apparently squeezed her sinus passages so tight that she spoke in a nasal whine. "Here—" She grudgingly handed Madge a brochure. "That explains everything, including the hours of the cafeteria and gift shop and a map of the galleries."

"And it's all free?" Madge asked, gaping at the number of rooms on the foldout floor plan. She could spend all day in here and not get to see everything.

"Yes," Dead Carp conceded in a tone of deep regret. "But contributions are always welcome."

"Oh," Madge said. "Maybe when I make my first million. Where do you think I should start?"

"*Chill*-drun"—the woman drew out the word as if she were referring to a lower order of invertebrates— "often enjoy the Egyptian tomb and the Arms and Armor exhibit."

"Arms and Armor? You mean like knights?"

"Those are the individuals most likely to have made use of such accoutrements."

"My brother Frankie loves that stuff. Thanks, Miss—" Madge peered at the brass name tag to keep herself from calling her Dead Carp. It read MISS ENID FITZBANE, HEAD OF SECURITY. *With a scowl like that on her face,*

Madge thought, *it's no wonder they put her in charge of scaring people away.* "Thanks, Miss Fitzbane. You've been swell. Which way to the Arms and Armor?"

"They are in the north galleries. Turn right upon entering—"

But Madge was already gone, the worn soles of her saddle shoes scuffing over the marble floor. She walked between two massive white columns that looked like the picture on the back of the ten-dollar bill. There was an Egyptian tomb you could actually go into! Frankie would love this. Maybe she could get permission to take him and the twins to the museum one day. She hadn't been allowed to take them out so far, because she wasn't an adult.

She walked past an Asian man and a girl about Madge's age. The man was wearing a somber gray suit, and the girl, who was wearing a navy skirt and starched white shirt that looked like a school uniform even though it was Sunday, was carrying a large briefcase that obviously belonged to the man. Madge felt a pang, recalling how she used to walk with her father to the corner carrying his lunch pail when he still went to work, before he'd Gone to Pieces. Madge thought of it this way because after they had come home from her mother's funeral, her father had sat down in her mother's rocking chair. It was where she had nursed the twins through chicken pox and where she would sit at the end of the day darning socks. No one but her mother had ever sat in it, but when Madge's father sat in it, the chair had fallen apart beneath him. It had gone to pieces and then *he* had gone—to the tavern down the street, where he started drinking and didn't stop for three weeks. He might still be drinking as far as Madge knew, because after three weeks, the nuns came from St. Vincent's and took Frankie and the twins away, and Aunt Jean offered to take Madge in.

The man strode past her, the heels of his shoes hitting the floor like angry slaps, and went up a flight of stairs to a balcony. He was saying something in a loud foreign language and the girl ran up the stairs after him crying, "*Otousan! Otousan!*"

Well, Madge thought, *envy is ignorance.* Still, she'd rather be fighting with her father than not know where he was.

Thoughts of her father had dampened her spirits. The gloomy coffins and leering dog-faced statues didn't help much to lift them. But then she walked into a lofty two-storied court filled with sunlight from a skylight. Brightly colored banners hung from poles suspended between the arches of the colonnade on either side. Four knights stood in the center of the hall in a diamond formation as if they were ready for battle. For a moment the walls melted away and Madge imagined herself on a green field, silk banners snapping in a brisk breeze, the sound of trumpets on the air—

"They're pretty keen, aren't they?"

The boy took her by surprise. Hadn't she been alone a moment ago? But he had such an open, friendly face that she wasn't frightened. He had reddish sandy hair that was cut too short over ears that stood out straight from his head, and freckles over the bridge of his nose. He was wearing an orange-and-blue-checked shirt under a forest-green sweater vest—*Sheesh, he must be color-blind!*—and carrying a sketch pad tucked under his arm.

"They're swell!" Madge said. "Are they supposed to be King Arthur and his knights?"

"I like to think that the one in front is Arthur," the boy said, his ears twitching, "and behind him are Lance-lot and Gawain and the one in back is—"

"Guinevere?" Madge asked. "It could be a girl under all that armor."

"I don't think there were any girl knights," the boy said doubtfully.

"What about Joan of Arc?" Madge challenged.

"I suppose. Do you like stories about King Arthur? I didn't know girls did."

Madge started to say that Frankie had liked the stories, but then she would have to explain where Frankie and the twins were. "Sure, I did when I was a kid. I don't really have time for that kind of malarkey now. They're just stories, after all."

"Of course I know they're just stories," the freckled

boy said, looking so crestfallen that Madge immediately felt sorry.

"But they're swell stories all the same. I'm Madge McGrory, by the way." Madge stuck out her hand to shake the way her father had taught her to.

"Walt Rosenberg." He shook Madge's hand, wincing slightly when she squeezed. "Would you like to see something really neat?"

"Sure," Madge said.

They walked into a dimly lit gallery behind the main hall, where there were helmets, shields, swords, and other objects having to do with knights and armor. The case Walt led Madge to contained a single sheet of paper sandwiched between two panes of glass. The paper was yellow with age and torn in places, and yet the ink looked as fresh as if it had been penned yesterday. A large ornate capital *A* filled the top left-hand corner. It was painted in colors that glowed like jewels—sapphire, emerald, ruby, and amethyst—and outlined in glittering gold.

"Oh," Madge said, her breath misting the top of the glass case. "It's beautiful. It's like a prayer book the nuns showed us once."

"Yes! Only this is a storybook. It's the last page of an adventure of King Arthur, one that isn't in any of the other books. Isn't that exciting?"

Madge looked from the brightly colored page to Walt. His eyes, which had seemed an unremarkable shade of muddy brown a moment ago, were now speckled with flecks of gold, as if the gold paint on the page had been dusted across his face.

"The last page? Where's the rest of the story?"

All the gold glitter fell away from Walt's face. "Lost," he said. "There were only a few copies ever made and they've all been lost."

"Oh," Madge said, looking back down at the beautiful page. A lost book wasn't as sad as her mother dying or her father falling apart or Frankie and the twins being stuck at St. Vincent's Home for Boys, but it suddenly seemed all of one piece. She had felt for a brief moment as if all she had lost had been restored to her—as it had been in her dream—and then cruelly snatched away. She squinted down at the page. "I can't even make out what it says—"

The sound of metal clattering, as if one of the knights had come alive, made Madge raise her head from the page. The noise came from a suit of Japanese armor at the back of the gallery. Madge peered into the gloom— and into copper-colored eyes.

"You!" she cried. "Did you follow me?" The boy from the park stepped out from behind the suit of armor. He was clutching a book to his chest. "And that's my book!"

She felt Walt straightening himself up beside her. "Hand that book over," he said, his voice cracking.

The other boy regarded Walt with his still-watchful

eyes and then handed the book to him. Then he looked from Walt to Madge.

"I found it on the bench where you left the sandwich. I didn't think you meant to leave it behind. Maybe you didn't mean to leave the sandwich, either."

"Oh!" Madge felt her cheeks go red. "I meant to leave the sandwich, but not the book. Thank you for returning it."

The boy shrugged and stuffed his hands in the pockets of his denim jacket. "Thanks for the sandwich." He started to turn away.

"It was just a leftover from the diner where my aunt Jean works. I could bring you more. My name's Madge— and this is Walt."

The boy nodded at Walt but he kept his eyes on Madge. "Joe," he said.

Walt, looking embarrassed, was fiddling with the brown paper cover on the book. He had torn away a piece of the paper, revealing the book's title. "Hey, I thought you said you didn't read this stuff anymore—"

Before Madge could explain that the book belonged to her brother, the sound of breaking glass behind her drew her attention. Joe, who had been facing that way, moved first, springing forward like Jesse Owens about to set another world record. Madge turned and saw the the man in the beige trench coat and gray fedora pulling the manuscript page out of its broken case.

Joe said something that sounded like "Stone Giant!"

"Thief!" Madge screamed. "Put that back!"

The man lifted his head. His eyes were shadowed by the brim of his hat, but Madge could feel a coldness radiating from them the way she could feel the chill of the East River when she walked by it. Instead of putting the page back, he turned and ran toward the stairs on the other side of the court. Madge and Joe and Walt ran after him. The boys were fast, but years of playing ring-a-levio had made Madge even faster. She should have caught him. But when she reached him, he seemed to vanish into a fog.

"Like the man in my dream," Walt whispered.

"You had that dream, too?" both Madge and Joe asked at the same time.

The man had reappeared at the other end of the court and was running down the stairs. Madge, Joe, and Walt ran after him, Madge in the lead, taking the steps two at a time. She was right behind him. She saw a bit of trench coat vanish around the corner at the bottom of the stairs—but when she reached the bottom, the thief had vanished. Madge was facing a long corridor with three closed doors. At the end of the corridor was another door marked EXIT—ALARM SOUNDS WHEN OPENED.

"Where'd he go?" Joe asked when he and Walt tumbled to the bottom of the stairs.

"He vanished again," Madge said.

"He can't have gone out the exit or the alarm would have sounded," Walt said.

A man who vanishes in a fog might not set off an alarm, Madge thought, but instead of saying that she turned to the door closest to her. "I'll open this one and you two open the others so he can't get away if we pick the wrong door." She spoke in the commanding tone she used when giving orders in ring-a-levio, and the boys did as she said.

"On the count of three," Madge said when the boys were in position in front of the other two doors. "One—"

"But what are we supposed to do if he's behind one of the doors?" Walt asked.

"Two," Madge said, ignoring Walt's question because she didn't know the answer. She could hear a sound coming from behind her door—a hissing sound, like a snake.

"Three!"

As they opened their doors, several things happened at once. Walt screamed, "He's here!" followed by the sound of something falling. Madge could hear the commotion, but she couldn't tear her eyes away from the sight in front of her. She had seen many strange things today, but this was the strangest. A short, rotund man in a three-piece tweed suit was standing on a footstool, holding a flaming blow torch up to a piece of paper hanging from a clothesline. As the man turned to Madge, she was horrified to see that he had the face of a huge pop-eyed bug. He gurgled something indistinguishable and flapped his hands around, which had the effect of lighting the paper and clothesline on fire. He became so agitated that, bug-man or not, Madge felt sorry for him. She ran forward to put out the flame, which she managed with a bucket of sand that the man was waving at. When she'd helped the bug-man to the ground, he took off the thing on his head, which Madge now realized was a gas mask, revealing a round pink face fringed with wispy white hair standing up like carpet fuzz.

"My dear, you gave me quite a shock opening the door like that, although I suppose I gave you one in return." He chuckled and put on a pair of wire-rimmed glasses. "You must wonder what I'm up to, lighting the medieval manuscripts on fire."

"Is that what you were doing, Mister?"

"I was trying, albeit poorly, to dry them," he said. "And it's Doctor. Doctor Dashwood Bean, curator of Arms and Armor, but everyone calls me Dash."

"I think I'll stick with Doctor, Dr. Bean—but hey, unless you don't care about *any* of your old books, you'd better come out in the hall. Some fella is trying to make off with that page that was under glass upstairs."

"The Kelmsbury King Arthur!" He looked more excited than upset.

"My friends are trying to stop him."

The gleeful look on Dashwood Bean's face faded. "Oh

dear, they shouldn't do that—" Just then a loud alarm sounded from the hallway.

"Oh no," Madge said, "he must be getting away!"

She ran out into the hall, followed by Dr. Bean. The sight that greeted her was almost as upsetting as the one of Dr. Bean setting pages on fire. Walt sat on the floor, his sweater vest unraveled and wrapped around his chest like a straitjacket. Joe, one eye turning blue and his lip swollen, was crawling around on the floor trying to gather something that looked like confetti.

"What happened?" Madge demanded. "How did he get away?"

"*Thstone Giant*," Joe lisped.

"I swear he kept vanishing," Walt said, trying to undo a knot in the green wool, "and somehow he got me all tangled up! We kept him from taking the page, but—"

"You did? Good for you!" Madge slapped Walt on the back. "Where is it?"

Joe sat back on his heels and held up his hands cupped together. They were full of confetti and gold glitter. "Here," he said. "We got it back, but I'm afraid it'th all gone to piethes."

4

FROM THE AIR

THE OLD GUY, whom Madge called Dr. Bean, did not look as upset by the destruction of a very old and very rare manuscript page as Walt would have thought he'd be. Instead he looked perplexed.

"Why, you're children!" he said, rubbing the top of his head as if trying to activate the brain cells inside. Then he turned to the tall woman who had just come out of the workroom "Ah, here's my assistant, Miss Lake. Vivian, someone's gone and stolen the Kelmsbury."

"Just as we thought," she said, straightening the hem of her sapphire-blue peplum jacket, which matched her eyes. She tossed her platinum-blonde hair, which curved over one eye in a perfect wave.

Walt stopped unwinding his sweater vest to gape up at her. "What do you mean *just as we thought*?"

"Yeth," Joe said, "what do you mean? That fellow thocked me in the jaw. Did you know he'd do that?"

Miss Lake tsked. "Let me get some ice for that, young

man." She turned on her three-inch heels, revealing perfectly straight stocking seams, and clicked her way into the Arms and Armor workshop. Madge helped Walt to his feet, and then he turned to help Joe up, which proved difficult because Joe wouldn't put down the shredded manuscript. They all ended up getting tangled in the green wool and covered with the bits of gold paint from the torn page. *We look like a third grader's Mother's Day card*, Walt thought. But when they turned to walk up the hall, Walt felt linked to the two others by more than just glitter and yarn. What they had done was like something out of *The Boy's King Arthur* or, another favorite of his, *The Three Musketeers. All for one, one for all!* But then his spirits sagged as he recalled that they hadn't in fact saved the page. And, as Dr. Bean had said, they were only children.

You're only a child, Walt's father had told him when he asked why he was being sent away, *and Germany is no place for children right now.* And then Walt had taken the train with a few hundred other children, all wearing tags with numbers on them, all crying about leaving their parents behind, to England, where his uncle Sol met him and brought him to America. He hadn't seen his parents since—had it really been two whole years now?— and whenever someone said, "You're only a child," Walt knew it meant he was about to lose something.

Walt's frustration vanished, though, as he walked into the workroom. Although they were in the basement there were windows high on the wall letting in sunlight through wavy glass. Full suits of armor stood at attention as if standing guard. Miss Lake handed Joe an ice pack and then went into a little alcove to make tea. The strains of Sammy Kaye's orchestra drifted from a radio. Dr. Bean cleared books and folders from five chairs surrounding a long table that was occupied by blank manuscript pages held down by stones, crystals, teacups, bronze daggers, and something that looked like a small meteorite. Walt gazed at the cluttered room in wonder, gaping at the suits of armor, tapestries depicting knights and ladies, and the vast array of swords and shields, helmets and breastplates, gauntlets and greaves piled on shelves and lying along a long low workbench. There was even an enormous anvil that looked like it had belonged to a medieval blacksmith. It was like an armory in here! There was a broadsword leaning against the wall that was almost as tall as he was. He wondered if anyone would notice if he picked it up—but then what if it were too heavy for him to lift? That would be embarrassing, especially in front of Madge, who had a grip like a stevedore. He turned away from the sword to a shelf that held wooden hat forms topped by plain rounded helmets.

"These look like they could be worn by soldiers today," he said.

"They *will* be," Miss Lake said, bringing a tray laden with a brown glazed teapot and mismatched china cups. "Dr. Bean has been commissioned by the British

Army to design a better helmet for the troops."

Walt whistled. "Keen! I told the fellows in the chess club that studying medieval armor would come in handy someday. Hey, Doc, did that page have something to do with the war? Was there a secret message written on it or something?"

"Something like that," Dr. Bean said. "But I really can't say any more."

"Oh, Dash," Miss Lake said, blowing on her tea. "Surely we can tell them a little. After all, they did keep Mr. January from taking the page."

"Mr. January?" Madge asked. "What kind of name is that? It sounds like a—"

"Spy name!" Walt cried. "I knew there was something underhanded about him. Is he spying for the Nazis?"

"Yes, Walt," Dr. Bean said gravely. "I'm afraid so. So you can see that this is a very dangerous affair—no business for children."

Walt clenched his fists at the word *children*. He was afraid his voice would crack, so he spoke slowly and softly. "I saw children rounded up by the Nazis, and my parents had to send me away with hundreds of other children because it was the only way to keep us safe. Hitler's already made this a *business for children* and if there's a spy working for the Nazis here in New York, I deserve to know what I can do to help."

Walt gulped and looked around, shocked at himself. How had he gotten the nerve to talk to Dr. Bean like that? The doctor would probably throw him out on his ear now. But instead Dr. Bean had gone very pale and Miss Lake put her hand on Walt's shoulder. "Well said, young man." Then, turning to Dr. Bean, "They did answer the call, Dash."

"Yes, Viv, but it must be a mistake. They can't be the ones."

"The book has never been wrong before," she said, pointing at the pages on the table. Although most of them were blank, it was possible now to see that there were traces of ink and gold glitter on some of them, as if they had once contained writing and pictures that had been washed away.

"I don't see how this mess could tell anyone anything," Madge said.

"The Kelmsbury is *not* a mess," Dr. Bean said indignantly. "At least it wasn't until it was immersed in water and ruined. I was trying to dry out the pages when you came in earlier."

"The same thing happened when Frankie was reading *Treasure Island* in the bathtub," Madge said. "Gee, Doc, you weren't reading this in the tub, were you?"

"I'm sure Dr. Bean wouldn't read an important old book in the bath," Walt said. "You wouldn't, would you?"

"I'd never . . . well—" He looked sheepishly at Miss Lake. "Not since the Caxton manuscript incident."

"Then how'd this book get in the drink, Doc?" Madge asked.

Dr. Bean drew himself up to answer, and Walt saw that Madge was goading Dr. Bean into telling them more than he meant to. Which was pretty clever. He wished he'd thought of it. "I'll have you know this volume was pulled out of the harbor down by Battery Park this morning by an associate of mine in the FBI. It was on the body of an Axis spy who drowned himself rather than be caught. We believe he was using the book as a cipher, that is—"

"A key to a code," Walt said. "I've read about them in spy novels." Walt peered at a page Miss Lake had picked from the pile. The letters were clearer on this page. There were still traces of color and gold outlining a large capital *A*. "Hey, this looks like the page from the case upstairs. But that can't be. The card on that case said it came from the only surviving copy of the Kelmsbury King Arthur."

Dr. Bean looked embarrassed. "I may not have been entirely truthful when I typed up that card. The truth is, we know of at least *four* copies of the Kelmsbury. Three of them are still in the hands of the enemy, but the museum has one copy. That's where the page in the display case was from. The rest of that book was . . . lost two years ago."

"Lost?" Madge asked. "You ought to take better care of your books, Doc."

"Well, perhaps *lost* is not quite the right word—"

"Hidden," Miss Lake said. "The book was hidden

in the museum by one of the board members, Sir Peter Bricklebank."

"Why would he hide a priceless manuscript?" Walt asked. "Was he crazy?"

"Not at all!" Dr. Bean said at the same time that Miss Lake conceded, "Possibly."

"Sir Peter could be a bit of a prankster," Dr. Bean explained. "But mostly he just wanted to make sure it didn't fall into the wrong hands. He took the book apart, except for the epilogue, which was the page we put on display, and hid it in four pieces and left clues that only the *right* people could figure out."

"And apparently Dash and I aren't the right people," Miss Lake said.

"Really?" Madge said. "But you two are so clever."

"Sometimes it's not enough to be clever," Miss Lake said, smiling sadly. "Sir Bricklebank didn't want anyone to find the book except for the people who were meant to find it—not even me and Dash—and he was very good at hiding things. But now it's imperative we find the book so we can break the code on the message that's been intercepted. We believe it outlines the plans for a sabotage plot."

"Do we know what they plan to sabotage?" Joe asked.

"No," Dr. Bean said, "we don't. We were able to confiscate the message from between the pages of the book." Dr. Bean took down a page from the clothesline and laid it on the table. Unlike the other pages, this one hadn't been washed clean of words.

"This handwriting is modern," Madge said, "but I can't make out what it says."

"That's because it's in code," Walt said, his voice breaking in his excitement. "Let me have a crack at it, Doc. I solve the code on the Little Orphan Annie show every week. . . ." He felt the blood rush to his face. Jeez! Had he just admitted in front of a girl that he listened to a kids' show on the radio? How could he explain that listening to the radio was the way he'd learned English so fast? Since coming to America two years ago, he'd listened to the radio every night, repeating the words until every trace of his German accent was gone. "I mean, I used to when I was a kid. Now I just do it with my cousin Rachel because she likes the decoder badge."

"Who wouldn't?" Madge said, beaming at Walt. "Frankie and I used to go to all our neighbors collecting Ovaltine lids so we could get one. Do we need a decoder badge for this message?"

"No, but we need the book," Walt said, looking sadly at the water-damaged pages. Then he looked back at the message and saw that the spy had already started writing letters over the coded part. He could make out a word— "Holy smokes! It spells *Camelot*." Walt looked up, his ears twitching with excitement.

"*Camelot* is the seventh word on this page," Joe said,

holding up the one page that still had visible writing on it.

"That would be an awfully big coincidence if the page we need is the same one that survived," Madge said.

"Maybe not," Walt said. "If the spy slipped the message into the book at the page he was using, the extra paper could have protected that page, isn't that right, Doc?"

"Yes, Walt," he agreed. "I think that's exactly what happened."

"I'm surprised you could read that writing at all, Joe," Madge said.

"I *can* read," Joe said.

Everyone turned to stare at Joe.

"No one doubted you could, young man," Miss Lake said, putting her hand on Joe's shoulder. "It's just that this page is from an eleventh-century manuscript. The writing is quite antiquated and yet you had no trouble reading it."

Joe shrugged. "All writing looked like that to me at first. I got pretty good at making out new languages at the Mush Hole, because we weren't allowed to use our own language."

"That doesn't seem fair," Walt said at the same time Madge asked, "What's a Mush Hole?"

"That's what everyone calls the school I went to. If you want me to read that page for you, I can."

Dr. Bean held up his hand. "Just because Joe *can*

read the writing doesn't mean he should. This book is very dangerous."

"Whaddaya mean, Doc?" Madge asked. "You mean like the books Hitler burned?"

"No! That's not what I meant at all!" Dr. Bean grabbed the fringe of hair at the back of his head until it stood up. "Vivian, help me out here."

"What Dash means is that there's a superstition attached to this book that it should only be read by the people meant to read it and even then it should never be read alone. But we're not alone, Dash, and the children are the ones who answered the call. Why don't we let them have a go? They won't be reading very much of it."

"So," said Joe, who had been flicking his eyes back and forth between the two adults, "what word do you need next?"

Walt looked back down at the page. "You said it was the seventh word, and this page . . . Hey, there's a symbol on the top of this page—a shield and the number seven. I bet the symbols are supposed to tell you which section of the book you need to decode each part of the message, and the number tells you which word to pick. . . . So I betcha the code is to pick every seventh word and write it over the letters in the message—leaving out any duplicate letters, of course, and then copying out the rest of the alphabet. . . ." Walt leaned over, his nose nearly touching the page, ears twitching, and worked out the code. He forgot to feel embarrassed. His uncle Sol said that he had a good head for numbers and he'd make a good accountant someday. Walt didn't want to be an accountant. He wanted to be a knight—or maybe a spy.

He finished trying to decode the message, but it didn't make any sense.

"It didn't work," he said glumly. "It's gibberish."

"Try using the key word and then skipping every seventh letter after that," Joe said.

"How . . . ?"

Joe shrugged. "I don't know. I can just see that sort of thing. Like the letters move around. . . . I know that sounds crazy."

"You see," Miss Lake whispered to Dr. Bean. "I think these children might really be the ones."

"But they're too young!" Dr. Bean wailed. "We can't allow it, Viv! You know what happens—"

"I'm going to give it another try," Walt said, determined to show Dr. Bean that they weren't helpless children, that they were the *ones*—whatever the heck that meant! "If I skip every seventh letter and make out a grid—it's called a Vigenère cipher, by the way," he added, hoping to impress Madge, but she had turned toward Dr. Bean.

"Doc, what did you mean about us not being the ones? Who are the ones and why are you so sure it isn't us?"

"I've already said too much," Dr. Bean replied. "If you don't believe me about what Miss Lake has called the 'superstition' about the Kelmsbury, listen to what's written on the last page." He leaned over Walt and read aloud:

At long last Arthur returned to Camelot with his companions, and they resumed their lives there, never telling anyone of the strange adventure they had shared in the Hewan Wood and the Maiden Castle or the grave portents told to them by the Lady of the Lake. They kept their secret through the terrible years that followed—through war, betrayal, exile, and death—for they knew that in the end, whatever they lost would be restored to them when they were reunited on the Isle of Avalon, and whenever great evil arose in the world, four brave knights would arise in their names to vanquish it.

Walt shivered. It was what he wanted most of all—to vanquish—*what a wonderful word!*—evil, which definitely meant fighting the Nazis and getting his parents out of France, where they'd gone after Walt was evacuated from Germany as part of the Kindertransport. At least that's where they'd been when he'd heard from them three months ago.

Dr. Bean straightened up and took off his glasses because the lenses had fogged up while he was reading. Then he put them back on and looked at the three of them as if he hoped they might have been replaced by grown-ups.

"There is no doubt that evil has arisen in the world. When I put the only surviving page from the book on display today, I thought it would call four knights to vanquish the evil, but something must have gone terribly wrong. No matter how brave and clever you three are, you are too young to battle the evil that has arisen now. I simply won't allow it."

Walt was opening his mouth to tell Dr. Bean that the book hadn't been wrong, but Joe spoke first.

"You're right, Doc, we're not the ones. I know I'm no hero."

Walt stared at Joe, surprised. The other boy was so tall and strong. He hadn't hesitated to run after Mr. January, and he'd been the first to tackle him when Walt opened the door. He sure looked like a hero to Walt.

"Honestly," Madge said, "the whole thing sounds like a bunch of malarkey to me. I mean, why would Nazi spies bother with using an old book to encode their messages?"

"It is believed," Dr. Bean said rather formally, as if he was offended at Madge calling his book a bunch of malarkey, "that a message encrypted using the Kelmsbury can never be broken."

"Well, that's not true," Walt said, his voice rising with excitement. "I've broken it. I've decoded your spy's message—at least this first part."

"Wow!" Madge said, slapping Walt on the back. "Good going, sport!"

The shivery feeling awoken by Dr. Bean's words swelled in Walt's chest.

"I suppose there's no harm in your reading it aloud with the rest of us here. Go ahead, young man," Dashwood Bean said, looking at Walt as if he might have been wrong about him.

Walt bent his head to the page and read, praying his voice wouldn't choose now to crack and that his English, which he'd worked so hard to remove any accent from, would sound right.

Your loyalty has been rewarded. Project Excalibur has begun. Decode each message below to receive your instructions. If you doubt our power, the events of today will put an end to those doubts. Remember that Project Excalibur will make today seem like nothing. . . .

His voice faltered. "I don't like to say the last part." He passed the page to Miss Lake.

"It says *Heil Hitler*," she said, taking out her handkerchief to wipe her eyes.

"Do you know what Project Excalibur is?" Joe asked.

"No," Miss Lake replied. "This was the first intercept."

"Do you know what it means about the 'events of today'?" Madge asked. "We've had the radio on for the last half hour, and the only news has been that Canada's been at war for two years, which everyone and their uncle knew already."

"Wait," Joe said, getting up from the table and walking toward the radio. "They're interrupting the broadcast."

He turned up the volume. A man's voice filled the workroom, which had suddenly become so quiet it seemed as if the wooden heads on the hat forms were listening as well as the five breathing occupants of the room.

"*. . . have attacked the Pearl Harbor, Hawaii, from the air. I'll repeat that: President Roosevelt says that the Japanese have attacked Pearl Harbor, in Hawaii, from the air.*"

"Hawaii!" Madge gasped. "But that's part of our country!"

"Yes," Dr. Bean said, looking at Miss Lake. "You see what I mean about the great evil. This is *not* something that children should be involved in."

Walt shook his head. He knew what the radio announcement and the coded message meant. He was looking at the suits of armor glinting in the watery light from the high windows but seeing instead an army of knights arrayed on a battlefield. "You're wrong, Doc," he said, not caring now if his voice cracked. "We've all got to do our part—we're at war."

Then a scream came from the floor above them.

5

PAPER AIRPLANES

KIKU LOOKED UP from her father's unconscious body and saw a crowd of people rushing from the basement stairs across the gallery floor. She recognized Dr. Bean and Miss Lake and that freckled boy who came to the museum every Sunday, but the other two kids— a redheaded girl and a dark-haired boy—were strangers. She felt ashamed that they should see her father, Curator of Far Eastern Art, lying on the floor, his suit jacket, which was always so neatly pressed, rumpled from his fall.

"What happened?" Miss Lake asked, kneeling beside her.

"We were listening to the radio," Kiku said, scanning the faces above her, "and then we heard about this terrible attack. It's what my father has always feared— a war between Japan and the United States. Just this morning he was angry at me. . . ." Her voice broke as she remembered the fight they had been having before the awful radio announcement.

It had all begun because of the surprise Kiku had planned for the new exhibit. Miss Lake had helped her late last night. Together they had come up with the idea of displaying some of the Japanese armor to tie the new armor exhibit to the Edo period Japanese screens in the balcony above the hall of Arms and Armor.

The Japanese armor was usually displayed in the basement. Kiku had often heard her father complain that because Far Eastern art was crammed into the basement and balcony galleries, the collection could not be presented chronologically or in any coherent order. And so Kiku, with Miss Lake's help, had come up with the idea of placing a few of the objects of Japanese armor in the first-floor gallery with a sign indicating that more Japanese art could be seen in the balcony galleries above. She had selected a suit of armor of the Edo period, which stood now in the rear gallery with a sign that invited visitors to continue their exploration of Japanese art on the second-floor balcony. She had steered her father, who usually retreated to the Far Eastern study room in the basement before the museum opened, to the Arms and Armor hall to show him her surprise.

He *had* been surprised. His eyes had widened as he read the sign Miss Lake had had printed. Then he had turned to her and in a low but penetrating voice asked, "What have you done, foolish girl?"

"I-I thought this would bring more visitors to the balcony. You are always saying that no one notices the paintings up there."

"Do you think *now* is the time to be noticed?" he asked.

Kiku felt the blood rush to her face. Her father made it sound as if she had deliberately tried to bring attention to herself, like the one time she had put on lipstick and face powder and he had made her scrub them off before leaving the house.

"B-but Mother always said that if the Americans understood Japanese culture better—"

He had turned deathly pale, and Kiku knew she had made a mistake to mention her mother. Three months ago her mother had gone back to Japan to visit her own mother, who was sick. Her father had been against her going. *This is our country now!* he had said. *If war breaks out, you may never be allowed back.* Now he spoke to Kiku in the same angry voice.

"And this is how you want them to understand us better? By setting up a suit of armor like a clothes mannequin?"

"But all the armor is displayed like that down here— and the armor is one of the most popular exhibits in the museum. All the children love the knights. I thought if they saw that we had knights too—"

"Do you think"—he enunciated each word slowly as if casting doubt on the idea that she was capable of thought—"that we should be drawing attention to our martial history while Japan invades China and forms an alliance with the Germans?"

"Oh!" The blood that had risen to her face drained down to the tips of her toes, leaving her feeling empty and light-headed. "I didn't think—"

"No, you did not think. What else have you done?" He had stormed up to the balcony to see the new cards she and Miss Lake had made, leading the curious visitor through the exhibit of fifteenth-century screens. He read each one aloud in a mocking voice, turning each description into a boastful declaration of war, his face turning the dangerous purple of storm clouds.

"I was only trying to bring more visitors to your exhibit," she kept saying, trailing after him. "You worked so hard!"

"Are we fishmongers in the market, hawking day-old fish?" he demanded. "Is this what you have learned in your American school? To sell yourself like a . . ."

He had finished the sentence with a word she had never heard before. And then his eyes had moved from her face to a spot two inches over her right shoulder and he told her that he could no longer look at her. He had grown blurred—as if he were the one vanishing into the mist of one of his favorite landscape paintings. *Scholar lifted into the clouds after the disappointment of a worthless daughter.* She had turned and run away from him, heading for the basement workroom, where she could hide behind the ancient screens awaiting restoration, wishing she *could* vanish so she'd never have to see that look of disappointment on her father's face again.

It was bad enough that the girls at school whispered behind her back. Trina van der Hoek called her a squinty-eyed Jap, and Gertrude Pillager had spilled yellow paint on her in art class and said no one would notice. People on the street stared at her as if she were an enemy spy. Now her own father had looked at her as if she were a stranger.

He had come downstairs eventually to restore a tear in a fourteenth-century scroll, but instead of talking to her, he had turned on the radio, to a football game between his beloved Dodgers and the Giants. She had thought that working on the scroll and listening to the game would calm him down, but then an announcer had broken into the game.

"We interrupt this broadcast to bring you this important bulletin from the United Press. Flash! Washington— The White House announces Japanese attack on Pearl Harbor."

He had stood up, letting the priceless scroll slip from his fingers and fall to the floor, unfurling like a waterfall.

"We must take down the suit of armor before anyone sees it," he had said, walking out of the workroom like an automaton. Kiku caught up with him on the stairs. "Perhaps it's a hoax," she told him. "Like when they said the Martians had invaded and it was just a play by Mr. Welles." Kiku bit her lip, thinking that it would be far better if the Martians *had* attacked than if it were true that the Japanese had. What would happen to her mother? She'd never be allowed to come back now! How would the girls at school look at her? And what would happen to her father and her?

She followed him up to the gallery and toward the back where a janitor was sweeping up glass. One of the display cases at the back of the hall, the one that had held that beautiful medieval manuscript page, was broken.

"He saw the broken glass case," Kiku told Miss Lake now, "and he said, 'It has begun.' Then he fell to the floor. . . ." *Like the scroll, unfurling, plummeting to earth.* "I didn't know what to do." She held out her hands to show her helplessness, and the girl with red hair gasped. Kiku looked down. Bits of glass were embedded in her hands.

"You did the only thing you could do," the redhead said, cradling Kiku's hand in hers and picking out the glass. Along with the broken glass from the display case, there were flecks of gold paint embedded in her skin. "You called for help. That was the right thing to do."

"There was nothing else you could do," Miss Lake said, pressing her hand to Kiku's father's neck and holding a silver vial of smelling salts to his nose. He stirred and murmured something Kiku couldn't understand.

"I think it was only the shock," Miss Lake said. "His heartbeat is steady. You ought to get him home."

"We ought to get him to the police."

Kiku looked up to see the new head of security glaring down at her father, her round glasses opaque in the glare of the ceiling lights, fisted hands on her narrow hips, her face as fierce as the ceremonial mask of the Japanese warrior. Since Miss Fitzbane had started at the museum last month, she had looked at Kiku and her father as if they were spies sent from Japan to steal museum artifacts. Even when Kiku recognized the creature on her pin as an amphisbaena and complimented her on it, Miss Fitzbane had snapped, "Some *chill*-drun are too smart for their own good!" Now she was staring at Kiku as if she was responsible for her own father lying on the floor.

"This man is now an enemy alien. He was fleeing the museum with confidential papers—look!" She pointed at the broken display case. "He's even broken into one of the exhibits."

"That wasn't—" the redhead began, but Dr. Bean stepped in front of Miss Fitzbane.

"There *was* a break-in, Miss . . . er . . ."

"Fitzbane," the woman spit out. "Which you would have remembered, Dr. Bean, if you ever bothered coming to any of the meetings I've called."

"Dr. Bean's been rather busy," Miss Lake said. "And as for Mr. Akiyama, I believe that Fred the janitor can confirm he only came onto the scene after the break-in. Would you please call the director and let him know we'll need extra security for the Asian exhibits? There could be a misdirected attack on them."

Miss Fitzbane glared at Dr. Bean and Miss Lake. "I shall speak to the director right away about having this enemy alien removed from the museum." She looked down at Mr. Akiyama, who, revived by Miss Lake's smelling salts, was sitting up and looking confusedly around him. Miss Fitzbane lowered her voice to a whisper that came out like the hiss of a snake. "He could be a *spy*."

"Kenji Akiyama has lived in this country since he was eighteen years old," Dr. Bean said. "Why, we were undergraduates at Columbia together! I will personally vouch for him." He turned and looked at Mr. Akiyama, who stood swaying between Miss Lake and Kiku, and spoke to him in Japanese. "My friend, the enemy I warned you about has arisen. Now is the time for us to stand together. Remember that a single arrow is easily broken, but not ten in a bundle." Kiku's father straightened his shoulders and bowed his head. Miss Fitzbane's face turned even whiter. Why had he spoken to her father in Japanese? Now Miss Fitzbane would think they were all spies. *We may all be arrested!*

As if to confirm her fears, a uniformed security guard appeared in the gallery. "There's a phone call for Dr. Bean," he said. "They said it was the War Department."

"The War Department!" Miss Fitzbane shrilled at the

guard. "They were probably having you on, Jenkins."

"I know you haven't been here long, Miss Fitzbane," Miss Lake said coolly. "So perhaps you don't realize that Dr. Bean is a consultant to the War Department."

Miss Fitzbane glared at Miss Lake. "I may not have been here as long as you, Miss Lake, but I've been here long enough to recognize an enemy when I see one."

Kiku was shocked. No one talked to Miss Lake like that! She turned to Miss Lake to see how she would respond and got an even bigger surprise. Miss Lake's lips had turned white and the icy blonde wave of her hair trembled. Kiku was sure she was going to tell Miss Fitzbane off, but instead she turned to Dr. Bean. "You'd better take that call, Dash. I can bring Kiku and her father home."

"We can go with her," the tall boy with dark hair said. He had been quiet since arriving upstairs, cautiously scanning the faces of the angry adults as if fighting the urge to flee. "It's like you just said, Dr. Bean: 'A single arrow is easily broken, but not ten in a bundle.'"

"Did he? I don't remember—" Walt began, but the redhead cut in.

"Yeah, we got to stick together." She put her arm around Kiku's shoulder. "Come on, let's get your pa home and make him a nice cup of tea."

Kiku nodded gratefully. "My mother always says there is no problem so big that it can't be solved over a cup of tea." And then her eyes filled with tears as she thought of what her mother must be thinking thousands of miles away in Japan, and she wondered once more if she'd ever see her again.

"My mother said that too," the redhead said, looking away. *Have I said something wrong?* Kiku wondered.

"I've always found that the answers to all life's problems are to be found at the bottom of a teapot," Miss Lake said, giving Dr. Bean a sharp look. "You three go with Kiku. I'll take you out the back exit and help you get a taxi. Here's cab fare." She produced a twenty-dollar bill.

"Jeez Louise," the redhead exclaimed. "Do you think we're taking him back to Japan?"

"Here," Miss Lake said, slipping the money into the girl's coat pocket along with a handkerchief. "You'll need this." Then she turned to Kiku. "You can trust Madge. She always says exactly what she means. And Walt"— she nodded to the freckled boy—"is stronger than he looks, and Joe will fight anyone who tries to hurt you or your father. What they all need is someone with a level head, so you'd better look after them, Kiku."

Kiku nodded, confused about why or how she could look after anyone, but she trusted Miss Lake, so she would *try* to trust the others. As they walked down the stairs, she turned to the dark-haired boy—Joe—and asked, "How do you know Japanese?"

"Me?" he asked, his eyes widening.

"Yes, that saying about the arrows. Dr. Bean said it in Japanese."

"Are you sure?" he asked. "I don't speak a word of it."

✳   ✳   ✳

There was a crowd outside the museum, jockeying for taxis. Everyone wanted to get home to be with their families or their sweethearts. "We'll never get one," Kiku fretted. But Madge stepped through the crowd, past a woman in a fur coat with half a dozen shopping bags from Bergdorf's and Saks, put two fingers in her mouth, and whistled over a Checker cab with its off-duty light on.

"I gotta get my uncle Syd to the hospital," Madge told the driver as Kiku gaped at her. "I think he's had a heart attack."

"Are youse blind?" the driver asked, pointing to his off-duty light. "I gotta get home to Canarsie to see my sweetheart before I enlist—" but then he looked at Madge's pleading eyes and he stammered to a stop. "Shucks, doll face, pile in. Which hospital?"

"Oh, we have to go home first." Madge nudged Kiku, who gave the driver her home address and then asked if it was all right if her father rode in the front because he got carsick in the back.

"This is your uncle Syd?" the driver asked, looking at Mr. Akiyama, who had closed his eyes. Anyone who didn't know him would think he was asleep, but Kiku knew that this was what he did when he had a headache. "He looks—"

"Chinese," Kiku said, remembering that her father had told her Americans couldn't tell the difference and no one was mad at the Chinese. "We are both Chinese. My cousin here"—she nodded at Madge—"her aunt was a missionary who married my father."

"Yeah, Aunt Jean the missionary," Madge said, giving Kiku an admiring look as she sat down next to her on the backseat. Joe and Walt sat on the jump seats facing them.

The cab driver just shook his head. "Whatever you say. I've been driving a cab in New York for ten years— there's nothing I ain't seen."

The traffic was jammed going down Fifth Avenue. "Jeez Louise," Madge said. "Everyone and their uncle seems to have decided to go home at the same time."

"They're scared," Walt said. "It's like when the soldiers came to our neighborhood back home. Everyone would hide inside their homes. They're afraid of another attack."

"An attack on New York?" Madge asked, shocked. "They wouldn't dare!"

"You heard what was in that message—" He clamped his hand over his mouth and looked at Kiku, his face turning bright red.

"What?" Kiku challenged him. "Are you afraid I'm a spy?"

"Of course not," Walt said, lowering his voice to a whisper so the taxi driver couldn't hear. "Only Dr. Bean told us some pretty crazy stuff."

"If it has anything to do with my father, you'd better tell me right now."

"It's not about your father," Joe replied. "It's about the page in that display case. It was stolen by a man in a trench coat."

"Did he have a gray hat and eyes that felt like ice picks?" Kiku asked.

"You saw him?" Walt asked.

"I-I dreamed about him last night," she said in a small, scared whisper.

"You too?" Joe, Madge, and Walt all said.

They stared at one another. The interior of the taxi suddenly felt very close, as if all the air had been sucked out of it.

"The Kelmsbury said four knights would arise in times of evil," Walt said. "You must be the fourth knight."

"You're not telling me you bought all that malarkey?" Madge asked. "About knights and prophecies and lost books and being called to vanquish evil? Besides, Dr. Bean said it couldn't be us because we're just kids."

"B-but Dr. Bean said—" Walt began.

"The doc seemed a nice enough fellow," Madge said.

"But with maybe a couple of screws loose."

"Dr. Bean *is* a bit eccentric," Kiku said. She was thinking about what Dr. Bean had whispered to her father about an enemy. What had he meant? Was there more to their friendship than a shared fondness for Japanese medieval armor and the Dodgers? "But he has always been kind to my father"—she leaned forward to check on her father in the front seat, but he still had his eyes closed—"and my father says that he's an honorable man. What else did he tell you?"

Walt leaned eagerly toward Kiku and in a hushed, excited whisper told her what the message from the spy had said. "We'll need the rest of the book to finish decoding it," he added.

"I liked looking at that page," Kiku said when he had finished. "There was something magical about it. Before Dr. Bean put it on display, it was in the Arms and Armor workroom and Miss Lake used to let me come in and look at it whenever I liked. But I don't know where the rest of the book is. Sir Bricklebank told me it was lost."

"Isn't that the fellow the doc said went crazy and hid the book?" Madge asked.

"He was rather odd," Kiku said fondly. "I once found a laundry ticket of his stuffed in a Ming vase."

"Of course!" Walt slapped his forehead. "You know your way around the museum. You'll be able to help us find the book."

Kiku smiled sadly at Walt. "I do know my way around

the museum, but I don't think that I can help you. You saw how Miss Fitzbane looked at my father and me. Do you really think he will be allowed to go on working at the museum? Or that I'll even be allowed back in? Look at all these people—"

The taxi had come to a stop near Rockefeller Center. A Salvation Army band was playing "The Star-Spangled Banner." People were hugging each other and crying. "We'll bomb them yellow devils to hell and back!" a man in a business suit yelled. People were looking up at the sky as if they expected to spot enemy planes flying overhead dropping bombs. . . .

And something *was* falling from the sky. White shapes fluttering down from the skyscrapers. Like enormous snowflakes. One of them sailed right through the taxi's open window into Kiku's lap. She started as if it were a bomb.

"It's just a paper airplane," Madge said, plucking it out of Kiku's lap and unfolding it. "Frankie used to love making these. Oh, look, there's a message inside."

Kiku took the paper airplane back from Madge. "It says, 'We are at war with Japan.'"

"It must be the fellas up in the newsrooms sending them down," Madge said. "In case we hadn't heard yet."

"It looks like everyone in the whole city's heard," Walt said. "Gosh, I wonder how my aunt Sadie's taking the news. I wonder if my cousin Ralph will sign up."

"By tomorrow all these young men will enlist," Kiku

said, wondering what her mother, thousands of miles away in Yokohama, must be thinking. "If I were a boy and I was old enough, I'd join the army to show everyone that I love this country as much as anyone. But no one will believe that. When they look at my father and me, they'll see the face of the enemy. I wish . . ." She thought of the moment this morning when her father had looked right through her. "It would be better if I were invisible." She crumpled the paper airplane up in her hand and let it fall to the floor of the taxi, feeling, as she let it go, as if she were the one falling from the sky.

6

RING-A-LEVIO

THE TAXI PULLED up in front of a building on Gramercy Park. It was a fancy building with an awning and a doorman in a red uniform with shiny brass buttons who came to open the door for them, but Madge didn't envy Kiku for living in such a swank place when she saw the look on the doorman's face.

"There are some men waiting for you in the lobby, Mr. Akiyama," the doorman said.

Mr. Akiyama opened his eyes and turned to fix Kiku with a hard stare. "Do not come in with me, Kiku-chan. They will only take you too. Dr. Bean is right." He moved his head to fix each of the kids with the same hard stare. "You are only children. You should not meddle with what you don't understand." Then he got out of the taxi with a surprisingly spry step for a man who had looked like he was at death's door a half hour ago and walked firmly toward the door of the apartment building.

Kiku started after him, but Joe grabbed her arm. "You heard what he said."

"Let go of me!" she cried. "I have to go with him. *Otousan!*"

The cry brought tears to Madge's eyes. It sounded like Frankie's cry when their father stood up from their mother's broken rocking chair and walked out of their apartment. "Da!" he had cried, but it had sounded just the same. Madge wanted to run after Mr. Akiyama herself. But then the front door of the building opened and her heart froze.

"It's him!" she shouted, grabbing Walt's arm. "It's Mr. January!"

The man in the trench coat was flanked by two men in dark suits. They held up badges to Mr. Akiyama. "We're here from the State Department," one of the dark-suited men said. "You're coming with us."

"Am I being arrested?" Mr. Akiyama asked.

"You are being detained as an enemy alien," the other dark-suited man said. "Is that your daughter in the taxi? She has to come too."

"Drive on," Joe hissed to the driver.

"No!" Kiku cried. "I want to go with my father."

"You won't be able to help him if you're arrested too," Joe said. "Drive!"

The driver looked out the window at the men and then at Joe's face. "Oh, what the heck! I don't suppose I'm ever getting back to Canarsie tonight."

He peeled away from the curb, tires squealing, Kiku wailing and pounding her fists on Joe's arm. Looking back, Madge saw Mr. January lift his head at the sound and watch them go. Even from this distance, Madge felt the coldness of those eyes on her.

"Where to, bud?"

"Make a right here," Joe said.

As the taxi went around the corner, Joe turned to Madge. "Have him go around the block. If I'm gone, keep on going."

"What do you mean if you're—"

But instead of answering, Joe opened the car door and stepped out of the moving cab.

"Holy smokes!" Walt shouted. "What does he think he's doing?"

"Providing a distraction," Madge said, watching Joe from the rear window. He had stumbled getting out of the taxi but recovered himself quickly and crouched behind a parked car just in time before one of the dark-suited men came around the corner. Joe popped out from behind the car and shouted something at the man and then took off running, the man in hot pursuit.

Madge laughed, then leaned forward to talk to the driver. "Go around the block, Mister. I've got an Andrew Jackson with your name on it if we're back before the suits and the girl's father leave."

The driver shook his head and swerved around a

parked fruit truck, muttering under his breath, "I hope youse kids know what you're doing."

"Joe's leading that man away while we go around the block so we can follow the others to see where they take your father," Madge said, squeezing Kiku's hand. "I've pulled the same trick myself in ring-a-levio. You get one of your players to lead the other team away from base and then you run around the block and free your teammates from jail."

"Jail?" Kiku asked. "Is that where they're taking my father?"

"They'll take him to Ellis Island," Walt said. "That's where they keep you if they think you're a danger to the country. I was there for a week when I came over from England because I had the measles—Look!" They had come around the block and were approaching the Akiyamas' apartment building. One of the dark-suited men was putting Mr. Akiyama in the back of a black Packard. Mr. January stood on the curb, looking up and down the street.

"Slow up!" Madge hissed.

"Faster, slower, I wish youse kids would make up your minds!" the driver complained while deftly maneuvering behind another taxi waiting at the curb.

"That's good!" Madge said. "Put your light on so it looks like you're waiting for a fare. Everyone, get down." She slid onto the floor, pulling Kiku with her. Walt stared at them and after a moment joined them on the floor.

"How will we know when it's safe to go?" Walt asked, peeling a piece of gum off the knee of his trousers.

"If you're waiting on that fellow who's got the girl's dad, they're pulling out now," the driver said.

"Follow them!" Madge cried, popping back up. She scanned the street, looking for Joe. He'd said to go on without him if he wasn't there, and that's what made the most sense, but she never liked losing a player so early in the game—

The door was flung open and a hot bundle of denim, flying hair, and copper eyes crashed into the backseat.

"What are you waiting for?" Joe asked. "Follow that car!"

✢   ✢   ✢

The taxi followed the Packard to Second Avenue, where it turned south. Their driver seemed to know exactly how far to stay back so as not to be seen.

"Usually I'm following some mook's wife," the driver admitted when Madge asked if he had experience "tailing." "This is a nice change of pace."

"Just shout out if they make any unexpected moves," Madge said. Then she turned to Joe. His denim jacket was torn and covered with garbage. There were egg-shells in his hair and he'd added a cut above his eyebrow to the black eye and swollen lip he'd gotten earlier. He smelled like week-old boiled cabbage. "What'd ya do? Catch a ride on a garbage truck?"

"I led him into a blind alley and knocked a couple of trash cans in front of him. We had a little tussle—"

"Did you . . . ?" Walt began, staring wide-eyed at Joe. "Is he . . . ?"

"I lost him a couple blocks away and doubled back. He didn't seem like the brightest bulb in the pack. In fact . . ." Joe narrowed his copper eyes. "He seemed like he was half asleep. Like he was just going through the motions."

"Huh," Madge said. "That's interesting. Maybe that will give us the chance we need to get Mr. Akiyama back."

"I don't understand," Kiku said.

"Madge is looking for weak spots in the enemy's team, right?" Joe asked.

"Oh, like in chess," Walt said, "when you see your opponent leave himself open."

"Yeah, I guess," Madge said, surprised at how good it felt to have the two boys looking at her like she knew what she was doing. It had been a while since anyone had looked at her like that. But Kiku was still frowning.

"No," she said. "I mean, why are you doing this for me and my father? We only just met and we're . . . I mean . . ." She lowered her voice. "We're Japanese. Everyone hates us now."

"I'm pretty sure you didn't have anything to do with

dropping those bombs on Pearl Harbor," Madge said. "And as for just meeting . . . we all just met, but something's going on here. I don't really understand what yet, but it's bad. That Mr. January is planning to do something bad to the city and we can't let him get away with it."

"It's like the page Dr. Bean read us said," Walt said. "Whenever evil arises in the world, brave knights will rise to vanquish it. We're the four knights. How can we vanquish evil if we don't help each other?"

"And I don't like to see anyone get pushed around," Joe said. Then he pointed toward the front window. "Look, that's the third turn they've taken in five minutes. I think they're trying to lose us."

It was becoming more and more difficult for the taxi driver to follow the Packard without giving himself away. He had followed them down Second Avenue, turned right on East Houston, and then south on the Bowery, driving through strips of light and shade beneath the elevated train track. From there the Packard had turned onto the narrow streets of Chinatown, which were crowded with food carts and Sunday marketers. As the big black Packard moved down the street, the crowds parted. Vendors closed up their carts and old women with baskets covered their heads and hurried home. Madge gazed at the shopwindows, where plucked ducks and silk banners hung beside signs hastily handwritten in English.

WE ARE CHINESE, the signs read. NOT JAPANESE.

The Packard continued south on Pearl Street and then Water Street.

"They're headed for the ferry," Madge said. "Maybe they really are taking him to Ellis Island."

"And then what?" Kiku asked. "Will they keep him there for the whole war? Will they say he's a spy and execute him, like they did those Italian men in Boston?"

Madge didn't know how to answer, but Joe did. "We won't let that happen. Look, they're stopping at that park."

"That's Battery Park," Walt said. "I came here on a class trip. The ferry to the Statue of Liberty is here and Ellis Island is just a short boat ride away. Look, they're getting out. We'll have to follow them."

Madge dug the twenty-dollar bill out of her pocket. There was something else in her pocket besides the handkerchief—something that crinkled—but she didn't have time to look at it now. The meter read $3.05, but she'd promised the driver the twenty. "Here," she said. "Treat your girl to a good dinner before you ship out." She looked at the driver's license on the dashboard. "Good luck to you, Alphonse!"

"Good luck to youse guys," Alphonse said, waving his hand out the window. "Whatever it is you're up to!"

The four crossed the street and entered the park. Mr. January and the dark-suited man were walking on either side of Mr. Akiyama, past a chestnut vendor and a stone castlelike building, toward a pier where a ferry was docked. The harbor was crowded with boats— supply ships bound for Europe, big cruise ships full of evacuees from Europe, and ferries going back and forth to the Statue of Liberty. Madge's old school, Our Lady of Perpetual Help, didn't do field trips, but she knew the park because her mother had taken her here once to catch the ferry for the Statue of Liberty.

"My grandmother came on a boat from Ireland during the Great Hunger," she had told Madge on the ferry. "Her mother died in the crossing, and she was all alone when she got here. They weren't going to let her leave alone without a responsible man to claim her so she convinced another passenger to say he was her brother. She found work in a factory and made enough money to send back to Ireland for her three brothers. They were big brawny men who worked the docks down in Red Hook, but when Peggy O'Shaunessy told them to wash their hands for supper, they said, 'Yes, ma'am,' like she was the Queen Mother. She raised five children and put food on the table for half the block as well." Madge's mother had given her a mischievous smile. "Some people called her bossy, but most just called her strong. Always remember you come from women who know their own minds like her—and *her*"—she had pointed to the statue in the harbor of the regal lady in green robes holding aloft a flaming torch—"and that you're just as strong."

Madge's eyes blurred with tears, remembering her

mother's words. When she blinked them away, the park in front of her was still blurry. A fog was moving in from the harbor. It had already swallowed up the ferry waiting at the dock.

"Funny," Walt said. "It was clear as a bell a minute ago. I could see the Statue of Liberty."

"Didn't Dr. Bean say that this is where they found that spy who killed himself?" Joe asked.

"Look!" Kiku cried. "They're taking my father to the ferry. We'd better hurry or we'll lose them in the fog."

Kiku led the way to the dock, ignoring Joe's pleas to stay farther back. They were only a few feet away when the men disappeared in the fog. Kiku let out a small cry and hurried forward, Madge, Joe, and Walt close at her heels. When the fog lifted, evaporating as quickly as it had descended, the four of them were standing on the dock in front of the ferry. An empty ferry.

SERVICE SUSPENDED DUE TO NATIONAL EMERGENCY read a sign hanging from a chain looped across the gangplank. A lone seaman was sweeping the ferry's deck.

"Hey," Walt called to him. "Did a couple of guys just get on board?"

"A fella in a trench coat, one in a black suit, and a Japanese man," Madge added in case there was any question about what men they were looking for.

The old seaman lifted his grizzled head and peered through rheumy eyes at the four young people. "Ain't no one come aboard and certainly no Jap. The harbor-master closed the ferry on account of the Japs bombing Pearl Harbor." His eyes rested suspiciously on Kiku. But Kiku didn't notice. She was looking around the park. Although there were crowds by the band shell and farther down the pier, this area was deserted.

Her father and his two captors had gone. Vanished with the fog.

7

FISH DREAMS

THEY SEARCHED THE park and even distracted the suspicious seaman long enough for Joe to get on board the ferry and search it, but there was no sign of Mr. Akiyama or his two captors. Finally even Kiku had to admit there was nothing left to do.

"Dr. Bean will know what to do," Walt said. "We'll go to the museum tomorrow. He'll call his friends at the War Department. I-I'll skip school so I can be there too."

The way he said it told Madge that Walt wasn't used to skipping school. Neither was she. If she had skipped at Our Lady of Perpetual Help the nuns would have come round and told her mother, but now that she was at public school she didn't think anyone would notice. "Me too. I bet a lot of kids'll be out, with everyone's fathers and brothers joining up."

"I don't have school," Joe said, "so I'll be there too."

Kiku nodded but made no move to get off the bench

where she sat, shivering in the cold. *She's afraid to go home alone*, Madge thought, remembering how she'd felt going back home after her mother's funeral—and she'd still had her brothers and father.

"Come on," she said, "you'll stay with me. Aunt Jean works the late shift at the diner. She won't even notice you're there."

"That's a good idea," Joe said, giving Madge an approving nod. "I'll meet you all back at the museum tomorrow."

His eyes roved around the park, lighting on a discarded bag of chestnuts. Madge gave Walt a nudge and widened her eyes at him. "Oh!" he said when he understood. "Would you like to come stay with me, Joe? You can have my cousin Ralph's bunk. He's away at college."

Joe looked doubtful, but then Walt added, "Really, you'd be doing me a favor. Aunt Sadie cooks when she's worried. I bet she's made enough kugel, gefilte fish, and blintzes to feed the entire neighborhood. If you don't come and help eat it all, I may die of overstuffing."

"Thank you," Joe said stiffly. "We can talk over our plans tonight." Then he turned to Kiku. "We'll meet at the museum tomorrow. I promise we'll get your father back."

He's just a boy, Madge thought as Joe and Walt turned away to walk to the South Ferry station to catch a train for Brooklyn, *so why do I believe he can find Mr. Akiyama?*

✳ ✳ ✳

Madge and Kiku took the IRT to Aunt Jean's apartment on Eighty-First and Lexington. A couple of toughs made remarks about Kiku on the train, but Madge told them to go soak their heads. Kiku just stared straight ahead of her like she didn't see or hear anything. No one else bothered them for the rest of the ride.

Aunt Jean should have gone to work already, but she was still there, standing at the bathroom mirror, fixing her mascara. Her eyes were red and puffy.

"What is it?" Madge asked, afraid something had happened to one of her brothers.

"Tony's going to enlist tomorrow and he wants to get hitched first."

"Oh," Madge said, wondering which of those two events had made Aunt Jean cry and what the right response would be. *I'm sorry? Congratulations?* Instead she said, "This is my friend Kiku. We're, um, going to do some homework together."

"Sure, kid . . ." Aunt Jean began, turning toward Kiku, who was trying very hard to blend in with the wallpaper. Madge thought Aunt Jean would pop a gasket. *Cause no trouble* definitely didn't include bringing home a Japanese girl the day the Japanese bombed Pearl Harbor. But Aunt Jean only blinked, rubbed her eyes as if she'd gotten a stray eyelash caught in one, and looked back at Madge. "It's been a long day, Margaret, don't fool with me."

Madge stared at her, not sure what she was mad at now. "But I wasn't—"

"Never mind," Aunt Jean said, turning back to the mirror and pinching her cheeks to bring color to them. "There are sandwiches in the icebox and some cannoli Tony brought from the bakery. Clean up after yourself and for Pete's sake, stay out of trouble!"

☆　☆　☆

Kiku loved the Murphy bed. "Every morning I have to fold my futon. This would be so much easier."

They were sitting cross-legged on the pulled-down bed. They'd eaten all the sandwiches and cannoli, both girls surprised that they had any appetite at all, and then Madge suggested they wash and curl each other's hair. "Who knows when we'll have the chance again?"

Kiku looked doubtfully at the rollers and bobby pins, but Madge coaxed her into trying it. They had washed their hair at the kitchen sink and then Madge, her own hair wrapped in a towel turban, sat behind Kiku, combing out her long silky hair. "Look," Madge said, "there's some of that gold paint from the book in your hair. You must have gotten it on you when you were kneeling next to your father."

"It looks pretty," Kiku said, holding her hand up to the light. "I wonder if the boys have it stuck on them too."

Madge snorted. "Walt won't be able to tell with all those freckles. I wonder how they're getting along. They're so different. Joe was awfully brave. . . ."

"So was Walt," Kiku said. "I've seen him at the museum before. He comes every Sunday and draws pictures of the knights. I think he's lonely."

"Well, now he's got Joe for company, and Joe will have something to eat."

Kiku laughed and then covered her mouth, looking embarrassed to be laughing with the world at war. "He did look half starved, but . . ." Her voice had grown somber again. "How long will Walt's family let him stay there? And you certainly won't be able to keep me here. What will happen if I go back to my apartment? Will those men come to take me away, too?"

"We won't let them," Madge said, giving a firm yank with the brush. "You said your father thought Dr. Bean was an honorable man. He'll help your father—and Joe and you. And in return, we'll help the doc find that old book he lost."

"But didn't you say that Dr. Bean didn't want our help—that it was too dangerous?"

"Pshaw," Madge said. "Adults are always saying things like that. What could be dangerous about an old book?"

"So you don't believe it's . . . magic?"

Madge snorted. "If that book's magic, I'm Joan Fontaine." She put down the brush and picked up a magazine. "Here, let's see if we can make me look like her."

✻ ✻ ✻

In Flatbush, Brooklyn, Walt's aunt Sadie was pushing another helping of something she called gefilte fish on Joe. "A big, growing boy like you needs more meat on his bones," she said, pinching Joe's arm.

"Ma," Walt's cousin Rachel said, "he's gonna think you're fattening him up for the pot if you keep poking him like he's a Thanksgiving turkey."

"Yeah, Ma, leave the boy alone," Walt's cousin Ralph said. Ralph had made an unexpected appearance. He wasn't supposed to come home from Harvard until next week, but when he heard the news, he got on the train from Boston because he wanted to join up with his friends from the neighborhood.

"And throw away your scholarship to college!" Aunt Sadie had been crying, one hand pressed to her large bosom, when they'd walked in. "To risk your life? For what? You know how they'll treat a Jewish boy in the army."

"You know how Hitler is treating our cousins in France?" Ralph had countered.

They had all looked guiltily at Walt, and Walt explained to Joe that those cousins were his mother and father. Then Walt introduced Joe as a friend from school whose parents had been called to Washington for "war business."

"*Nu*, he's skin and bones!" Walt's aunt Sadie had cried, pushing Joe into a chair at the food-laden table. When Joe's uncle began to say a prayer in an unfamiliar language, it meant nothing at first, but as he listened, he found the words about being thankful for the food became clear. *How do I understand what it means*? he wondered, but then he took a bite of a blintz and forgot everything but the delight of eating a fresh meal lovingly prepared. He'd never tasted food like this before—a noodle dish with raisins and sweet cheese, a kind of fish that didn't look like it had ever swum, crisp blintzes covered with heavy cream they all called "sour" but that tasted fresh to Joe. The minute Joe finished one dish, Aunt Sadie gave him something else to eat, her eyes shining with happiness at every bite he took.

After dinner, Ralph said he was going out to see some friends. He told Joe he was welcome to his bunk since he didn't plan on getting back until late and he could camp out on the couch. "If I get back at all," he'd added with a wink at Walt.

"I bet he's going to see his sweetheart," Walt said later when they were in their bunks. "Probably all the girls will be going nuts over the guys who are enlisting."

"You sound jealous," Joe said from the upper bunk.

"I am!" Walt admitted. "I wish I was old enough to enlist! Don't you?"

Joe didn't answer right away. He was thinking about how it had felt to hit the principal. He clenched his hands, remembering the impact of knuckles on flesh. It had felt good—and then it had felt bad. And the bad feeling had lasted longer than the good. He rubbed his hands and noticed there were still bits of the gold paint from the book on them. That was what the feeling of hitting the principal had been like, a stain that wouldn't rub off. He wondered if that's what it would feel like to kill a man, maybe many men, in war. How long would that bad feeling last? How hard would it be to get rid of that stain?

Instead of saying all that to Walt, he asked a question. "Hey, what was that gefilte fish we ate, and where do you catch it?"

Walt laughed. "Well, it's not exactly a fish. . . ." Walt went on to explain the intricacies of Jewish home cooking with Joe interjecting questions—"What's kosher?" "Why don't you eat meat at the same meal as dairy?"—until he heard Walt snoring and realized he'd fallen asleep.

It must be nice, Joe thought, *to close your eyes at night and not see the face of the man you may have murdered.*

✳   ✳   ✳

When Joe finally did fall asleep, it wasn't the principal's face waiting for him. It was a grotesque iron mask carved to look like a snarling boar. Ivory tusks curled up from its fanged mouth. The worst part was the glimpse of flesh beneath the blackened metal—the red mouth, the strangely pale eyes. It looked like pieces of a man were trapped inside an iron cage. Even the voice that came out was hollow and booming, as if it came from the bottom of a well.

"I've come to challenge your best knight," it said, "to a contest unto death."

Joe stirred and felt the clash of metal on his own limbs. He knew *he* was the best knight, but it was not a welcome knowledge. Still, he would rise to the challenge, even though there was something wrong about the knight. From behind him came a woman's voice.

"Don't fight him."

"I may not refuse a challenge," Joe heard himself saying. Only his voice was deeper, older. Everything about him was different. Except for one thing: he still carried the memory of striking a man and the knowledge that he would pay for it.

"I will accept your challenge, knight!" he shouted. "May I know the name of him I fight against?"

"You will know it at the moment of your death," the knight replied. And then he sprang forward, faster than a man should be able to move in such heavy armor, swinging his sword in the air. Joe raised his own sword just in time to meet his opponent's. The impact of metal on metal sent a shock through his limbs, but he fought on, meeting the knight blow for blow, all the time with those strange pale eyes locked on his, no matter which way he turned.

Finally, he saw his chance, an opening in the knight's armor just below the edge of his helmet. He swung his sword at it and cleaved the knight's head from his body. The head rolled toward him and came to rest at his feet. He reached down and tore the helmet off. To his horror, the knight's face came off with the helmet, blood and flesh clinging to the iron visor. But even more horrifying, when he looked back down, he saw another face behind the first, grinning up at him—

Joe awoke, gasping in fright. Beneath him he heard Walt murmur, *"Der Mann hat zwei Gesichter."*

Exactly, Joe thought, too sleepy to wonder what Walt was dreaming—or how he'd understood the German for "the man has two faces."

8

AT THE BOTTOM OF A TEAPOT

KIKU WOKE UP in the unfamiliar apartment with a start. The first thing she remembered was why she wasn't home with her father. The second was the awful dream she'd had about two knights fighting. One had worn silver armor and carried a shield with three diagonal stripes on it. The other wore a helmet with a grinning boar's face carved on it. She'd known that there was something wrong with the boar's head knight. She'd begged the knight in silver not to fight him, but he had anyway (*He never listens*, she'd thought in the dream, as if she knew him), and when he had at last defeated the other knight, severed his head, and removed his visor, she'd been horrified to see that there was another face behind the first one.

Ugh! She threw the blankets off as if worms might be crawling on the sheets.

Madge moaned and sat up, curler papers sticking up

all around her head. "Where's the fire?" she complained, rubbing her eyes.

"I'm sorry," Kiku said. "I had a terrible dream."

"You too?" Madge asked, getting up and shuffling over to the icebox. "Must have been the liverwurst. . . . Hey, there aren't any new sandwiches. I wonder if Aunt Jean came back."

While Madge went to check her aunt's room, Kiku got up. She took the curlers out of her hair and saw that it was as straight as ever. She wasn't surprised, but she was a little disappointed. She felt *different*, as if there was something fizzing through her blood. But when she peered at herself in the bathroom mirror, she looked just the same: straight black hair, bangs that were getting a little too long because her mother wasn't around to trim them, plain brown eyes. Her same ordinary face, only after yesterday, it was a face that everyone would stare at. The face of the enemy.

"What did you expect?" she asked the reflection in the mirror. "That you were going to wake up someone different?" She *had* been someone different in the dream.

But that was just a dream.

She rinsed her mouth with tooth powder, washed her face, and dressed. When she came out, Madge was pouring bitter-smelling coffee into two mugs that said SUNNYSIDE DINER on them. Oatmeal was bubbling on the stove.

"Aunt Jean didn't come home last night, so I figured,

what the heck, I'd cook us some breakfast. I hope coffee's all right. We're out of tea."

Madge was talking fast, moving around the tiny kitchen, avoiding Kiku's eyes. *Maybe she's sorry she invited me to stay*, Kiku thought. Trying to keep out of the way, she went over to make the bed, but Madge came over and pushed the bed up against the wall, jamming all the sheets and blankets in higgledy-piggledy.

"What difference does it make?" she asked. "There's no one here to care."

*　　*　　*

The museum didn't open until ten, but Kiku had the key to the staff entrance. "My father always let me carry it," she told Madge. "He said it was to teach me responsibility, but now I wonder if he worried that he might be taken and I would need it."

The staff entrance was in the basement. She led Madge through a maze of corridors, and Madge stopped to peer in the little glass windows in each door even though they were all dark.

"Jeez Louise, this place is as big downstairs as it is upstairs. What's in all these rooms?"

"Mostly storage for holdings that aren't on display. The museum owns far more than it can exhibit at one time. There are workrooms and offices, too, for different curators, but no one seems to be in yet. I suppose everyone's still stunned at the war news. I hope Dr. Bean is in."

When she opened the door to the last corridor, she saw that the door to the Arms and Armor workroom was wide open.

"Oh good," Madge said, going on ahead. "Dr. Bean must be here."

Kiku stood in the hall, halted by a feeling that something was wrong. Dr. Bean never left his door wide open like that.

A cry from Madge made her run down the hall, where she found her standing in the middle of an utterly transformed workroom. The table and chairs lay on the floor with their legs up in the air like a bunch of dead sheep. Tapestries had been torn from the wall. The armor was piled in heaps—breastplates, greaves, gauntlets, and visors strewn around the room like body parts from some horrible massacre. Pages from the drowned book and what looked like pieces of today's *New York Times* floated over it all like ashes over a bonfire. Kiku knelt to pick up one of the pages and found that it wasn't paper—it was a silk scarf. A white silk scarf with the monogram **VdL** stitched in blue.

"It's Miss Lake's," Kiku said.

"Holy smokes!" a voice declared from the doorway. "What happened here?"

Kiku looked to the doorway and saw Walt and Joe.

"The real question," she said, holding up the scarf so they could all see the spot of blood on it, "is what happened to Dr. Bean and Miss Lake!"

✳︎　✳︎　✳︎

"Quick!" Madge said. "Get in here and close the door."

"I think it's a little late to close the door," Walt pointed out, following Madge's directions nonetheless. He was looking sadly at the piles of armor that yesterday had been arrayed so neatly along the shelves. "Who would do this?" he asked.

"Mr. January, of course," Madge said. "He must've come back looking for something."

"But what?" Walt asked.

"The message that was taken from the spy," Joe said. "If Mr. January found out his spy was dead, he'd want to get his message back before anyone could decode it and find out about the sabotage plot."

"How would he know Dr. Bean had it?" Kiku asked. She had begun sorting through the chaos of broken armor. Miss Lake always kept it all neat and polished. She would be devastated to see it like this—but then she thought of the spot of blood on Miss Lake's scarf and was afraid that Miss Lake might never see the workroom again. *I won't let that happen*, a voice inside her head said. She shook her head to clear away the unfamiliar voice and focused on what Joe was saying as he knelt to help her.

"Maybe someone at the museum overheard us talking yesterday."

"Or in the taxi," Madge suggested. "Here—let's get the table righted and these shelves up."

"Wait," Walt said. "Shouldn't we be calling the police before touching any of this?"

"And tell them what?" Joe asked. "That a man in a trench coat, who we saw disappear in a fog, broke in here to find a message from a Nazi spy that's been encoded using a magical book?"

"They'd never believe us," Kiku said. "And they'd arrest me."

"And me," Joe said, helping Walt to flip over his end of the table. "But if you two"—he nodded to Madge and Walt—"want to go to the police, then you should do what you think is right. Just give me a chance to clear off."

"Yes," Kiku said. "I, too, would like time to . . . *clear off.*"

"Oh, for Pete's sake!" Madge cried. "No one's clearing off. We're in this business together, right?"

"Yes, but . . ." Walt turned so white, his freckles stood out like spots of blood. "If we don't tell the police, who's going to stop the attack on New York?"

The four of them stood staring at one another across the chaos of scattered armor. For a moment, Kiku had an idea she'd stood like this before, looking at her friends across a battlefield strewn with weapons and pieces of armor . . . *and the bodies of the dead and dying.* She shuddered at the image.

"We are," Madge said. "We're going to stop the attack on New York."

"But how?" Kiku demanded. "We don't have the message. We don't have *anything.*" She bit her lip to keep from crying, but Madge must have seen the tears in her eyes, because she pulled a handkerchief out of her coat pocket. As she passed it to Kiku, something fell out of it—a piece of paper folded into the shape of a bird. It fluttered toward the floor. As she watched it fall, Kiku remembered the paper airplanes they'd seen yesterday and the messages written on them.

"Hey," Madge said, reaching for the paper bird.

But Kiku had already caught it. "It's an origami crane," she said. "I taught Miss Lake how to make them. I think it has writing on it."

"Open it up," Walt said.

Kiku unfolded the crane with trembling fingers.

"It's the spy's message!" Walt cried. "She gave it to you, Madge!"

"Did she say anything when she gave it to you?" Joe asked.

"Only that I would need it," Madge said. "I thought she meant to blow my nose."

Walt laughed, but then looked stricken. "She must have known that Mr. January would come for it. And that she and Dr. Bean would be taken—"

"And that they'd take my father too." Kiku's eyes widened. "My father hasn't been taken to Ellis Island— he's been kidnapped. Just like Dr. Bean and Miss Lake!"

"She must have been afraid that might happen, too," Walt said. "So she gave the message to Madge for safe-keeping."

"So we could decode the rest of it," Joe said.

"But we need the book for that," Kiku said. "And it's hidden."

"Miss Lake said that Sir Peanut Brittle guy left clues," Madge said, still staring at the spy's letter. "But we don't have the clues."

"Are you sure she didn't give you anything else?" Walt asked.

Madge emptied her pockets. She had three gum wrappers, a broken pencil stub, a brass button, and a buffalo nickel, but no other piece of paper from Miss Lake. Walt examined the handkerchief for writing, but there was only Miss Lake's initials—**VdL**.

"She must not have had time to give the clues to you," Kiku said. "Which means . . ."

"They're still here somewhere," Joe said, looking around at the disordered workroom.

"Unless Mr. January found them," Madge said.

"No," Kiku said. "Miss Lake would have hidden them. She knew we'd come looking for them after Madge found the letter in her pocket."

"You're right," Walt said. "*She* thought we were the ones meant to find the book—that we're the knights in the story even if we are just kids."

"I don't know about us being knights—" Madge began, but Kiku, thinking of that image she'd had of the four of them standing on the battlefield, heard the voice in her head: *You have to make them believe.*

But how? she thought, but she was already opening her mouth to speak. "If Miss Lake believed we're the knights, then that's good enough for me." She looked around at the others and they each nodded, even Madge, who said, "Then what are we doing standing here gawping at each other? Let's start looking!"

✻   ✻   ✻

They spent the morning sorting through the mess. Kiku said that they might as well try to put it back the way it belonged, in case anyone came down looking for Dr. Bean, and Walt eagerly revealed that he had practically memorized where everything went.

"You must have an eidetic memory," Kiku said.

"Yeah, I've got an I-get-it memory too," Madge said. "Tell me something once and I get the picture. But something about this picture isn't adding up."

They had reassembled the shelves and put back each piece of armor, looking inside every joint and hinge for loose paper. They'd felt under the torn tapestry linings and hung them back on the walls. They'd gone through Dr. Bean's drawers and found a box full of keys.

"Gee," Kiku said, "Dr. Bean's got keys for every gallery and display case in the museum."

"Ha!" Madge laughed. "The doc's a sly one. I bet he and Miss Lake had them so they could search the museum for this darn book. Those might come in handy."

They'd tried to move the anvil to look underneath it, but when the four of them couldn't budge it, they figured no one else could have. Joe had thumped the walls looking for hollow hiding places. They had tested sword hilts to see if they unscrewed, and peered inside helmets—Walt getting one stuck on his head for a claustrophobic moment—for secret compartments, but the only paper they'd found in the whole room was the shreds of the water-ruined book, a torn-up newspaper, and a ledger Miss Lake kept of repairs and their costs. They had gone through each page, holding the paper up to the light for invisible writing. Walt suggested applying lemon juice to the ledger, but he couldn't find any in the alcove where Miss Lake kept the tea things.

"What about those cookies" Madge asked.

"You think the clue is in the cookies?" Walt asked.

"Nah, but I'm starving. I'd murder a cup of tea."

"What did Miss Lake say?" Kiku mused. "That the

solution to all life's problems could be found at the bottom of a teapot. . . ."

Kiku's eyes widened and met Madge's equally wide eyes.

"It couldn't be," Joe said. "It's too obvious. Wouldn't they have looked?"

Walt had already lifted the heavy glazed teapot off the shelf in the alcove. "At least they didn't break it," he said, putting it down on the table. They all leaned toward the teapot, but no one made a move to take off the lid.

It's because there's nowhere else to look after this, Kiku thought. *And if it's not there, we'll have to admit that we can't find the clues, and if we admit that, we'll know we're not the ones meant to find the book. That Dr. Bean was right. We're only children.*

She needed to believe she could be someone other than the girl everyone saw when they looked at her, but she wondered why it was so important to the others. Of course Walt needed to find that spy after all he had seen in Germany, and Joe—well, anyone with eyes to see could tell he was running from something and if he couldn't stop here, he'd have to keep on running. But why was it so important to Madge?

Then she remembered how disgruntled Madge had been this morning when she'd found out her aunt Jean hadn't come home. For all her brave talk, Madge was afraid that the magic wouldn't turn out to be real.

She needs it more than any of us, the voice in her head said.

"Here," Kiku said. "I'll look—"

As she put her hand on the teapot, Madge reached out and laid her hand on top of hers and then Walt put his hand on hers and Joe rested his on top of all of theirs.

Why, it's warm, Kiku thought. As if it were full of tea. It even smelled like the *sencha* her mother liked.

"It smells like the Barry's Breakfast tea my mother used to make," Madge said.

"Huh," Walt said. "I think it smells like the honey my grandmother used to stir into her glass of tea."

"It smells like the sweetgrass my grandmother uses to weave her baskets," Joe said as he lifted the lid.

"There's something in there!" Kiku cried.

"A rolled-up piece of paper!" Walt said.

Kiku reached her hand into the pot and drew out a slim scroll no bigger than a cigarette. It was tied with twine. She picked the knot apart, amazed that her fingers weren't shaking. *It could still be all a sham—*

But when she unrolled the scroll and read the first line, she knew it wasn't.

9

TWO-FACED

SEEING THE LOOK on Kiku's face, Joe took the paper out of her hands and read aloud: "'The story of the Two-Faced Knight is the first chapter of our heroes' adventure.'"

"The Two-Faced Knight," Walt repeated. "I dreamed about a two-faced knight last night. When his helmet came off . . ."

"His face came with it," Madge said, shuddering.

"And there was another face beneath it," Kiku said, "that grinned up at the knight who killed him."

"That was me. I was the knight who slew him," Joe said. Then he felt his face go hot. It sounded like he was bragging, like he thought he was a knight. "I mean . . . it was me in the dream."

They were all staring at him, but then he realized it wasn't because they thought he was bragging.

"We all had the same dream," Walt said. "Just like we all dreamed about Mr. January."

"What does it mean?" Kiku asked.

"I think it has something to do with the book," Madge said.

"You mean you don't think it's just a bunch of malarkey?" Walt asked.

Madge shook her head. "Not anymore. When I was watching the knights fighting, it felt . . . *real*. Like something I had lived through. And when the silver knight slew the Two-Faced Knight, I felt relieved." She turned to face Joe. "But that's not how it felt to you, did it?"

Joe looked down, ashamed. How did she know that killing the Two-Faced Knight in the dream had felt like striking the principal all over again? Could they all see the stain of that, like the gold dust that still clung to his hands?

Madge startled him by touching his hand. "I think it's because of the gold dust. It's on my hands too. Maybe it's how the book works its magic on the people who read it. I think it's made us all have the same dream—"

"We all dreamed about Mr. January before we touched the gold dust."

"True," Kiku said, "So we must have been connected somehow even then because we were all called by the book."

"But now the gold paint is making the connection stronger," Madge said, "like we're becoming the people in the book. Joe was the knight with the diagonal-striped shield—"

"That's Lancelot's shield!" Walt said excitedly. "Does that mean Joe is Lancelot?"

"I'm nothing like Lancelot," Joe said. "He was a brave knight who went around saving people and I . . . I . . ." He hesitated. "I hit the principal because he was beating my sister Jeanette."

"That sounds just like the sort of thing Lancelot would do," Walt said.

"But then I ran," Joe said, fighting back tears. "And I left Jeanette in the Mush Hole. That's not something Lancelot would do."

"Lancelot wasn't thirteen," Kiku said. "And I'm sure your sister didn't want you to stay and get in trouble. I'm sure she's fine."

"Yeah," Madge said. "And when we find Dr. Bean, I bet he'll be able to talk to your school to make sure."

Joe nodded, grateful for their assurances, but none of them knew how bad the Mush Hole was. "We should probably read the clue before we worry about who's who," he said. He looked down at the paper in his hands and read it out loud.

The story of the Two-Faced Knight is the first chapter of our heroes' adventure. A fitting place to start, for who amongst us is not two-faced? One face we present to the world, the other we keep to ourselves. But if we never show our true face, we will never see the truth

in others. Only the true of heart may set out on this
road, so the first chapter lies in a place where only the
truthful dare go.

Joe stopped and turned the paper over to make
sure there was nothing on the other side.

"Is that it?" Walt asked. "No wonder Dr. Bean and
Miss Lake couldn't figure it out. It doesn't tell us where
the first part of the book is at all!"

"It's a clue," Joe said. "We have to figure out the place
where only the truthful dare go."

"Like the confessional," Madge said. "Maybe we're
supposed to look in a church."

"But Sir Bricklebank hid the book in the museum,"
Kiku said. "There's lots of religious art in the museum,
but I don't think there's a confessional."

"What about a Bible?" Joe said. "People put their
hand on the Bible to swear to tell the truth."

"I suppose. Are there Bibles in the museum?" Madge
asked Kiku.

"I think so. We'll have to look through each one."

"There are other things that people swear truth by,"
Walt said. "In a book of Norse myths I read once, the heroes swear by a drinking cup called a *bragarfull*."

"All right," Madge said, "we'll look at all the beer
mugs and Bibles. Jeez Louise, I wish Sir Peanut Brittle
had drawn a map."

"Kiku knows the museum well enough," Joe said. He wanted to let Kiku know that he was grateful for what she'd said about Jeanette, but when he looked at her, he saw that all the color had drained from her face. She was staring at a scrap of newspaper she'd picked up from the floor.

"What's the matter?" he asked.

Kiku shook her head and handed Joe the scrap of newspaper.

"What is it?" Madge asked, craning her neck to read over Joe's shoulder.

"Read it to them," Kiku said. "They should know."

"It says"—Joe cleared his throat—"that *Mayor La Guardia directed that Japanese nationals be confined to their homes pending decision as to their status . . . 2,500 Japanese nationals living in New York, some of whom are Japanese who were born in the United States, to be taken into custody* and that . . ." He hesitated, but Kiku nodded for him to go on. ". . . *the Public Safety Director of Newark ordered policemen to board all trains in Newark and to take into custody 'all suspicious persons of Oriental character.'*"

"So you see," Kiku said, her face so pale she nearly faded into the whitewashed wall behind her, "I can't really help you look for the book. Maybe . . . maybe I should just go home." She faltered. *Because she has no home to go to*, a voice said inside Joe's head.

"You can't," Walt said. "We've got to do this together or not at all. All for one . . ."

"One for all," Joe finished for him. One of his teachers—who hadn't lasted long—had read to them from *The Three Musketeers.* "Walt's right. We're all in this together."

"Yeah," Madge said, looking uncomfortable, "but maybe you should stay down here and tell us where to look."

Kiku nodded. "That's a good idea. I'll plan out where to search. I've got some maps of the museum and catalogues of the exhibits in my father's office. I'll get them and come back here." She smiled, but it wasn't a real smile. She looked like Jeanette had when she would try to please the teachers. Joe thought of what the clue had said. *One face we present to the world, the other we keep to ourselves. But if we never show our true face, we will never see the truth in others.*

"I'll stay here with Kiku and run messages back and forth," he said. "That's what I'm best at anyway. Running."

10

THE EGYPTIAN BOY

"DO YOU THINK Joe and Kiku are mad at us?" Walt asked as they walked around the Egyptian gallery. They had decided to go through each of the galleries looking for items that had something to do with truth telling and that had an opening that could be reached into. Walt had out his notebook to write down objects that looked promising. He had devised a rating system based on size, openings, and cultural lore relating to lie detection.

Madge's method was slightly different. She had already stuck her hand into a canopic jar (*You know they kept organs in that*, Walt had pointed out) and now she had her head in a sarcophagus. Walt's question was partly to get her to take her head out before the guard saw her. But also he felt bad about leaving Kiku and Joe behind in the workroom.

"Why should they be?" Madge asked, her voice echoing inside the sarcophagus. "It's not our fault the Japanese bombed Pearl Harbor."

"No, but it's not Kiku's fault either, and I feel like we should be standing by her more. You know, to show we don't think it's fair to round up people just because they're Japanese."

"But some of those people could be spies," Madge said, batting a cobweb out of her hair. "They could even be part of Mr. January's group who are planning to attack New York."

"But a lot of them are probably innocent people like Mr. Akiyama and Kiku. It just doesn't seem fair."

They had stopped in front of a painting of a young boy with dark liquid eyes that reminded Walt of someone. "News flash, kiddo," Madge said, "the world isn't fair. Not everyone is your friend. I'd think you of all people would know that. And that you'd want anyone connected with Hitler rounded up and put away where they can't do any harm."

"Yes, but it reminds me of how the Jews were treated in Germany," Walt said, looking at the boy's dark brown eyes to avoid looking at Madge. "First they said we couldn't have jobs in the civil service and universities, then we couldn't be citizens. Then they rounded up 'enemies of the state.' No one spoke up for us or tried to stop it. I . . ." Walt felt his face go red, and he looked away from the painting. He'd realized who it reminded him of. "A boy I went to school with before I was kicked out said, 'Don't worry, it won't be so bad. They're just putting you someplace together to be safe.' *Safe from what?*

I wondered. That's when my parents got me on the Kindertransport list to be taken out of Germany. So I'd be safe. My mother wrote a few months later that they had managed to get to France, where they were supposed to be safe, but then the Nazis invaded France. I haven't heard from them in three months, and I'm beginning to suspect that they're not *safe* at all."

"But that's completely different," Madge said. "We're not Nazis. We won't hurt those people. And if they're really not spies, I'm sure they'll be A-okay."

"Maybe," Walt said. People acted differently when they felt threatened. He remembered how the old shopkeeper on the corner who used to smile at him and give him free candy had stopped looking at him. "Still, I feel weird that Kiku has to stay downstairs while we're up here. I guess the least we can do is find this thing for her. And I don't think it's here. I'm going to go check out the Roman art. They were big on swearing the truth. Are you coming?"

Walt walked away quickly, hoping Madge wouldn't see that his eyes were filling with tears. She had nearly caught up with him in the Great Hall when a voice shouted at them. "You two *chill*-drun! Stop!"

The sharp bark sounded like the German soldiers when they ordered someone to halt in the street. He'd seen an old man who hadn't stopped get shot in the head. Madge grabbed his arm and tried to pull him toward the columns on the south side of the hall, but

Walt couldn't move. He stood frozen as Miss Fitzbane marched toward them, the heels of her alligator shoes going off like the gunshots that had killed that old man, her bulging girdle swishing like an angry cat's tail behind her.

"Just follow my lead," Madge whispered. *What in the world does she mean?* Walt wondered, staring at the sweet smile on Madge's face as she beamed up at the head of security. "Hello, Miss Fitzbane, how nice of you to remember us."

"What are you doing here?" Miss Fitzbane demanded, the light flashing off her round glasses making her look like Professor Strange in the Batman comics. "Why aren't you in school?"

"Canceled," Madge replied quickly, giving Walt's arm a pinch. "So we could be with our families and pray for our country in its time of need."

"Neither of which do you appear to be doing." She focused on Walt. "What about you, boy, do you have a tongue in your head?"

"Um, well, I . . ."

"Walt's family is in France, so he could hardly be with them. He wanted to come here because it's where he feels most peaceful. Isn't that so, Walt?"

Walt stared at Madge. "Actually . . . yes."

"Plus we wanted to check in with Dr. Bean to see if everything was hunky-dory after what happened yesterday."

"And did you find Dr. Bean? I haven't seen him yet today."

"He's gone to talk to his friends at the FBI about getting poor Mr. Akiyama released," Madge said. "But he asked us to help him with a special project at the museum—a scavenger hunt." Madge nudged Walt and plucked his notebook out of his hands. "We're making notes on it now. Doc thinks it will help keep kids' minds off the war."

"And have *chill*-drun running helter-skelter all over the museum, no doubt. I'll have to have a word with him."

Miss Fitzbane was turning toward the north galleries, but Madge slid in front of her. "Like I said, the doc's not here."

"I will leave him a note in his office," she said, plucking an enormous ring of keys from the alligator handbag on her arm. "And make sure all is *hunky-dory*, as you put it."

She sidestepped around Madge and started off toward the north galleries. "What'll we do?" Walt whispered. "If she finds Kiku and Joe in there . . ."

"You go head off Miss Fishbone and delay her. I'm going to go through the basement and warn them."

Madge took off toward a staircase on the southwest side of the hall, leaving Walt to head off the indomitable and scary Miss Fitzbane. That was something that Madge—fairly indomitable and a little scary herself—

would be much better at. How those stories had flown from her lips! What a spy she would make! Why had she trusted him with this job? It was clear that she thought he was a naïve boy—*News flash, kiddo!*—and then he'd gone on about all the bad things in Germany.

He'd never told anyone about that because it embarrassed him that he'd done nothing. He remembered when they came to take Jacob Goldblatt's father. Jacob Goldblatt had been his best friend, but Walt had hidden in a wardrobe when he'd heard the soldiers marching down their street. Afterward, he had seen Jacob crying on the stairs and he hadn't gone up and comforted him because he was afraid that if people saw them together the Nazis might come and take *his* father away. That's who the Egyptian boy had reminded him of—Jacob Goldblatt staring out at him through those ancient brown eyes. Well, he'd failed Jacob. He wasn't going to fail Madge and Joe and Kiku.

"Uh, Miss Fitzbane!" he squawked when he'd caught up to her—which happened to be right next to the portrait of the Egyptian boy who looked like Jacob. She turned around, her skirt hissing, and glared at him.

"What is it, young man? I don't have all day."

He opened his mouth, willing a story to come to his lips the way they came to Madge's, but those shiny round glasses seemed to mesmerize him into silence.

Miss Fitzbane clucked her tongue impatiently. "Are

you trying to catch flies or do you have something to say?"

Walt gulped. He could feel the blood rising to his face. Why was it always so hard for him to speak up when he most needed to? He looked away from Miss Fitzbane into the eyes of the Egyptian boy.

It's because you want everyone to like you, a voice inside his head said. What the heck did that mean? He looked back at Miss Fitzbane and noticed her name tag for the first time. HEAD OF SECURITY, it read beneath her name.

"This must be a difficult time for you," Walt said. "I mean, making sure the museum is safe now that we're at war."

"You have no idea," Miss Fitzbane snapped. "Three of our night guards quit today to enlist! Who's going to protect all this?" She held up her long bony hands to indicate the statues and sarcophagi. "And where am I going to find replacements when every able-bodied man is running off to war? It's an enormous responsibility."

Walt whistled. "Jeez Louise—" That's what Madge would say. "I bet! But I notice you're always down here. I bet the director stays up in his office."

"Well, yes," she sniffed, touching the pin on her lapel. It was a weird pin shaped like a lizard with wings and with a human head at the end of its tail. It gave Walt the creeps. So did looking at her glasses. They seemed always to catch the light so you couldn't see her eyes. "That's only befitting his dignity. I like to keep . . . an *eye* on things." When she said *eye*, her hips twitched, and Walt got the queasy feeling she had eyes back there. *Yech!*

"I'm here every Sunday, you know, and I've seen you prowling—I mean patrolling the galleries," he said.

"Well, I have to." She leaned closer to Walt. Her breath smelled like the dead mice he threw out for Aunt Sadie when they got caught in a trap. "You'd be surprised at how many guards I find napping. . . ." Miss Fitzbane went on to outline the grave security risks to the museum, from sleeping guards to unlocked exit doors. Unfortunately the unlocked exit door led her back to the subject of Dashwood Bean. "He has been known to disable the alarm and prop the door open to smoke his pipe!" she exclaimed. "I'll add that to the note I plan to leave him."

She was off again, alligator shoes clicking through the Egyptian galleries toward the Arms and Armor gallery and down the stairs. Walt could only follow, hoping that Madge had had time to warn Kiku and Joe. At the foot of the stairs, Walt thought he glimpsed a door closing in the hallway. He opened his mouth, and Miss Fitzbane wheeled on him as if she'd seen him.

"Catching flies again, boy?" she demanded. "Civilians—especially *chill*-drun—are not allowed in this section of the basement."

"I-I just wanted another look at the workroom," Walt stammered. "Dr. Bean said he'd give me a tour."

"Well, you'll just have to wait." Miss Fitzbane was

sorting through the keys on her enormous ring. Had they had time to get out? Would Miss Fitzbane notice anything amiss about the workroom? Had they put back everything in its right place?

Miss Fitzbane opened the door and flicked on an overhead light. The workroom was empty, the tabletop bare except for a piece of paper held down by a medieval dagger. Walt thought he could still detect the aroma of honey and tea he'd smelled earlier, but Miss Fitzbane didn't seem to notice. She picked up the note. Walt read over her shoulder.

To whom it may concern,

I will be out today, attending to matters of the gravest national security. Miss Lake has accompanied me. Please refer any questions to my new assistant, Miss Margaret McGrory (who has been kind enough to take this note down from my dictation in her excellent hand).

Sincerely,

Dr. Dashwood Bean,
Esquire

"Assistant?" Miss Fitzbane sniffed. "We'll see about that!" She sniffed again. "What is that smell?"

Walt shook his head. "I don't smell anything."

"Humph. Well, tell your friend Miss McGrorrrr-y

that she shouldn't expect a salary. I've heard the girls in accounting saying that Dr. Bean is far over budget."

She shooed Walt out the door, but paused behind him on the threshold, hips twitching, glasses flashing as she scanned the workroom suspiciously. When her eyes came to rest on Walt, he felt a chill run up his spine, but she only sniffed at him, as if she suspected he was the source of the peculiar odor in the room, and locked the door behind them.

✫　✫　✫

Walt had to follow Miss Fitzbane back upstairs, but as soon as she left the Arms and Armor gallery, he ran back downstairs and knocked lightly on the door he'd glimpsed closing before. "Hey, guys," he whispered, "the coast is clear."

The door behind him opened and three faces peered out. "Is she gone?" Madge whispered—at least she tried to whisper. She had a carrying voice that could have been heard as far as Fifth Avenue.

Walt nodded and they all came down the hall. Joe was carrying a stack of books; Madge balanced four teacups and saucers. Kiku unlocked the door to the Arms and Armor workroom.

"Phew! That was close," Madge said, collapsing in a chair. "Did she buy my note?"

"I think so," Walt said, looking at the books Joe was

laying out on the table. They were museum catalogues and guides to the exhibits. "She said not to expect a salary."

"We'll see about that," Madge said, grinning. Then she slapped Walt's arm. "Good diversionary tactics, Freckles. How'd ya do it?"

"I asked her about security precautions for the museum—Hey, did you know that three of the night guards quit to enlist?"

"Hm," Kiku said, rattling the keys in the box they'd found in Dr. Bean's desk. "That will make it easier for us to sneak around when we go get the first chapter."

"You know where it is?" Walt asked.

"Kiku's figured it out!" Joe said, beaming at her. "She knows where the first chapter is hidden."

"Well, I don't *know*," she said, blushing. "But I have an idea. I was looking through the Greek and Roman collections because they were always swearing to the truth."

"Hey, that's what Freckles was saying," Madge said. "We were on our way over there when we ran into Miss Fishbone."

"It's just as well you were delayed. There are some things you should know about this statue before anyone tries to get the chapter out of it." Kiku slid a catalogue across the table for Walt and Madge to see. It was open to a page showing a black-and-white photo of a lion carved out of marble. Its mouth was wide open in a menacing snarl.

"Jeepers, he looks angry!" Madge said.

"*She,*" Kiku corrected her. "She's a lioness, made in Greece around 400 BC. But she was found in a Roman ruin in Great Britain. They think she was meant to guard a tomb. There's a superstition about her . . ." Kiku hesitated.

"Go on, tell them," Joe urged her. "They ought to know."

"It's something Sir Bricklebank once told me. I thought it was just one of his fanciful stories, but then there was the incident . . . and now that we know he hid the book in the museum, I figure it might be important . . ."

"Go ahead and spill it!" Madge cried, fidgeting with impatience.

"Well . . . it was believed that if you put your hand in the lion's mouth and told a lie, the lion would come to life and bite your hand off."

"Holy moly! Why would anyone chance it?" Madge asked, looking with terror at the open mouth. "I wouldn't put my hand in that thing on a bet."

"I guess the threat was enough to make anyone afraid to lie. There's a legend that a Roman centurion put his hand in it to swear his loyalty to the Emperor and he took out a bloody stump."

"Holy smokes!" Walt said, his eyes wide. "And you think this is where Sir Bricklebank hid the first chapter?"

"It makes sense. It's certainly worth a try. Only the Greek and Roman gallery is near the information desk in the Great Hall, where Miss Fitzbane sits during the day, and I'm afraid she's already suspicious of us."

"We should wait until night," Joe said.

"You mean stay here after the museum is closed?" Walt asked, his eyes widening. "But isn't that against the law?"

"So is poking around ancient artifacts, I suppose," Madge said. "But what about the guards?"

"Walt just said that three of them quit," Kiku said. "That leaves only two and it will be Jenkins and Carson, the two oldest guards. On nights I stayed here with my father I noticed that they usually spent the night playing pinochle or taking turns napping. It won't be hard to avoid them. And the only other curators who stay late are Dr. Bean—who's not here—and Monsieur Dupin, curator of European Sculpture and Decorative Arts. He spends his time in Marie Antoinette's bed."

"In *what*?" Madge asked.

Kiku smiled. "Well, it's not *really* Marie Antoinette's bed, but it is of the same period. He thinks he's her reincarnation. He's a little . . . eccentric. He won't give us any trouble."

"Well, then," Joe said, "it's settled. We'll stay the night. Of course, if you two have to get home . . ."

"My aunt Jean won't notice I'm gone," Madge said— with a trace of bitterness, Walt noticed.

"My aunt Sadie will, but I can run home and sneak out. I'm not going to miss seeing the Lion of Truth! But what was the incident you were talking about, with the statue?"

"Oh," Kiku said, "a little boy stuck his hand in it and said it bit him. The parents sued the museum because . . . well, the tip of his pinkie had been cut off."

11

THE LION OF TRUTH

MADGE THOUGHT SHE should go home just in case Aunt Jean decided to put in an appearance. She found a note toothpicked to a tray of sandwiches in the icebox.

Gone to Niagara Falls with Tony to get hitched! Be back Friday. Lois will meet you at the diner back door to give you leftovers. Wish me luck! XOXO Jean

PS Stay out of trouble!!!

"Meet me at the back door," Madge muttered, slamming the icebox. "Like I'm an alley cat or a tramp!"

She opened the icebox again and took out half a sandwich and a half-full bottle of milk. She sat chewing a liverwurst on rye without tasting it and then washed it down with the milk. When she was done, she left the unwashed milk bottle and a plate full of crumbs on the counter.

"What the heck!" she said out loud. "There's no one here to notice."

She went into Aunt Jean's room and tried on her face powder, which made her sneeze, and then went through her closet looking for something she could wear tonight that would make her feel like a proper spy. Like Madeleine Carroll in *Secret Agent*. In the front of Aunt Jean's closet were her extra waitress uniforms and the two good dresses she wore when Tony took her out to the movies on her nights off. Behind that row were silk dresses and scarves that Madge had never seen her aunt wear. She remembered, though, that Aunt Jean used to dance in vaudeville. When Madge was little, they'd sometimes go to New Haven to see her in a preview. Her mother told her once that Jean had lived in Greenwich Village with "the bohemians." That must've been when she wore the high-waisted trousers Madge found at the back of the closet. Well, Jean wouldn't miss them now that she was marrying Tony.

Madge put on the trousers and found that not only did they fit but they made her instantly feel more grown up. She practiced strutting around the apartment in them, hands in her pockets. She felt swell. She added a wool sweater, a navy peacoat that belonged to Frankie, and a tam-o'-shanter her mother had knitted for her that she pulled low over one eye. She gave herself a once-over in the mirror. She looked like a girl who could take care of herself, which was just as well, since apparently no one else was going to.

*   *   *

Joe stood behind the museum waiting for Madge's arrival and watching the shadows that lurked outside the circle of light from the lone streetlamp. He'd spent enough time in the park to know that even though he didn't see anyone that didn't mean there wasn't anyone hiding in the trees or brush. Or that every birdcall was made by a bird.

The men who lived in the park had their ways of moving through the woods without a sound and communicating with one another. Joe had learned about the signs they used the first time he'd hopped a train outside of Buffalo. The hoboes didn't care that he was running away from the Mush Hole or that he'd hit the principal. They were all running from something they weren't proud of. They taught Joe the language of hobo signs—symbols scratched in the paint of a fence or carved into trees that told a man which houses to ask for a handout and which to avoid, where it was safe to make camp, where there was a policeman or train guard who had it out for tramps. Following the signs had felt a little like walking in the woods with his *Tóta*, the way she would show him where a deer had lain down in the grass, where the ruffed grouse burrowed into the snow for warmth, and where to find the best berries in summer. It had made him feel like if he could just get home, he might someday learn his own language again.

He heard a rustling noise coming from the bushes near the tall stone spear that rose out of the trees. Kiku had told him that it was called Cleopatra's Needle, although it didn't look anything like the needle his *Tóta* used to mend his clothes. There were figures carved into it that looked like the pictures on the big stone coffins in the Egyptian wing of the museum. At the top was a row of birds wearing some kind of hats. Joe could almost figure out what the signs meant, but then he heard the rustle again and a stomping noise that reminded him of how the grouse sounded when they beat their wings to attract a mate in spring.

Thump . . . thump . . . thump . . .

Suddenly he remembered that this was where the name of his home came from—Akwesasne—the land where the ruffed grouse drums. The word unlocked a part of Joe's brain where other words waited: *niáwenhkó:wa*, which was how you thanked someone and *Katsi tsienhá:wi*, which meant "she is carrying flowers" and was his *Tóta*'s Mohawk name. He remembered how he used to say, "*Konorónkhwa, Tóta*" as he went off to bed. It meant "I love you." And she would answer, "*Konorónkhwa . . .*" and then she would say his full name. Joe whispered "*Konorónkhwa, Tóta*" at the memory. He could almost hear his grandmother answering and saying his name when someone jumped out of the bush and yelled, "Boo!"

Joe turned to find Madge standing behind him. She was carrying a large paper bag.

"Boo yourself," he said. "I could hear you a mile away. No one ever taught you to walk quietly, did they?"

"Why would they?" Madge asked.

"In the Mush Hole, we'd sneak down to the kitchen at night to get food. We'd go barefoot so the teachers wouldn't hear us."

They both looked down at their feet. Joe was wearing the soft leather moccasins that his grandmother had made for him. He'd hidden them outside the school before he went back the last time. They were the only thing he'd taken with him when he ran away. Madge was wearing hard-soled saddle shoes. After he unlocked the door using the key Kiku had found and followed Madge into the museum, he saw that the sound they made came from a loose sole.

"I could sew that for you," Joe offered. "I noticed there were some thick needles in the workroom."

"That would be swell," Madge said, and then in a lower voice, "Hey, can I ask you something?"

"Sure," Joe said, surprised that brazen Madge would be so hesitant.

"You've been on your own for a while, right?"

Joe nodded. It had only been a few weeks since he'd

left the Mush Hole, but it felt like a lifetime.

"Well . . . do you get used to it? I mean . . . do you miss having someone waiting for you to get home from school and sewing your buttons on and all that stuff?"

Joe stared at her, thinking about how a few minutes ago he'd been on the edge of tears just remembering his *Tóta*'s name. "I think it's something you could get used to," he said, thinking of the hard eyes of the tramps he'd met in boxcars and camps, "but I don't think I'd *want* to get used to it. And we won't have to. We've got each other now. That's part of reading the book together—it means we'll look out for each other." He poked the hole in her coat where a button had fallen off. "I can sew that for you, too."

"Thanks, Joe," Madge said, blushing. "And I've got something for you." She handed him the paper bag she was carrying. Joe unfolded a thick wool peacoat and a knit cap. "They're from when my dad was in the navy, but he's not home to use them. You can't walk around New York in that thin jacket."

Joe thanked her as he put on the coat.

"What does *niá:wen* mean?" Madge asked.

Joe looked at her, puzzled.

"*Niá:wen*," she repeated. "Isn't that what you just said?"

"It means *thank you*," Joe said, "in Mohawk."

*   *   *

Kiku looked up when Joe and Madge came into the workroom. They looked like they were sharing a private joke. She saw Walt looking at the two of them with a funny expression on his face; then he burst out laughing. It took Kiku a moment to realize why, but then she saw it. Walt was dressed in the same outfit—dark trousers, black turtleneck, and beret—as Madge.

"I guess I'm not the only one who's watched *Secret Agent*," Madge said, grinning at Walt. Then she handed Kiku a round box. Kiku opened it and took out a red felt hat with a beaded veil. "For going out," Madge said. "No one will think you're a 'suspicious person of Oriental character' in that."

Kiku went to the mirror in the alcove to try on the hat. She looked like someone else in it, like one of the models in the fashion magazines she'd seen last night at Madge's. When she turned around, Walt gasped. "No one would recognize you!"

"We've all put on other faces," Joe said. "Let's hope that doesn't make us two-faced."

*   *   *

The maze of basement corridors seemed even longer and more confusing to Madge in the dark. There were dim emergency lights every twenty feet or so, but some of these had burned out, and Kiku thought it was better if they didn't use a flashlight in case one of the guards was patrolling the basement.

"Just stay close to me," she said. "I know the way." When they reached the stairs, Kiku whispered to the others that they shouldn't talk once they were upstairs.

"We can use hand signals," Walt suggested.

"Great idea, Freckles," Madge said, "only it's too dark to see anything."

"How about birdcalls?" he said. Walt pursed his lips and made a sound like a dying pigeon.

"That sounds like a mourning dove," Joe said.

"Yeah, that's swell if we were out in the woods," Madge said.

"Birds get into the museum all the time," Kiku said. "We'll make the cooing sound when we find the lion. If anyone sees a guard coming, whistle like this." Kiku whistled a tune that was far more elaborate than Walt's coo.

"Sure," Madge said, rolling her eyes. "Then I'll sing the aria from *Madame Butterfly*."

The long sculpture gallery was slightly better lit than the basement, but that only made the shadows cast by the statues seem spookier. *All these Greeks and Romans like to hold up their arms*, Madge thought, *like they're trying to hail a cab.* It made their shadows stretch out across the polished marble like jagged exclamation marks and made Madge feel uneasy. And why were there so many naked ones? Here was a woman with one breast bared and here was a girl wearing a nightie that didn't leave *anything* to the imagination. Even creepier were the statues missing body parts. She passed a woman in a long draped dress who didn't have a head. It made her think of the dream they'd all had last night of the knight who lost his head but kept on talking. The thought made her feel faint for a moment. She stumbled and put her hand out to brace herself—and touched cold marble.

Jeepers! She wasn't supposed to touch the statues. What if it was one of the creepy ones? But this one wasn't creepy. It was one of those flat ones, like a gravestone, but the statue on it was rounded and lifelike: a little girl holding two doves. She remembered something about doves her mother had told her—that they stood for the spirit, the part of yourself that never died. She reached toward one of the doves and ran her finger along the curve of its rounded breast, remembering the way her mother would cup her face with her hand when she had a fever. No one touched her like that anymore.

You don't need anyone to take care of you—you will take care of the others.

There was that voice again, sounding more and more real inside her head. She took her hand away from the dove and noticed that a bit of the gold dust had come off on the marble. Then she heard a cooing.

Nerts, it's Walt, she thought. *He's found the lion.* She turned away from the dove girl and hurried after the others. As she ran, she could have sworn she heard the rustle of wings, but it must have just been her imagination.

She found the other three standing around the crouching lion. It looked even fiercer in real life. Madge could see its ribs under its marble skin and had to remind herself it was just stone.

"What are you all waiting for?" Madge whispered. "Someone's got to stick their hand down there and see if the chapter's there."

"Sure," Walt said, "only . . . what if the superstition is true?"

"Oh, for Pete's sake," Madge said, "I'll do it. I've got long fingers. My mother always said I could have played the piano if we could afford one, and I was jacks champion in the fourth grade." Madge wriggled her fingers in the air. They sparkled in the emergency lights. *That durned gold paint*, she thought, wiping it off on her handkerchief before reaching toward the mouth. The same gold paint that had gotten on the dove a minute ago before she heard the flutter of wings . . .

It was only paint. It couldn't bring a statue to life. And besides, the lion only bit off your hand if you were lying and she didn't plan on telling any lies while sticking her hand in there.

Only she'd been telling lies of one sort or another since her mother had died. Stories she made up on the spot like the one she had come up with today when they ran into Miss Fishbone in the Great Hall. Stories that turned her into a different girl—tough girl Madge, not little Margaret McGrory from Brooklyn who'd lost her family.

"Do you think," Madge asked, fingers inches from the gaping mouth, "it cares if you've told lies *before* you put your hand inside?"

"That's not in any of the stories," Kiku said.

"And it's not like you've told any really bad lies," Walt said. "Have you?"

"No, but . . ." Madge thought of all the things she hadn't told them. Didn't the nuns call those lies of omission? "What about the things you haven't said? Is it lying if you're keeping something to yourself?"

"I hadn't thought of that," Kiku said, looking worried.

"I guess if it was something really bad," Walt said, biting his lip.

"It might be safest to make a clean slate," Joe said.

"Here goes then," Madge said, screwing up her eyes and thrusting her hand into the gaping mouth. "Right before my mother fell down in the kitchen, she was scolding me for burning the oatmeal. Only the oatmeal wasn't burned, and I was angry, so I said she never trusted me and I . . . I didn't say it but I thought to myself, *I wish I could live by myself.* And then she fell over and died. The doctor said it was from a blood clot that flew to her brain, but I've always thought maybe it was me wishing her gone."

She waited, breath held, eyes screwed shut.

"We all say terrible things we don't mean," Kiku said, laying her hand on top of Madge's inside the lion's mouth. "I told my father I wished we weren't Japanese. That I hated the way people looked at me so much I wished I could disappear."

"I told my parents that if they sent me away, I'd never come back," Walt said, putting his hand on top of the girls' hands.

"I left my sister behind in the Mush Hole because I was afraid to stay and face what I'd done to the principal."

They stood with their hands lying on top of each other's inside the lion's mouth, staring at the fierce face, waiting for it to come alive and chomp off their hands. For a moment Madge thought that the cold marble was growing warm, but then she realized it was only the warmth of her friends' hands. They *were* her friends, she thought, because when you tell someone the worst thing about yourself and they still stand by you, that's how you know.

"Hey," Madge said. "I think I feel something." She wriggled her fingers farther into the mouth and drew out a rolled-up sheaf of paper. Joe looked over her shoulder and read the title out loud: "The Two-Faced Knight; or How Our Heroes Forged the Bond of Friendship in the Mouth of the Lion."

12

KNIGHTS AND LADIES

"HEY," WALT SAID, "that's kind of like what we just did."

"That must be why Sir Bricklebank put the first chapter here," Kiku said. "He knew it was important that we meet at the Lion of Truth just like *they* did." She was staring at the lion's face, which was glowing in the dim emergency lights. *As if it's alive*, Kiku thought. Was its mouth stretched wider than before? For a moment when all of their hands were in the lion's mouth, she had thought she felt the marble grow warm. No, that was just her imagination. She looked nervously around her at the other statues. The disembodied head of a Roman senator glared at her from one of the side galleries.

"What are we waiting for?" Walt said. "Let's go back to the workroom and read it!"

"Yes," Kiku said, carefully tucking the pages into her skirt pocket. She turned to lead the others back to the stairs, but there was no need to show them the way;

there was a trail of gold dust showing where they had
come from.

✳   ✳   ✳

When they got back to the workroom, Kiku laid the
pages down on the worktable and they all gathered
around in a circle, leaning toward the pages as if warming themselves around a bonfire. On the first page there
was a painting of knights and ladies seated in a pavilion,
watching a jousting contest. In the front row there was a
man wearing a crown.

"That must be Arthur," Walt said, "and the lady on
his left would be Guinevere."

"And that's Lancelot," Madge said, pointing to the
knight on the field. "The fellow who looks so pleased with
himself. His shield has three diagonal stripes across it."

"Who is she?" Kiku asked, touching her fingertip to
the figure of the lady sitting on Arthur's right. She was
wearing a pendant with a half moon on it and there was
a falcon riding on her shoulder.

"I bet that's Morgaine, Arthur's half sister," Walt
said. "She was a witch. There are a lot of different stories about her. Some think she was evil and plotted
against Arthur, and others think she helped Arthur and
that the real evil one was their other half sister, Belisent.
And this boy"—he pointed to a figure in tunic and tights

kneeling in front of Arthur—"this must be Arthur's squire."

"He doesn't look happy," Madge remarked.

"Maybe we'll find out why if we read the chapter," Kiku suggested, "but I can barely make sense of these letters."

"I can," Joe said. "At least I think I can, but . . ." He paused and looked up. "Should we? Remember what Dr. Bean said about how dangerous it was to read the book? We could just use the chapter to decode the next message. We don't actually have to read it."

"Oh," Kiku said, feeling a great swell of disappointment. "You're right, you know, only . . ." She looked up at the others and saw the same glow of excitement in their eyes. *They all want to read it*, the voice said inside her head. "Dr. Bean only said that about the book being dangerous because he didn't believe we were the knights and clearly we are the knights. We found the chapter when Dr. Bean and Miss Lake couldn't. That must mean we're the ones who are supposed to read it. And I think that if we read it together, it will be safe."

Madge nodded. "I think Kiku is right."

"Well, I know that I *want* to read it," Walt said. "Heck, it's a story about King Arthur I haven't read before!"

"All right," Joe said. "We're agreed. But we'll only read the chapters together." He spread his hands over the pages to smooth them flat. A bit of gold paint got on his hands, Kiku noticed, and as he spoke, his voice sounded different. As if someone else were speaking through him.

He drew the pages toward him but left them flat on the table so the others could see the pictures as he read.

THE TWO-FACED KNIGHT; OR HOW OUR HEROES FORGED THE BOND OF FRIENDSHIP IN THE MOUTH OF THE LION

Many are the adventures of King Arthur and his brave knights that have been told elsewhere by bards more skillful than I, but none have told this tale, for it was sworn between the king and his three companions who accompanied him on this adventure never to speak a word of it. It is not a tale meant for any but the four destined to take up the battle in their names. Before you read further, ask yourself if you are true of heart and if you are in the company of friends.

Joe's voice grew hoarse at the last words. He paused and looked up from the page and met Kiku's eyes.

"I think that's all been settled," Kiku said. Madge and Walt nodded, and Joe bent his head back to the page and, after a moment, began reading again.

It began on a spring day in the early years of King Arthur's reign. Arthur had newly come to power and united the warring tribes of Britain. There were still many dangers to face—invading Saxons and Northmen, and rivalries still festering in the hearts of chief-

tains and petty kings and queens—but Arthur, with
his gifts of kingship, had been able to draw them all together to swear allegiance and celebrate their alliance.
A feast was given and a tournament held, which Arthur
watched with his beautiful and loyal lady Guinevere on
one side and his sister Morgaine on the other—

"It *is* Morgaine," Kiku said.

Morgaine was known throughout the kingdom as
a wise and clever sorceress. She was feared by some,
but she had pledged her fealty to Arthur. His older half
sister Belisent had also come—

"That must be the dame with the sour puss," Madge
said, pointing at a lady dressed in green wearing a hat
that looked like a dunce's cap and scowling at Arthur.
"What's her beef with Arthur?"

"Well, if you'd let me go on," Joe said.

"No one's stopping you, sport," Madge replied.

. . . although it was whispered that she was angry
that Arthur had been crowned king and not one of
her sons. Belisent bore for Arthur the grudge of the
displaced sister and aggrieved daughter. She believed
that Arthur's father was responsible for her own father's death. That hatred rankled in her breast as a
serpent bites its own tail until, it was whispered, she

had through spiteful witchcraft become that horrible monster—the lizard with two heads.

"Look," Kiku said, pointing at the picture, "you can see a lizard tail peeping out from underneath her dress."

"Yech," said Madge. "Why did Arthur even let her come to the party?"

"I guess he didn't want her any angrier," Joe said.

In appeasement, King Arthur offered to make her youngest son his squire, but when Mordred begged King Arthur to allow him to take part in the tournament, the king said he was too young—

"That must be the kid with the unhappy mug," Madge said.

And Mordred went away with rancor in his heart, because youth does not like to sit idly by.

"I'd be sore too," Walt said, "if I wasn't allowed to joust."

Joe turned the page to a series of three pictures. In each, a knight in brilliant armor was shown dueling, jousting, and in the last, receiving a prize from the queen.

In all the contests, Lancelot prevailed as the bravest and most skilled knight. His only fault was his habit of

boasting, which only grew greater when Queen Guinevere bestowed upon him her garter—

"Her garter!" Madge cried. "You mean she took it off her leg? Wouldn't her stockings fall down?"

"Maybe they used them differently back then," Kiku said, blushing. "But still, I bet that didn't make Arthur very happy. Lancelot looks awfully pleased with himself."

Lancelot was just about to be named victor of the day when a new knight rode onto the field. He was wearing a helmet shaped like a boar's head, and indeed his demeanor was much like a boar, as he immediately charged at the company, announcing that he would fight their best knight unto death. Lancelot, always bravely ready to put himself in the way of danger and sure of his right to be called the best knight, gave battle to the stranger and fought valiantly. He offered the boar-faced knight every chance to stand down, but the boar-faced knight taunted him thus: "What gives you the right to be called the best knight in the kingdom when you cannot best me?"

And then, his pride wounded, Sir Lancelot swung high his sword and cleaved the knight's head from his neck.

"Golly!" Madge said. "He's got a temper on him!"

But lo! A wondrous strange thing occurred. When Lancelot removed the helmet from the fallen knight, his face came off with it. Beneath it lay a horrible grinning skull that spoke thus: "I lay a curse on this land and its descendants. You will be wiped from the face of the earth, while I will live forever no matter what you do to me."

"Is there nothing we can do to evade this fate?" asked the good lady Guinevere, looking first to Arthur. When she saw he had no answer, she looked to Lancelot. But Lancelot was still too angry to speak.

"There is one way," spoke the wizard Merlin to King Arthur, "but you must make a great sacrifice. You must travel into the Hewan Wood and, if you survive the terrors of the wood, you will come to the Maiden Castle. The lady of the castle will tell you what you must do to save your land, but it will be at a dire cost."

"A dire cost indeed," spoke the two-headed knight. "Everything you value most will be sorely tested in the Hewan Wood, and if you come to the castle, you will find the dreaded Beast of the Wood, who will tear the flesh from your bones."

With those words, the knight closed his eyes and ceased to speak. Lancelot bent to pick up the helmet and found to his surprise that it was empty. Indeed, when they looked, they found that the suit of armor was empty as well. The knight with two faces had vanished without a trace.

"That's creepy," Walt said, shuddering.

"You said it," Madge said. "If I were them, I wouldn't go to the Hewan Wood."

"Yes, you would," Kiku said. "You'd be the first to head straight for the woods. And that's what they did, right?" She looked at Joe, who was still looking down at the page.

Arthur stood and spoke to his assembled subjects: "I will go into these woods and save my land, no matter what danger lurks there."

"No, my lord," spoke Lancelot, "as your champion, it is right that I perform this quest."

"Leaving me alone and unprotected?" asked Guinevere, looking from Arthur to Lancelot. For truthfully, Guinevere was weary of being left alone in the castle while the men went off to battle. "I would rather go with you."

"My lady is too eager to put herself in danger," spoke Morgaine, "when clearly it is I who ought to go, as I am the only one amongst you who knows sorcery."

The four argued thus until the sun went down and the rest of the court, weary of their sparring, returned to their beds. At last Arthur spoke: "Enough! We shall go together or not at all."

And so the four set forth for the Hewan Wood. They traveled many days, following fearsome signs: marks of blood on the trunks of trees, bones hanging from branches, cast-off remnants of armor. At last they came to a place where the path was blocked by a fierce lion carved in stone. As they came to a halt, the lion opened its wide gaping mouth and spoke.

"Beware all who come to the Hewan Wood. Only those true of heart may pass here."

"We are all true of heart," spoke Arthur, "and we have come because an enchanted knight with two faces cursed our land, and the wizard Merlin told us we must come here to save it. Tell us how we may prove ourselves so that we may pass."

"You must each place a hand in my mouth and tell the secret you are most afraid of telling. If you lie, by word or omission, you will lose your hand and your chance to proceed."

"Just like we did!" Walt said. "Hey, I bet that means we're going to become like them!"

"I don't know about that," Madge said. "So what were their secrets?"

"It doesn't say," Joe answered. "It just says . . ."

They each did as was asked. It would not be chivalrous to tell the secrets of such august knights and ladies. Suffice it to say that they spoke from their hearts and when they were done, their friendship for each other was stronger than ever.

"Well," Madge huffed, "I don't call that fair. We had to tell our secrets."

"But would you want them put into a book for strangers to read?" Kiku asked.

"I suppose not," Madge admitted. "What happens next, Joe?"

Joe turned the page and read.

When they had told their secrets, the Lion of Truth stepped aside and disclosed a dark and narrow path so entwined and embowered by vines and branches that it might have been a tunnel. Arthur went first, then Guinevere and Morgaine, and Lancelot took the rear. As soon as they had passed, the lion stepped back in front of the path and turned again to stone. There was no going back now and so they went onward into the Hewan Wood.

"That's it?" Madge asked when Joe looked up from the page.

"That's the end of this chapter," Joe said, "but there's something else here—a note in pencil."

"That's Sir Bricklebank's handwriting," Kiku said, reading over Joe's shoulder. "I think it's the clue to where to find the next chapter."

"That can wait," Walt said. "We've got to decode the next part of the message. There are two numbers beside the crown symbol—a six and a five. I bet that means to start with the fifth word on the sixth page. Joe, can you help me make out the letters?"

While Joe and Walt worked to decode the next part of the letter, Madge went to the alcove to put the kettle on for tea. Kiku followed her. She opened a cabinet and asked Madge if she could reach a tin of cookies on the top shelf. As soon as Madge stepped behind the open cabinet door, Kiku laid a hand on her arm. "There's something I want to talk to you about."

"Spit it out," Madge replied, folding her arms across her chest and leaning back against the counter. "Something you don't want the boys to hear?"

"I don't want to worry them. It's just . . . what Walt said about us becoming like the characters in the story. Do you think that's what will happen to us?"

Madge laughed. "Walt's a swell guy, but he's got a big imagination. He'd love it if this book somehow turned us all into the knights of King Arthur's Round Table. When I used to read the stories from *The Boy's King Arthur* to Frankie, he always wanted to play knights and ladies afterward. Of course he always had to be King Arthur, and the twins would be Lancelot and Gawain—or Perceval or Galahad, whoever's story we'd read that day. Ma would be the Lady of the Lake and she'd hide the bread knife under the kitchen tablecloth and say it was Excalibur."

Madge swiped at her eyes, and Kiku, seeing how much she missed her family, squeezed her hand. After a moment Madge went on again. "But it was just a game and so is this. I certainly don't think you or I will turn into Lady Guinevere. Sheesh, she can't even make up her mind who she likes best—Arthur or Lancelot. And neither of us is a witch . . ." She looked at Kiku's stricken face. "Is that it? You think you're going to turn into Morgaine?"

"It's just that in the stories Morgaine betrays King Arthur, and I wouldn't want . . . I mean, the girls at Spence aren't very nice and my father never let me go to parties. You three are the first friends I've had and I'd never, ever do anything to hurt Walt or Joe or you—"

"Of course you wouldn't! No one would think that of you for one minute."

"No? Not even of a *suspicious person of Oriental character*?"

Madge turned an alarming shade of red. "Now that's what I call malarkey. I can believe all this magic stuff before I would believe you'd do anything underhanded."

"But you just met me!" Kiku whispered, her eyes filling with tears.

Madge pulled out her handkerchief and dabbed at Kiku's face. "I don't think you're suddenly going to become Morgaine any more than I'm about to become Queen Guinevere or that Freckles over there"—they both looked around the cabinet door at Walt, who was so absorbed in his task that he'd raked his short red hair into peaks like whipped egg whites—"is King Arthur. Now Joe on the other hand . . ." Madge lifted an eyebrow. "Joe makes a pretty good Sir Lancelot. But do you think he and I are going to run off together? Jeepers, we're only thirteen years old!"

"I guess you're right," Kiku conceded. "And Miss Lake wouldn't have left the clue if she thought it was really dangerous for us to read the book."

"Exactly," Madge said. "So as long as we make sure we always read the book together, we'll be A-okay." She turned away to pour boiling water in the teapot, but then Walt shouted so loudly that she nearly dropped the kettle.

"Holy smokes! You two better get over here. We don't have much time!"

13

THE TENTH OF DECEMBER

WALT'S HANDS WERE shaking as he held up the notebook. "Listen to this."

> *As you read this, our plan has already been set in motion. Pearl Harbor was just the first step; now we will make the American people tremble in their own beloved city, New York. None will escape the next attack. The tenth of December will be a day even more notorious than the seventh—*

"The tenth of December!" Madge cried. "That's only two days away."

"Does it say what the attack is?" Kiku asked. "Or where it will take place?"

"No," said Walt. "It says: *We must make sure none but the faithful know where the attack will take place. I have used separate sections of the book to encode the messages below to tell you where, how, and when the attack will be."*

"That means we have to find the other chapters of the book to read the other messages—and fast!" Kiku said. "Give me the clue Sir Bricklebank wrote at the end of the chapter. I'll start looking for it right away and try to find them all before you three return in the morning."

"Return?" Joe asked, looking up. He'd been studying the pages, running his hands over them as if he were trying to absorb the words into his skin. And he practically had; his hands were covered in flecks of gold paint. "Where do you think we're going? I'm sure not leaving you here alone."

"No way," Madge said. "It's pretty creepy here at night with all those statues and coffins upstairs."

"And we have to read the book together," Walt said. "I'm staying here tonight."

"Won't your aunt Sadie worry about you?" Kiku asked Walt.

Walt shrugged. She would, but how could he leave now when his adopted city was threatened by the very people who had driven his family out of their home? And when he was about to embark on the biggest adventure of his life? He understood what Guinevere said about being tired of always having to stay at the castle while Arthur and Lancelot went off on quests. He wanted to be part of the quest. "I'll call her and tell her I'm staying at a friend's house to do a homework assignment."

"And I don't have to worry about Aunt Jean," Madge said. "She's gone to Niagara Falls with Tony."

"So it's settled then," Joe said. "We'll stay here until we find the remaining three chapters, then we'll take the information to the police in the morning." *His voice sounds different*, Walt thought, *as if each word means something else. Maybe it comes from being as big and strong as Joe.* Walt wished he felt that strong. But maybe doing this thing—finding the rest of the book and decoding the messages and saving New York—would make him feel that way.

"What are we waiting for?" Walt asked. "Let's read the clue."

Joe read the clue out loud.

To find the next chapter
You must wander through the Hewan Wood
Cut off from all you love
Just as our heroes did.

The trees grow close.
The thorns spring thick as doubt.
To find your way, you need a guide
To rise above the dark and fly free.

"That's easy," Madge said, looking proud of herself. "It's a bird. Are there any bird statues in the museum?"

"Hundreds!" Kiku said. "It would take days to check them all out."

"There must be a way to narrow it down," Walt said. "It's not just a bird, but a bird that rises above the dark. Hey, I think I noticed a lamp shaped like a duck in the Roman gallery."

"Hm," Kiku said, "I've got a catalogue of the Roman gallery right here." She thumbed through the catalogue and then held it up for the others to see. The black-and-white photograph showed a clay sculpture of a fat duck with a hole in its back.

"It looks kind of small to hold a whole chapter," Madge said.

"Sir Bricklebank could have folded the pages up real small," Walt said.

"Would he, though?" Joe asked. "It would ruin them. The old paint on the pages cracks and falls off—especially the gold."

"Yes!" Madge said. "We all have a bit of it on our hands. Have any of you noticed anything odd about your hands? Like when you touch things?"

Walt frowned and looked down at his hands. "No. What do you mean?"

Madge shook her head and picked up another catalogue. "Nothing. Hey, this place is full of birds. What about this one? It looks big enough to hold a chapter."

"That's an Egyptian falcon sarcophagus," Kiku said, consulting the caption under the picture.

"A sarcophagus?" Joe said. "I thought those were the big coffins."

"It's any kind of coffin," Kiku said. "This statue probably held the remains of a prized hunting bird, the favorite of some king who wanted it buried with him." Kiku shuddered. "The pages could fit in there, but it doesn't fit the poem."

"Sure it does," Joe said. "*Rise above the dark* could mean surviving after death." He ran his finger along the realistically carved feathers on the picture. "The man who carved this statue and put the bones of that bird in it must have thought he was giving a kind of eternal life to it."

"Huh," Madge said, leafing through the catalogues. She picked up one with a picture of a copper dove covered with beautiful enamel work. "This is like the dove that hangs over the altar in our church. My mother told me once that it's supposed to stand for the Holy Spirit, the part of yourself that lives forever . . ." Madge's voice faltered, and Walt took the catalogue from her.

"It's called a Eucharistic dove," he said, reading from the catalogue. "This one's from the thirteenth century. Madge is right, it could be any of these three."

"Or this one." Kiku touched her finger to the picture of a black crow, its head tilted at a quizzical angle. "It's a Japanese *okimono* from the Edo period. My father told me that they were sometimes hollow inside so you could burn incense as an offering to your ancestors. That's like 'rising above the dark'"

"So we have four birds," Joe said. "And there are four of us. We can each go find one and bring it back here to examine."

"Do you think we should move them?" Madge asked. "I mean, won't we set off an alarm or something?"

"The individual cases aren't alarmed," Kiku said. "And I don't think we should stand around trying to figure out how to open them. I've got all the keys to the display cases." She spread out the keys that they'd found in Dr. Bean's desk. "I can give you each the key you need."

"Okay, then," Walt said. "We can each grab one of these birds and meet back here."

"Are you sure we should split up?" Madge asked, her voice sounding nervous. "I thought we were supposed to do this together."

"We're supposed to read the book together," Kiku said, "but we really ought to split up to save time. But if you're scared of being alone in the museum . . ."

"What, me?" Madge said. "Afraid of some statues and mummies? Nah. It's not like they're gonna come alive or anything!"

14

BIRDS OF A FEATHER

WALT VOLUNTEERED TO get the duck lamp. It might be small, but he wouldn't put it past Sir Bricklebank to stuff a chapter inside it. Next to Arms and Armor, the Greek and Roman galleries were his favorite rooms in the museum. He liked the statues of athletes and heroes and the vases that told stories from Greek mythology. He especially liked a big marble sarcophagus that had scenes from the adventures of Theseus on it. There was Ariadne giving Theseus the thread that would lead him out of the labyrinth, and Theseus slaying the Minotaur.

Walt would have been embarrassed to admit it, but he liked to imagine himself as the Greek hero who had saved all the boys and girls sent to be killed by the Minotaur. In his daydreams, he was no longer a skinny, noodle-armed weakling but a muscular hero brave enough to face the fierce monster. Instead of hiding in the wardrobe when the Nazis came, he burst into the Goldblatts' apartment and knocked all the soldiers to the floor. Then, instead of getting on the train to safety with a bunch of crying kids, he led all his friends and family onto the train, and they all got out of Germany together, just like Theseus leading the Athenian youths to safety.

But that was just a daydream. He'd never be that strong. He'd always be the helpless boy who had to be lifted bodily up onto the train by his father because at the last minute he'd refused to go. He'd been so angry and ashamed that he'd hidden his head in his hands while the train pulled out, refusing to join the other children at the windows shouting their good-byes to their parents. Only when the train picked up speed did he realize he had lost his chance to see his parents for the last time. He'd squeezed in between the other children and pasted his hands to the window, but they entered a tunnel and so the glass only gave back his own reflection: the face of a scared and crying boy.

He blinked at his own reflection in the museum case now and saw the duck lamp. Madge had been right. It was way too small to hold a whole chapter. Still, he used the key Kiku had given him to unlock the case and take it out. It fit in the palm of his hand. The duck's head was turned back to form the handle, its wide flat tail pierced to hold the wick. It looked like something that had been made for a child. Walt would take it back to show the others even though it didn't have the chapter inside. He put it in his pocket and was just closing the case when he heard voices.

"Mr. Jenkins, what have I told you about napping on the job?"

"Uh . . . that I shouldn't do it, Miss Fitzbane?"

"So get up instantly! Have you patrolled the Roman galleries?"

"Not lately . . ."

"Then don't just stand there gawking at me—go to it! Where is your cohort?"

"My co—?"

"Mr. Carson?"

"Uh . . . he's usually na—patrolling the Egyptian—"

"I will go check on him. You take the Roman gallery—and make sure you look behind all the statues. I'm afraid those *chill*-drun Dr. Bean let in might be sneaking around. If you find them, bring them to my office immediately."

"Yes, sir . . . uh . . . I mean ma'am."

Throughout the conversation, Walt had stood frozen in the shadow of a Roman gladiator, but now, as he heard the guard's footsteps approaching, he realized he would be caught. He looked around for someplace to hide. He could try standing behind one of the statues, but most of them were missing body parts where his would stick out. If the guard caught him, he would get all of them kicked out before they could find out where the attack was going to take place. The only place he could see big enough to hide was the sarcophagus, but it was covered with a marble lid that must weigh a ton. He'd never be able to move it.

Try, a voice said inside his head. *You're stronger than you think.*

That's ridiculous, he thought, but he found himself clutching the edges of the marble lid nonetheless. Maybe if he could just slide it far enough for him to squeeze inside—

The lid popped up easily in his hands, as if it were the top of a Cracker Jack box. He stared at it dumbfounded and noticed that his hands were covered with that gold paint from the book.

Could it be—?

He didn't have time to wonder. He jumped inside the sarcophagus and pulled the lid over him as quietly as he could, hoping that whatever had given him superhuman strength would last long enough for him to get out.

✻ ✻ ✻

Joe was in the Egyptian gallery, looking for the falcon sarcophagus. According to the catalogue, it was near the statue of Haremhab, but how was he supposed to know which of these statues was Haremhab? It was too dark to read the little plaques attached to each one, and some of the statues were in pieces. One was the bottom part of a woman's face carved in yellow stone, her lips so beautifully curved, it seemed she might speak at any moment. It made him uneasy to be in a room with all these things having to do with the dead. It wasn't just the mummies—those were creepy enough—but as he looked around, he realized that everything was supposed to honor the dead, from the little jars with animal heads to the cunningly crafted model of a boat. They were all supposed to represent the things the dead person had needed in life and would still need in death.

Was it right, then, Joe wondered as he walked between the rows of tomb offerings, that these things were here and not in the tombs where they had been found? Hadn't these things been taken from their people just as Joe's language had been taken from him at the Mush Hole? When he'd gone home the second time he'd run away, he had realized he no longer understood everything his *Tóta* said to him. It had made Joe feel like a ghost in his own family. But it had also made him, just for a moment, proud that he had moved so far ahead of his family. And he hated the Mush Hole for making him feel that way.

At the end of the room there was a short, squat statue of a man sitting cross-legged. Joe knelt in front of it and saw that the man held a scroll open on his knees, the surface carved with dozens of those little pictures he'd noticed earlier. More than the tall striding statues and cat-faced gods, this statue felt comfortable to Joe. The broad plain face seemed to smile at Joe as if he'd been waiting here for him. *I wonder*, Joe thought as he touched the pictures incised into the glossy black stone, *what your name was.*

The figures on the scroll began to move beneath Joe's fingertips. The snake crawled toward a bird that flapped its wings and soared over the head of a man fishing. They formed themselves into words that Joe heard in his head: *I was Haremhab, royal scribe of Tutankhamen and Aya and finally king myself.*

Joe rocked himself back on his heels and sat staring at the smiling scribe. "How can I hear you?" Joe asked out loud.

You have the gift of language, the voice inside his head said. Joe realized that the voice did not belong to the scribe—but it didn't belong to him either.

Yes, it does, the voice said. *It belongs to who you truly are and who you were always meant to be. You've always known that you were special—even when they stole your language. Now all of it belongs to you!*

Joe looked around at the mummies and found he could read the words on their tombs: *I was the great king . . . All bow to me . . . I will live forever . . .* all boasts.

None a greater warrior than you, the voice said. And suddenly Joe saw himself in a bright green field, mounted on a horse, a crowd of people in colorful costumes cheering him on as he charged at another knight on horseback. He drove his lance into the knight's chest and watched as he fell to the ground, and he heard the shouts of the crowd, saw the bright fluttering ribbons that the women showered on him—

This is what you deserve—fame, honor, love—

And then he heard a keening cry, and a snow-white falcon landed on his hand. Joe opened his eyes and stood up. He still heard the cry of the falcon. It came from a bronze statue perched on a pedestal. As Joe laid his hand on the bird's back he heard the voice inside his head say: *The chapter is within the falcon. You are the one to find it because it is meant for you alone.*

Before he could object to what the voice was saying, he heard another voice, this one outside his head. "Honest, Miss Fitzbane, there's no one here. If there were a bunch of kids in the museum, dontcha think me and Jenks woulda noticed?"

"From the smell of whiskey on your breath, Mr. Carson, I don't believe you'd notice a stampede of hippopotami. Now, find those children and bring them to me."

Joe could hear the guard and Miss Fitzbane heading toward him. He grabbed the falcon and dashed inside the big tomb. He held his breath until Miss Fitzbane and the guard had passed. When they were gone, he started to come out, but then the voice inside his head said: *Stay and read the chapter first. After all, you're the only one who can read it. Why do you need the others?*

Joe could think of half a dozen reasons why he needed Madge and Walt and Kiku, but his hands were already unlocking the mechanism on the falcon's belly and slipping the pages out.

⁂ ⁂ ⁂

Kiku found the little *okimono* crow quickly, but she didn't go straight back downstairs. It was exciting to have new friends, but she wasn't used to spending so much time with people. Besides, night was her favorite time at the museum. Often when her father worked late, she would wander through the empty half-lit galleries, able to stand as long as she liked in front of a favorite painting and get lost inside it without worrying about some nosy tourist or, lately, Miss Fitzbane looking at her as if she were planning to steal one of the paintings.

How could she explain that she was playing her favorite game: vanishing inside a painting? That if she looked long and hard enough at a painting, she began to feel herself dissolving into that world—into the tawny gold wheat fields of a Brueghel, where she could feel the hot sun on her skin and the prickle of rough grass on her back, or onto the deck of a whaler painted by Turner, where she could smell the salt and feel the ocean spray on her face. She could be anyone in these moments—a pampered *duchesse* or a tired Parisian laundress or Joan of Arc hearing the call to arms. What a relief it was to feel her own self—the bookworm who always knew the answers but was too afraid to raise her hand, the awkward girl shunned by her haughty schoolmates, the girl left behind by her mother because she was too babyish to make the long trip back to Japan, the clumsy daughter who never seemed to do anything good enough for her father—fade away. Just now she would like to forget the girl whose face had become the face of the enemy to all around her.

She walked slowly past the cases of porcelain vases and statues of Buddhas until she reached her favorite Chinese landscape, *Mountain Market, Clearing Mist.* There were tiny figures walking along a path at the bottom, but Kiku let her eyes rest on the towering craggy mountains wreathed by great swaths of fog so that the mountaintops seemed to be floating. When she looked at this painting, she didn't feel like any of the figures in it; she felt like no one. She closed her eyes and pictured herself floating free of her body, her life, and her self.

If only, she thought, *I could feel like this forever.*

She was so lost in the floating feeling that she didn't notice Miss Fitzbane and Mr. Carson walking up the stairs to the balcony until they were almost on top of her. She wheeled around to face Miss Fitzbane, prepared to tell a story. She would tell her she had come to find something she had lost. She knew that Miss Fitzbane would turn her over to the police, but maybe she could at least convince her that she was here on her own and Miss Fitzbane wouldn't catch the others.

Miss Fitzbane marched right up to her and stopped inches from Kiku's nose, the glow from the emergency lights flashing off her glasses.

"See, I told you," Mr. Carson spluttered behind her, "there's no one up here."

Miss Fitzbane took off her glasses and stared straight at Kiku. Her eyes burned yellow like a cat's. Mr. Carson, standing right behind her, was staring at Kiku too.

"Is there something wrong with that painting, Miss Fitzbane?" Mr. Carson asked.

Miss Fitzbane leaned closer so that her nose almost touched Kiku's. Kiku stayed perfectly still, breath held.

"I've always liked this one. Those little guys climbing the mountain look like they're having a good time." Mr. Carson jabbed his finger toward Kiku's nose. Was this some kind of a joke? Miss Fitzbane didn't look like she was joking. And neither did Mr. Carson. He was so scared that he was trying to sneak a flask out of his pocket to take a swig.

"Put that back in your pocket, Mr. Carson," Miss Fitzbane said without turning around, "and come with me to the Medieval galleries. We'll look for the *chill*-drun there."

Miss Fitzbane sniffed the air, her nostrils flaring like a hunting dog's, and turned around, her skirt making a hissing noise. Kiku stayed perfectly still while they walked away. *What was that about?* Why would Miss Fitzbane pretend not to see her? Why would Mr. Carson? He had pointed at Kiku as if he could see the painting behind her. Kiku turned to look at the scene on the painting. There were the tiny figures at the bottom of the painting that Mr. Carson had been talking about. He had seen them right through her. As if she were invisible.

Kiku held up her hand, half expecting not to see it, but there it was, sparkling with gold paint and trailing a bit of mist. *Your own cloak of invisibility*, said the voice inside her head. *Fitting raiment for a sorceress.*

Then she remembered what Miss Fitzbane had said. She was on her way to the Medieval galleries. That was where Madge had gone. She had to go warn her to keep out of Miss Fitzbane's way.

✷   ✷   ✷

Madge was glad when she got past the mummies, but the Great Hall wasn't any better to walk in alone. She could hear her footsteps echoing under the high ceiling, and she expected any minute for the guards or that creepy Miss Fitzbane to come running out or—worse—those mummies. What if the gold dust had gotten on them and they came to life like Boris Karloff in *The Mummy*?

She walked past the Grand Staircase. It looked like the steps of an ancient temple—like the one Fay Wray was dragged up in *King Kong* on her way to being sacrificed.

That's what this kind of felt like, Madge thought as she walked through the hall of Medieval Art, like she and Joe and Kiku and Walt were supposed to give up a piece of themselves to find the Kelmsbury and stop Mr. January. She'd known that it would be dangerous, and Madge wasn't afraid of facing danger. She knew how to run and how to fight. But she wasn't sure she knew how to hold on to herself—not when she had lost so much already.

Madge walked past a painting of an emaciated saint and a tapestry of a woman wearing something that looked like a pillow on her head. She walked past altars and crosses and panes of stained glass and statues of saints and Madonnas. Here, too, was something she had lost. She had gone to Mass every day in Catholic school and to church on Sunday with her mother. When people asked her what she was, she told them "Irish Catholic" like the two were inseparable and as bonded to herself as her red hair and blue eyes. But she hadn't been able to make herself go to church since her mother's funeral, and looking now at these suffering saints and sad-eyed Madonnas, she thought that this, too, all came down to sacrifice. Which made her kind of mad. Hadn't she lost enough?

She found the dove in a glass case. It was far more beautiful than the black-and-white photograph had suggested. Its neck and breast were bright copper etched with little feathers, its wings inlaid with blue, green, yellow, and red enamel. Bright blue-black glass eyes regarded Madge steadily as she used the key Kiku had given her to open the glass case. Holding her breath, she reached inside and cupped the bird in both hands. It felt cool and light, like her mother's gloved hand had felt in hers that day in church when she'd told Madge, *The people you love and who love you, Margaret, are always with you.* But that wasn't really true. Her mother had been with her one moment, stirring the oatmeal, chiding Madge for letting it burn (which Madge *hadn't*) and then she was falling to the floor and out of Madge's life forever.

If only I could have done something, Madge thought as she took the bird out of the case, *if only I could have held on to her—*

You still have her, a voice inside her head said. *All that you've lost can be restored. Only you can't do it alone. You bring out the best in others and they bring out the best in you.*

Pshaw! Madge thought, cradling the bird in the crook of her elbow as she walked back toward the Great

Hall. Now she was imagining voices in her head. Sheesh! The next thing she'd think she was turning into Queen Guinevere—

You're not— the voice began, but Madge told it to put a lid on it. Walt was coming into the Great Hall from the Roman wing at the same time that Joe was entering from the Egyptian wing. What the heck were they doing? The guards were going to see them! She could hear Miss Fitzbane yammering away at one of the guards. And there was no place to hide in this big open space.

Walt reached her first and grabbed Madge's hand. "Hurry! We can hide behind the information desk!"

But when Joe reached them, he grabbed Madge's other hand and told Walt to stick out his other hand. "What for?" Walt asked, but then his eyes grew wide and he stared at his hand as if something was attached to it. The air shimmered around them, gold specks falling down over their heads like snowflakes. Madge heard Kiku's voice coming from the empty space between Walt and Joe. "Just hold still and imagine you're floating."

Do it, the voice said. She closed her eyes and pictured herself on the beach at Coney Island where her parents sometimes took her. She remembered how it would feel to walk into the surf with her mother and father on either side of her, holding her hands, lifting her up as the waves rolled over her. She could hear Miss Fitzbane squawking at the guard and the *swish-hiss* of her skirt as she walked by. She cracked open one eye and peeked to see Miss Fitzbane and the guard disappearing into the Medieval galleries. They'd walked right past them as if they were—

"Invisible!" Walt whispered. "Kiku can make us invisible. It's the book! It's given us all powers."

"Joe can understand languages," invisible Kiku said.

"Yeah," Walt admitted. "I think I got superstrength."

"Jeez Louise," Madge sighed. "I got zilch." She shifted her arm to adjust the copper dove—and the bird tilted its head and looked up at her with its bright blue-black eye.

"Hey!" Madge cried.

The dove flapped its enamel wings and rose up into the air.

15

BORIS KARLOFF

"HOLY SMOKES!" WALT whispered. "We'd better catch it before Miss Fitzbane and the guards come back!" He let go of Kiku's invisible hand, and the gold flecks surrounding them came down like a summer rainstorm—along with the lovely image he'd had in his head a minute ago when Kiku had asked them to picture themselves floating. He'd imagined himself riding the carousel in the park where his parents had taken him when he was little. He'd been able to smell the sugary aroma of caramel corn in the air and hear the tinny music as he was lifted up, up, up on the back of a charging white horse—and then it had all vanished. Madge and Joe were back in focus now. Only Kiku remained invisible.

"Nerts," Madge said. "We'd better catch that bird and scram before Fishbone comes back. Come on, Boris," Madge cooed to the dove, who had landed on the information desk and was cocking its head at them with a strangely intelligent glint in its beady eyes.

"Boris?" Kiku asked, making Walt jump at the sound of her voice.

"Yeah, as in Boris Karloff in *The Mummy*. Only I'm afraid this bird isn't as smart as that monster."

"He looks smart to me," Kiku said.

"He looks hungry," Joe said.

"Hm." Madge dug in her pocket and drew out a crumb from a doughnut she'd slipped in there earlier. She held it out to the bird. Boris flew straight to her hand, eagerly ate the crumb, and then looked up at Madge as if he wanted more. "Poor guy. I don't suppose he's had anything to eat since the thirteenth century. Let's get back to the workroom and get him a bite before Miss Fishbone comes back."

✶　✶　✶

As soon as they got to the workroom, Boris jumped off Madge's shoulder and dived for the sandwich crumbs they'd left on the table.

"Here . . ." Madge opened the sandwich bag. "What do you think a thirteenth-century dove would prefer—pastrami or deviled ham?"

"I think the real question is how he came to life in the first place," said Kiku, who was visible again. "How does this magic work? And how long does it last?"

"And why can we each do different things?" Walt asked, walking over to the big anvil. He rubbed his hands together, placed them on either side . . . and lifted it over his head.

"Jeez Louise, Freckles!" Madge cried. "You've turned into Superman."

Walt put the anvil back down, trying to look properly serious, but then gave up and grinned. "I was wishing I was strong enough to lift up the lid of the marble sarcophagus to hide from the guards and suddenly I was."

"And I was wishing I could be invisible," Kiku said.

"I was wishing I hadn't lost my own language," Joe said.

"And I was wishing I could have kept my mother alive," Madge said. "But Boris didn't come to life right away. It only happened when the four of us held hands."

"Try it again, Madge," Kiku said. She took the *okimono* crow out of her skirt pocket and handed it to Madge. "It doesn't have the chapter in it—I checked already. See if you can bring it to life."

"Okay," Madge said, regarding the statue warily. "I just hope he doesn't bully Boris." She held the crow statue in her hands. "Nope," she said after a few minutes.

"Try it with all of us holding hands," Walt suggested.

Madge wedged the crow statue in the crook of her elbow and they all held hands again, but the crow remained stubbornly inert.

"Huh," Walt said. "That's funny. There must have been something different when we did it before."

"It doesn't matter," Madge said. "Now I don't have to worry about bringing the mummies to life by accident."

"There's a lot we have to understand about these powers," Kiku said. "I mean . . . what if I couldn't make myself *visible* again? How would anyone ever find me?"

"And what else might the gold paint do to us?" Madge asked.

"We need to know more," Walt said.

"Maybe the next chapter will tell us," Kiku said, "but it's not in the crow or the dove . . ."

"It's in the falcon," Joe said, taking the statue from the inside pocket of his jacket. "Um . . . at least that's what it told me."

"Sheesh," Madge said, slapping Joe on the back. "That's quite a talent you've got, sport. What are you waiting for?"

Joe opened the mechanism on the belly of the falcon, and a sheaf of papers fell out, uncurling in a cloud of gold dust. Walt saw Madge brush a little of the dust into her palm and rub her hands together under the table. *She does mind about not having a power*, Walt thought. And then, so the others wouldn't notice what she was doing, he slapped Joe on the back just like Madge had. "Yeah, what are we waiting for . . . *sport*?"

Joe gave Walt a funny look, then cleared his throat, and began.

THE HEWING

After our four had passed the Lion of Truth, they thought they'd endured the worst of the tests, but their trials were only beginning. The Hewan Wood was so named for a terrible battle that had been waged there, in which the soldiers had hewn each other to pieces until the ground was soaked with blood. The place came to be known as the Hewing and then the Hewan Wood. As they stood on the edge of the wood, they could hear the ghostly cries of the soldiers in the wind and the clank and clatter of sword and blade in the movement of branch against branch.

"This is a cursed place," Morgaine said. "We should leave here at once."

"And forfeit the safety of our land?" replied Arthur. "No, but perhaps I should go alone."

"I will never abandon you, my lord," spoke Guinevere.

"Nor I," said Lancelot.

"If one goes, we shall all go," said Morgaine, "for there is strength in our bond of friendship."

At that the very trees seemed to shake with laughter, for the magic of the Hewan Wood is that it cuts asunder the ties that bind us one to the other. No sooner had they set foot on the path than the trees began to whisper in their ears.

To Guinevere they whispered that Arthur loved his country better than he loved her. Why could he not be more like Sir Lancelot, who always put her first?

To Arthur they whispered that Guinevere did look upon Lancelot with too favorable a glance.

To Lancelot they whispered that he who was the better swordsman should be king.

To Morgaine they whispered that the others thought she was a witch and did not trust her. *Use your power*, they whispered, *show them what you can do.*

They had come to a place in the wood where the path split in two. There was a spring here, bubbling up out of a cleft in the rock. A dove carved from stone rested in a niche in the rock above the spring.

"What a beautiful bird," Guinevere exclaimed, reaching for the bird.

"You shouldn't touch that," Morgaine said. "It must be sacred to the old people of the forest."

She thinks she knows everything, the trees whispered to Guinevere.

"Oh, I don't think they would mind," Guinevere said, cupping the bird in her hands.

She takes whatever she wants, the trees whispered to Morgaine, *but you can show her that not everything belongs to her.*

And so Morgaine whispered a spell that made the dove come to life in Guinevere's hands.

"Oh! I've made it come to life! How precious!" Guinevere cried.

But then the dove flew out of her hands and down the path that stretched to the right. Guinevere cried out and chased after it.

"Come back!" Arthur cried. "We must stay together to finish our quest."

All he thinks about is his quest, the trees whispered to Guinevere. *If he wants you to come back, why doesn't he come after you?*

"I'll go after her," Lancelot said.

But Arthur said that he would go after his lady and bade Lancelot stay with Morgaine to ensure she did no more magic. Morgaine, angry at Arthur's chiding, would not stay as he bade but set off down the left-hand path with Lancelot following. And so divided, the four wandered through the Hewan Wood until Arthur and Guinevere at last came to the Maiden Castle, which stood on an island in a lake guarded by an old man who sat before it on a rock.

"Good sir," Arthur said, "I have come to the Maiden Castle to learn how I may save our land and people."

"Do you come alone that you say 'I'?" the old man asked him. "I see a lady by your side and do you not have other companions? You may not enter the Maiden Castle alone."

"No," Arthur admitted, "I come with my lady Guinevere and my good friend Lancelot and my sister Morgaine, but alas we were separated in the wood."

"Were you? Then whom do I see behind you?"

Arthur and Guinevere turned to see Lancelot and Morgaine come from the forest. They rejoiced each to see the others and were sorry they had argued. They each spoke of what had irked them into rash words and told each other the adventures they had had in the forest. When they were sealed again in amity, they turned to the old man and found in his place a tall and imposing sorcerer in a midnight-blue robe, whom they recognized as Merlin.

"You have done well to heal the rifts between you. You will need each other in the Maiden Castle. If you succeed and make it to the top of the tower, the Lady will bestow a talent suited to your need and nature, but always remember that you are strongest when you use your powers together. Then, and only then, will you defeat the great evil that has risen in your kingdom. But remember that with every gift comes a burden and a danger. Be careful how you use what you are given."

And then, with a swoop of his cloak, Merlin vanished into the mist that rose from the lake, and the four were left to go forth into the castle with pure

hearts and friendship sworn, but with also a foreboding at what Merlin had told them, for one among them already felt a darkness growing within and knew it would lead to betrayal.

"Huh," Madge said, "that last part is kind of creepy. But it's not like anyone here would betray the others."

"But what if we weren't . . . *ourselves*," Joe said. "What if the book gets into you somehow? What if the gold dust doesn't just give us powers, but also turns us into the people in the book?"

"Into Arthur, Guinevere, Morgaine, and Lancelot?" Walt asked. "Would that be so bad?"

"I guess I'd be Morgaine," Kiku says. "The witch who betrays Arthur."

"Well, I certainly don't want to be Guinevere," Madge said. "She ran away with Lancelot and hurt Arthur." She was looking at Walt.

"What? Do you think I'm supposed to be Arthur? That's ridiculous. I'm not a leader. Madge is more likely to be Arthur . . ."

They went around and around like this until Madge slapped her hand on the table. "Enough! I don't care if I'm the Queen of Sheba. Arguing like this isn't going to make it any better and it's not going to stop the attack on New York. All this business with the gold dust is just . . ."

"Malarkey?" Joe asked.

"No, I guess not," Madge admitted. "But it's kind of

beside the point. We found the chapter so we could decode the next part of the message, so let's get to work on that. Joe and Walt, you can start decoding the message. Kiku, you start on Sir Peanut Brittle's next clue. It's that scribbled bit at the bottom, right? I'm going to make us all a pot of strong tea to keep us awake."

They all nodded, even Boris, who bobbed his head up and down and cooed.

"You know," Walt said, as they got up to go, "Madge really does make the best King Arthur."

16

WHERE HEROES DIE

WALT WROTE THE seventh word on the twelfth page over the first word of the coded message and tried to concentrate on decoding. It had been exciting to be able to lift that heavy sarcophagus lid and to see Madge's eyes grow wide when he hoisted the anvil over his head, but now that he thought about all the powers he might have wished for, he was sorry he hadn't had more time to choose.

"Hey, Joe," he said, keeping his voice low so the girls wouldn't hear him. "What would you have chosen if you'd known you were going to get a power?"

Joe shrugged. "I don't think it works like that. The book said the gift they each got was according to their need and nature."

"Huh. I can see how I might've *needed* to be stronger, but I don't see what it's got to do with my nature."

"What would you have wanted, then?"

"To fly," Walt said without hesitation. "Then I could

fly across the ocean and pick up my family. While I was at it I'd swoop down and give Hitler a sock to the jaw just like Captain America did."

"Would you kill him?" Joe asked.

"Oh," Walt said, surprised at the bluntness of the question. "I don't know . . . I mean he sure does deserve to die, but I think I'd just tie him up and deliver him to President Roosevelt. Then he could be put on trial and everyone would know the terrible things he's done and he'd have to let all the people go from the labor camps and ghettos."

"It sounds like a good plan," Joe said. "Let's get this message decoded and save New York and then see what we can do for the rest of the world."

"All right," Walt said. He lowered his head to the page and then it popped up again. "Hey, Joe, you never said what superpower you would want."

"Oh, that's easy," Joe said. "I'd like to be able to turn back time."

✳   ✳   ✳

When Walt had the message decoded, he called Kiku and Madge over to the table. Madge poured them all cups of strong tea while Walt read the message out loud. "I've got it decoded," he said, "but I don't really understand it. It says:

> *The weapon you and the other operatives will use is one my colleagues in Germany have found to be effective in the killing of all vermin. Right now, these vermin are being incorporated into concentration camps in Germany, Poland, and France. We will do the same to the people of New York. When the American people see their own dying, it will undermine their will to fight.*

"Like heck it will!" Madge said. "And what does he mean by *vermin*?"

"Pests," Kiku said. "Rats, cockroaches . . ."

"I don't think that's what he means," Joe said, looking warily at Walt. "When I look at the word, I can tell he meant something else. Maybe it's like understanding languages. I can understand what the person who wrote it *really* meant."

"So what does he mean?" Madge asked.

"I-I . . ." Joe looked regretfully at Walt. "I think he means Jews. And when he says they're being incorporated into concentration camps . . ." Joe touched the words on the page, and all the blood drained from his face. "I can see something else. I'm not sure if it's something that's happening now or if it's what Mr. January *wants* to happen in the future. I-I . . ."

"What is it?" Walt said, his face drained of all the boyish happiness that had been there a moment ago.

"I can see hundreds of people being marched at gunpoint, herded like cattle onto trains, forced behind barbed wire . . ." Joe shuddered and drew his hand away from the page as if it were on fire. "I also saw poison canisters and rooms filled with gas. They plan to kill all those people."

"No," Walt said. "That can't be . . ." But he was thinking of the things that his uncle Sol and his friends whispered when they thought Walt wasn't listening—that Hitler wanted to wipe the Jewish people from the face of the earth.

"Wait," he said, staring at Joe. "The message says this is happening in Germany, Poland, *and* France. Are you saying that they plan to kill Jews in France, too?"

Joe lifted his eyes to meet Walt's as if it took a great effort to move them. "I think so, Walt . . . and I think they mean to do the same here in New York. They mean to kill us all."

Walt looked down and his eyes lit on a scrap of newspaper that had been left on the table. *Arrests of 12,850 Revealed in Vichy*, read the headline. *Jews who entered France since January 1936 are ordered rounded up.* His parents had fled Germany only two years ago, in 1939, which meant—

The room began to spin.

"I-I think I need some air," he stuttered. Then he fled the room.

✶   ✶   ✶

Madge got up to follow Walt, but Joe stopped her. "Trust me," he said, "no fellow wants a girl watching him puke."

"Oh," Madge said, sitting back down. "I guess you're right. Will you go see if he's all right?"

"I'm on my way," Joe said, glad for an excuse to get out in the air. Along with the horrible images he had seen when he touched Mr. January's note he had heard a voice. An awful voice—

He followed Walt out the back exit, but he waited a few minutes when he heard him throwing up in the bushes. No one really wanted *anyone* to watch them throw up, especially not Walt, who was a little touchy. Joe didn't blame him. In the Mush Hole, it had been hard to hold on to any bit of himself. The teachers shaved the students' heads—to protect against lice, they said, but he suspected they wanted to get rid of their braids as soon as possible—and daily checked behind their ears and under their fingernails as if they suspected they were hiding weapons there. When your body wasn't your own, you started feeling like you had nothing. When people treated you like vermin, you began to feel like vermin.

And you left your sister Jeanette there. If you joined me we could get her out—

Joe shook his head to dislodge the voice. It was different from the one he'd heard when he read the chapter on his own. It was a bad voice.

To distract himself, he looked up at the tall stone spear that rose up from a stone base. When he had looked at it earlier tonight, he hadn't understood what the figures meant, but now he did. There was a lot of "Praise be to this god" and "Protect us from that demon," but Joe could now also hear the grunts and groans of the men who had cut the stone from the quarries and dragged it across the desert. He could hear the cries of the Roman soldiers who moved it to commemorate their own victories and the clash of other armes that came when the Roman Empire fell. Men were always killing each other. What was the point of knowing all languages if the stories he kept hearing were all about the terrible things that people did to other people?

So that you can control them. There was that awful voice again. But it couldn't be right. How could he control anyone when he was just a runaway Indian boy living off discarded food in the park?

I will make you powerful, so powerful that you can go back to the Mush Hole and take Jeanette out of that place. Why not? These people are not really your friends. They're just like the people who put you in the Mush Hole—

"Shut up," Joe screamed out loud. There hadn't been any noise for a few minutes, so he walked softly into the bushes and found Walt squatting on the ground, his arms wrapped around his knees.

"How ya doin', sport?" Joe said, sitting down next to him.

"Okay, I guess . . . I knew things were bad over there. I've heard my uncle Sol and his friends whispering, and there were rumors about the camps. But this . . ."

"Maybe I shouldn't have told you."

Walt shook his head. "No, I had to know. The world has to know. People just can't sit by and let this happen. We have to do something."

"We are. We're finding out where they plan to attack New York and stopping them." Joe put his hand on Walt's shoulder, and Walt sat up straighter. *It's like it says in the book*, Joe thought, *we are stronger when we use our powers together, like when we joined hands in the Great Hall*. When Kiku had asked them to picture themselves floating, Joe had remembered how he'd felt when he first came to the city and he found out his brother wasn't at the boardinghouse. Lost. Alone. Cut off from everything and everyone that he knew. He had found the park and hidden in the wooded parts. That first night he had huddled in the cold, so hungry that he felt himself leave his body and float over it. He had looked down at himself and thought he didn't even recognize this boy anymore.

Then one of the tramps had given him a half-full can of beans and showed him how to read the signs that other tramps left for each other. The tramps had invented a whole language and a brotherhood—a brotherhood of the lost. He'd thought that might be the closest he ever got to feeling like he belonged anywhere since going to the Mush Hole. But then when he joined hands with Madge and Walt and Kiku in the Great Hall, he'd felt connected to them. How long would that last?

"You're right," Walt said now. "We should get back to the girls and read that next clue. You know Madge, she'll be chomping at the bit."

"Yeah," Joe said, thinking that he *did* know Madge even though they'd only met yesterday.

Walt began to get up, but Joe saw that he was still shaky, so he got up first and held out his hand to Walt. He was afraid Walt wouldn't take it, that he'd think it meant he was weak, but he did—and Joe felt a bolt of power shoot through his arm. Walt sprang to his feet, bouncing on his toes and squeezing Joe's hand so tight, Joe thought it would break.

"Didya feel that?" Walt asked, grinning, but then the smile slipped from his face. He was looking over Joe's shoulder.

Joe spun around and saw the silhouette of a man in a trench coat and fedora slipping into the shadows.

"It's him," Walt growled. "That monster!"

Joe could feel the heat coming off Walt, and when he turned, he barely recognized the mild-mannered boy from Brooklyn. His fists were clenched, biceps bulging, his chest puffed to twice its former size. He was growing before Joe's eyes, muscles coiling for a spring.

He was going after Mr. January, and Joe had a feeling that for all Walt's superhuman strength, he'd still be no match for "that monster." "Hold off," Joe said, reaching for Walt's arm to hold him back. "You can't take him on yourself."

Walt flung up his arm to fend off Joe's restraining hand—and his clenched fist rammed into Joe's jaw so hard that Joe heard his teeth click together and he tasted blood. *He didn't mean to do it*, was Joe's last thought as he fell to the ground, and once again he felt himself floating free of his body.

✳   ✳   ✳

"Do you think it's true?" Madge asked. "The things Joe said about what's going on over in Europe?"

"If Joe said that's what the words mean, then it must be."

"I didn't mean that Joe would lie about it," Madge said miserably. "It's just so . . . unbelievable. That human beings could treat other human beings like that. Imagine knowing that could be happening to your family—"

"My mother's in Japan," Kiku blurted out. "She went to stay with my grandmother because she was sick, and now that we're at war with Japan, they'll never let her back in the country. And you heard what they were saying on the street about 'bombing those yellow devils to hell.'"

"Oh!" Madge cried. "I didn't know. I hadn't thought about it like that. . . . I guess I wasn't thinking very much at all. When this is all over and we find Dr. Bean and Miss Lake, I bet they'll know how to help your mother." She reached over and squeezed Kiku's hand, and Kiku felt a jolt of electricity pass between them.

"Then we'd better work on finding the book," Kiku said, squeezing Madge's hand back. "Why don't we read the clue to find the next chapter? Maybe we'll have it figured out before the boys come back."

"Do you think we should? Aren't we supposed to read them all together?" Madge asked.

"That's just the chapters," Kiku said. "I don't think it applies to the clues. Here." She picked up the page and read it aloud.

These pages lie
In wood where none may go,
Beneath the page where heroes die,
And all you see and know
May be a lie.

"Well, that's a gloomy little ditty," Madge said, making a face. "Remind me not to ask Sir Peanut Brittle to write my Christmas cards."

"It's certainly puzzling," Kiku said, wrinkling her brow. "Wood could mean a picture frame or the furniture in Decorative Arts. And there are lots of heroes depicted in paintings, but what does he mean by *all you see and know may be a lie*?"

"Beats me," Madge said. "Hey, maybe Joe could 'hear' what Sir Peanut Brittle meant. Come to think of it, maybe Joe can read the rest of the coded message and we won't even *need* to find the other chapters. I'm going to go find him. He and Walt have been gone awhile."

"Mmmm," Kiku murmured. She was staring at the pages they had just read through.

"I'll bring the boys back," Madge said. "Maybe you should drink some tea. You look a little . . ." Madge searched for a word that wouldn't hurt Kiku's feelings. The truth was Kiku looked the way Madge's father did after he'd had a couple of drinks down at the tavern. Her eyes were glassy and remote. ". . . peaked," she said, choosing a word her mother would use when Madge was overtired.

"Mmmm," Kiku murmured again. "You do that."

Madge rolled her eyes and left Kiku staring at the pages of the old book, which she seemed to find more interesting than Madge. No one wanted her around tonight. She seemed to keep saying the wrong thing. The nuns at school were always telling her, "Think before you speak, Margaret!" but everything she thought leapt straight to her lips. Talking was the way she thought things through.

"And you'll figure this thing out," she said aloud as she walked down the hallway to the exit door. As she opened it she remembered that Joe had the key but she didn't. If she went out and didn't find the boys she couldn't get back in—but that wasn't going to be a problem. She saw Joe right away. He was lying unconscious on the ground, and Walt was nowhere to be seen.

17

TROMPE L'OEIL

KIKU BARELY NOTICED when Madge left the room; she was too busy staring at the pages of the Kelmsbury. She wasn't reading it—she knew she wasn't supposed to do that. She was only looking at the pictures, specifically the ones in the margins where the artist had painted the dense undergrowth and intertwining branches of the Hewan Wood. She noticed sparks of gold paint in among the deep green and leaned closer to make out a figure drawn in delicate gold filigree. And then, as she stared at the figure, it moved.

The figure was slithering from branch to branch.

Kiku blinked. It was a trick of the eye, she told herself. A trompe l'oeil. Her father had shown her many examples in the museum.

She looked closer. The figure was a small person with catlike eyes, pointy ears, and an elfin face. A fairy. As she stared at it, the fairy blinked its eyes and slipped over the edge of the page and onto the next.

Kiku stood up quickly, upsetting the chair she'd been sitting on. It clattered to the floor so loudly she was afraid the guards would hear it and come. She waited for a moment, breath held. She was seeing things. She should go find the others. Where were they? Why had they left her here all by herself? Hadn't Dr. Bean said it was dangerous to read the Kelmsbury alone?

But this was rereading. They'd already read this chapter together. And that gold fairy was perhaps an important clue that only she was supposed to see. Maybe this was part of her power. Not just to vanish—but to vanish into a painting where she could see things that the others couldn't.

She sat back down at the table and turned the page. The next page showed Guinevere chasing the dove and Arthur chasing her, and the one after that showed them arriving at the castle. But what had happened to Morgaine and Lancelot in the woods? Why hadn't the writer shown that part of the story? Was it because they weren't as important?

Kiku turned back to the page where they had split ways. The picture on the center of the page followed Arthur and Guinevere, but the margins were full of drawings, too, and those, she saw now, followed Morgaine through the woods, where she met the gold fairy who gave her something—something too small to see.

What could it be? And why didn't the book tell *this* story? Why was Morgaine's story in the margins, when, quite frankly, it looked more interesting? Or maybe Morgaine's story was in the next chapter.

She turned to the last page where Sir Bricklebank had penciled in the next clue and read it again.

These pages lie
In wood where none may go,
Beneath the page where heroes die,
And all you see and know
May be a lie.

It wasn't even a good rhyme. The first and last lines ended with the same word—although, Kiku realized now, the word didn't mean the same thing in both lines. One meant to lie down, and the other meant to tell an untruth. And what kind of painting told an untruth but a trompe l'oeil? There were quite a few trompe l'oeil paintings in the museum and many painted on wood—but only one that she knew of that was made entirely of wood.

That must be where the chapter was. She could tell the others when they came back.

Or she could go get it now herself. She could turn herself invisible and go find it. She'd have it here waiting when the others finally decided to come back.

She gathered up the pages and weighed them down with the dagger and, for good measure, a heavy brass globe. As she placed it on top of the last page, she thought she saw the gold fairy wink at her—but that could've just been another trick of the eye.

The most famous example of trompe l'oeil in the museum was the *studiolo* of Federico da Montefeltro, Duke of Urbino, brought from Gubbio, Italy, two years ago and installed in the Italian Renaissance gallery. It was one of Kiku's favorite places in the museum, a tiny room lined in wood panels designed to look like the cabinets and bookcases of a Renaissance study. But what was so special was that the cabinets were made to look like they were open so you could see what lay inside them.

Only it was a trick. The books and lutes and other objects were all illusions fashioned out of strips of wood—*intarsia*, it was called. It was done so cunningly that it seemed as if you could reach out a hand and pluck one of the books from a shelf. Kiku had stared at them for hours trying to understand how the craftsmen had created the illusion. She remembered now that when the *studiolo* was being installed she would often find Sir Bricklebank there as well. He had told her he thought there might be hidden compartments in the panels. He could easily have placed a chapter in one of those.

She passed Mr. Carson napping on a sarcophagus in the Egyptian galleries, and Jenkins sitting on a bench in the Great Hall, but neither of them saw her, even though Jenkins looked right at her. She padded softly into the Medieval galleries and stopped in front of one of her favorite tapestries. It was called *Hawking Party* and showed a man and lady seated on the same horse and another lady seated on her own horse with a hawk perched on her hand. A man in a flowing orange shirt and brown leggings stood before her, holding out his hand. What Kiku loved most about the tapestry was the millions of flowers and plants stitched all over the dark green wool so that the figures seemed to be floating in a sea of woodland flowers. If she squinted her eyes, she could imagine herself surrounded by that magical forest. She could almost smell the ferns and trees—

Kiku turned away from the tapestry and found herself on a forest path. She was *inside* the tapestry. Standing in front of her was a small person, a few inches shorter than herself, dressed in a tattered gray-green tunic that looked like it had been stitched from leaves and was the same color as the person's skin. She couldn't tell if it was a boy or a girl. It smiled and revealed a mouth full of sharp, pointy teeth. Then it turned and skipped down the path, disappearing around a bend.

She should go back. If she followed the path back the way she'd come, she would come back to the museum—*wouldn't she?*—but if she went on, she might never find her way back. It had been a mistake to come looking for the Kelmsbury alone. As punishment she might be lost in this twilight land forever.

Or perhaps this is the only path to find the chapter and you are the only one who could find it.

The voice had a point. She remembered once coming

upon Sir Bricklebank standing in front of a painting of a woodland scene. When she had asked him what he was looking for, he'd said, "The way back in."

So perhaps Sir Bricklebank had been in these woods before and perhaps he'd hidden the third chapter here.

Taking a deep breath to calm the beating of her heart, she walked forward and rounded the bend. The little green person was just disappearing around the next bend. Kiku walked faster to catch up, afraid of being lost in these woods. There was no way of telling direction; the light filtering through the leaves was even all over, as if it didn't come from the sun, and the trees all looked alike. And somehow she had gotten off the path. She was crossing a field of bluebells. In the center of the field was a tiny stone cottage. The green person was sitting on the front step, chewing on a stalk of grass. It laughed at Kiku when she arrived, panting for breath, and cocked its thumb over its shoulder. "Go on," it said in a surprisingly husky voice. "He's waiting for you."

Kiku stepped inside the one-room cottage. She had thought she was beyond surprise, but she was amazed to find herself in a beautiful room paneled in fine wood, fitted with cabinets holding rare musical instruments, books, globes, and even a parrot in a cage. All of which she'd seen before. She was inside the *studiolo*, only what were tricks of the eye in the museum version were real here—as real as the old man in tweed who sat on a bench, paging through a book.

"Sir Bricklebank?" she asked.

The old man looked up from his book and smiled. "Ah, you're Mr. Akiyama's daughter, aren't you? Only you've grown since I saw you last."

"You've been missing for two years," Kiku said.

"Two years?" He pulled a pocket watch from his vest pocket and frowned. "But I've only been here an hour. . . . Never mind. I knew the risks when I came. Oh dear, you haven't had anything to eat, have you?"

"No!" Kiku shook her head.

"Then you should be fine." He gestured to a cup of tea and a plate of cookie crumbs. "My host offered me refreshments when I came, and I'd forgotten the rules, but no matter. I am content to remain here. There's an excellent selection of books in the Duke's collection."

"So this *is* the *studiolo* from the museum?"

"In a manner of speaking. It was crafted by a magician in the Duke of Montefeltro's employ to coexist in our world—or perhaps I should say *your* world—and another world, a world some would call Faerie."

A snorting noise from below caused Sir Bricklebank to pause. He looked down at the green person, who was squatting on a footstool, thumbing through a copy of Virgil's *Aeneid*. "Oh, excuse me; my friend Moth objects to the use of the term Faerie as too whimsical. Moth prefers Avalon, although frankly I don't see how that's much better. At any rate, we could talk all day, which would be several years in your world, about the physics of alternate universes and be none the wiser. Tell me what is happening in your world that has brought you here."

Kiku, unsure of where to begin, decided to start with the attack on Pearl Harbor, then went on to tell Sir Bricklebank about her meeting Madge, Joe, and Walt, what Dr. Bean had told them about the Kelmsbury, the dead spy, her father's abduction, the attack on New York, and how they had found the first two chapters.

"Ah, so my clues worked! I designed them, you see, so only the four true knights could follow them." He chuckled. "I'll bet Dash and Vivian were peeved they couldn't find the chapters."

"I think they were a bit . . . *concerned*," Kiku said cautiously. "Why didn't you want them to find the Kelmsbury? I mean, we're all on the same side, right?"

"Oh, yes, of course!" Sir Bricklebank exclaimed. "But Dash can be a bit of a know-it-all. If it had been up to him, he wouldn't have given you the chapters. So I had to hide them in a way that only the true knights would be able to find them. And here you are!"

"But have I ruined it all by coming here alone?"

"Not at all. You were meant to come by yourself, just as Morgaine . . . oh, but you haven't read the third chapter yet. You'll see. Even the closest of friends aren't meant to do everything together, and the best friendships are those that allow us to grow as individuals. But then you're used to being on your own, aren't you?"

"Yes," Kiku admitted. "I-I don't have a lot of friends."

"Ah, I thought I recognized a soulmate. I, too, have often been a solitary creature, but I have made a few friends over the years and so have you now. When you bring the third chapter back your friends will be pleased that you found it."

"They won't be angry that I found it on my own? Or see it as a betrayal? The second chapter says that one of the knights will betray the others. Does that mean one of us will betray our friends? Is that how the Kelmsbury works? Are we *becoming* the characters in the book?"

"Oh dear." Sir Bricklebank ran his long fingers through his silver hair until it looked like he'd stuck his finger in an electric socket. "I don't really know how it works. I know it's not healthy to read the book alone— too many voices in your head! I thought it would be safe if you all read it together." He sounded upset.

Moth stood up and stroked his arm, making a soothing sound, and hissed at Kiku, "You've stayed long enough, girl. Take what you came for and go."

"And leave him here?" Kiku asked.

"This is where he belongs," Moth began, and then, holding up a hand to shield the next words from Sir Bricklebank, added, "It's where he's always belonged. He just forgot."

Sir Bricklebank, calmer now, was feeding a cookie to the parrot. He did look as if he belonged in the little *studiolo*, as if it had been made for him.

"If you're sure," Kiku said.

"It's time to give her the chapter, Sir Peter," Moth said, nudging Sir Bricklebank.

"Oh yes, the chapter. Now, where did it get to?" He riffled through some loose papers on his desk, opened a cabinet and tossed out a lute, a number of quill pens, and what looked like an original Shakespeare folio.

"Um," Kiku said, "your clue said something about it being under where heroes die."

"Right! How clever of me! I meant Virgil's *Aeneid*, of course. Now, where did it go?" He stared down at the book Moth was holding. "Oh dear, you've moved it, haven't you, Moth? Now, where was it before? The lectern, I think . . ."

On the side of the lectern there was a small triangular opening out of which a slender roll of papers protruded. Sir Bricklebank drew it out and smiled. "Here it is!" he proclaimed, handing the rolled-up pages to Kiku. She looked down at the pages to make sure he'd given her the right ones and read the title: *In Which Morgaine Makes a Journey of Her Own in the Hewan Wood.*

"Oh, I suppose this must be the right one."

"You see," Sir Bricklebank said. "You were meant to make this journey on your own, but you don't have to read it alone. Take it back to read with your friends."

"I will, Sir Peter. Are you sure you don't want to come back with me?"

He shook his head sadly. "It is too late for me, dear. But do let me know how things turn out. You can leave a note for me right there." He tapped the small triangular opening on the side of the lectern.

"All right," Kiku said, unsure how she would leave a note on what would be a flat surface back in her world. "I'll try. I guess I'd better go . . ." She turned to face the open doorway, but all she saw there was forest. "But how will I get back?"

"Just go the way you came," she heard Sir Peter say. She looked back and saw that he was already bending over one of his books again. And then she noticed something strange. Where Sir Peter had raked his hair back, one pointed ear protruded, and when she looked down at his feet, she noticed they were cloven like a goat's.

"You see," Moth said, "he *does* belong here."

"You mean he was always . . ."

"One of us," Moth explained, "from the very beginning, the last of the people of the hills and the oldest of the old things. How do you think he had the power to hide the chapters so only the true knights could find them?"

"Oh, I see," Kiku said, although she didn't really.

As she turned to leave, Moth pointed to the pages in her hand. "Are you sure you want to read that?"

"Yes, of course," she said. "We have to in order to stop Mr. January from attacking the city."

"Perhaps," Moth said, "but if you and your friends read all the chapters the spell will be complete and you will suffer the same fates as the first knights."

"But then what can we . . ." she began, but before she could finish, Moth grinned and gave her a shove out the door.

"Oh!" Kiku cried, tripping over the doorstep. "But who—?" But when she looked back, she saw that the room was empty. All the objects that had been three-dimensional a moment ago were flat pictures on the wall. And when she turned around, she saw that she was standing in the Italian Renaissance gallery of the museum. The woods had disappeared.

Had she imagined it all? But she held the third chapter in her hands. She tucked it into her skirt pocket, where she could feel it nestled against her hip like a bird safe in its nest. She turned to go back, but a figure stepped out of the shadows to block her way.

18

THE RAMBLE

WHEN JOE CAME to, he was staring up into Madge's sky-blue eyes. His head hurt—but when she put her cool hand on his brow, he felt better. He remembered his *Tóta* putting her hand on his brow and singing him a song when he was sick. . . . *Sénta'wh Sóse Tehsakóhnhes, Konoronkhwa kwah tsi nén:we . . .*

"What happened?" Madge demanded.

"Mr. January . . ." he began. His tongue felt swollen.

"Mr. January did this to you?" Madge's fists clenched like she wanted to go hit somebody.

"No. Walt saw Mr. January and took off after him. I tried to stop him."

"And Freckles *hit* you?"

"He didn't mean to," Joe said, struggling to his feet. "He just struck out when I tried to stop him and my face got in the way of his fist."

"Golly, who'd've thunk it—Walt the he-man! I'm sorry about your face, but you gotta admit—it's pretty funny."

"It's not going to be funny if Walt catches up to Mr. January and gets himself killed."

"No," Madge agreed, her face sobered. "We'd better go find him."

Joe looked into the shadowy park. He'd spent the last few weeks living here and knew there were many dangers besides Mr. January. "Maybe you should go back inside and wait. Keep Kiku safe."

"Kiku's fine," Madge said, heading into the woods. "I left her lost in a book. What trouble could she get into?"

✳   ✳   ✳

"Miss Fitzbane," Kiku said, trying to keep her voice calm. "What are you doing here?"

Miss Fitzbane grinned. In the month that Miss Fitzbane had worked in the museum, Kiku had never seen her smile, and now she saw why. She had terrible teeth— small, pointy, yellow, and so crowded together that it looked like she had three sets of teeth instead of the usual one.

"I could ask you the same question."

"Oh!" Kiku said, wishing she could turn invisible *now*, but she couldn't summon up that floating feeling with Miss Fitzbane's glasses trained on her. "I'm looking for something I lost."

"Really?" Miss Fitzbane took a step closer, her skirt swishing. *What does she wear under there?* Kiku wondered. *A slip sewn out of sandpaper?*

"Um . . . yes . . . a file card with a description of a vase. I was . . . er . . . helping Monsieur Dupin with an exhibit and I thought I dropped it here."

"Hmph." Miss Fitzbane took another step closer and wrinkled her nose as if she could smell Kiku's lie. Kiku could smell something herself, but it was Miss Fitzbane's breath—a horrible combination of dead fish and bone-meal. Kiku understood now why Madge kept calling her Fishbone. "And did you find it?"

"What? Oh, the card! Um, no . . . I didn't. I must have left it downstairs."

"I thought I saw you put something in your pocket just now." She took another step closer, and Kiku stepped back into a display case. The paper in her pocket crinkled.

"Oh, that! It was just a map of the galleries I was looking at."

"Are you sure?" Miss Fitzbane asked, craning her neck like an old turtle. "Do I need to call the police to search you? I'm sure they'd be interested in an *enemy alien* lurking around the museum at night."

"P-please don't, Miss Fitzbane," Kiku stammered, trying very hard not to cry. "My father's already been taken, and this is the only place I have to stay. I promise I'm not hurting anything. C-could you please just look the other way?"

"The other way?" Miss Fitzbane parted her thin

lips and showed her awful teeth. "Well, I'm not entirely heartless. I suppose I could . . . only I'd want something from you in return."

"F-from me? What can I give you?"

This time when Miss Fitzbane smiled, Kiku was quite sure there were more teeth in her mouth than there should have been. "Just a little information. Nothing that you'll miss."

*　*　*

They were able to follow Walt because his footprints were the only ones made by Chuck Taylor All-Stars with Walt's initials carved into the soles and there were broken branches all over the place.

"It looks like a tornado went through here," Madge remarked, staring at the dark woods warily. The Ramble was where the tramps lived. She could hear sounds in the underbrush, dry leaves shifting underfoot, and branches creaking overhead. Patches of moonlight and shadow skittered along the ground like mice. With all that she had learned about the world in the last twenty-four hours, she suspected that the Ramble was home to creatures more dangerous than tramps.

The trail led them in circles and wobbly loops that doubled back on themselves like a ball of tangled yarn until Madge had lost all sense of direction. She didn't even feel like she was in the city anymore.

"It's like Mr. January was trying to confuse Walt," Joe said, "by doubling back on his path."

"I haven't been so dizzy since I rode the Cyclone at Coney Island. Look—what's this?" She was pointing at a sign carved on a tree—a wavy squiggle between two parallel lines. "What does this mean?"

"It's hobo language," Joe said. "Tramps leave each other signs to tell each other where to find food, which places are safe, which aren't . . ."

"Huh," Madge said, "and you can read it because of your power?"

"No," Joe said. "I can read it because I'm a tramp. Hey, is that Walt's beret?"

"It is!" Madge said, glad Joe had changed the subject. *You made him feel bad by reminding him he doesn't have a home*, the voice admonished her as she stepped off the path into a clump of prickly bushes to grab the hat from an overhanging branch. "It's got something sticky on it—Jeepers! I think it's blood!"

"That doesn't mean it's Walt's blood," Joe said, examining the beret. "Remember, Walt's got superstrength."

"Yeah, but I think Mr. January's got his own powers. Here—it looks like they went through here next . . ."

They stuck to the trail of broken branches, came out of the Ramble, and followed Walt's muddy footprints across a road and up another path until they emerged at the foot of a castle beside a lake. Fog lay over the water and around the base of the castle. That sense of having left the city far behind had never been stronger.

"I've a feeling we're not in Kansas anymore," Madge joked, trying to make herself less afraid.

"It's okay," Joe said, "I know this place. It's called Belvedere Castle. I come here sometimes because there are always school groups visiting." He pointed to a sign drawn on a tree—a circle with an *X* in the middle. "That means 'good chance to find food.' Kids throw out their half-finished lunches."

He needs to know he'll have someplace to go after all this is over, the voice inside Madge's head said.

But how can I offer him that? Madge said back to the voice, adding to herself: *Sheesh! Now I'm talking to myself!*

Just do it! the voice replied.

"Hey, Joe," Madge said, laying her hand on Joe's shoulder. "When this is all over, we'll figure out someplace for you to stay."

"Sure," Joe said, shrugging her hand away. "Look, I think I see Walt!"

Well, that didn't go so well, she told the voice as she followed Joe to a bench at the edge of the lake. *So unless you have more helpful suggestions—*

Look, the voice replied, *at what's in front of you.*

There was Walt, sitting on the bench beside a man who was unshaven and dressed in rags. A tramp who was dabbing at Walt's hand with a very dirty rag.

"There you are," she said to Walt. "You gave Joe quite a scare, hitting him like that." She looked down at Walt's right hand. Even though the tramp had cleaned away the blood, she could see that the knuckles were swollen and bruised. "Did that happen when you hit Joe—or Mr. January?"

"Mr. January," Walt said, turning his gaze from Madge to Joe. "I'm sorry I hit you, Joe."

"I know, sport, no hard feelings."

Walt nodded. *Boys!* Madge thought. It was always easy for them. They didn't hold grudges like girls did. "Here, let me take a look at that." She reached out for Walt's hand, but then the tramp looked up.

"Meg, is that you?"

Madge froze and looked at the tramp. "Da?"

"*Da?*" Joe repeated.

The tramp dropped his head. "I'm sorry you have to see me this way."

Walt moved over so Madge could sit down next to him. For a moment she felt too stunned to move. She'd thought for months what she would do and say if she saw her father, but now that he was in front of her she wasn't sure what to say, which wasn't like her at all. Finally she sat down and said the only things she could think of. "I'm glad to see you, Da. I've been so worried about you."

"You shouldn't worry over me, Meg. You should go on

and live your life. Is Aunt Jean treating you all right?"

"Sure, Da, only I wish you'd come home."

He shook his head. Then he looked at Joe and Walt. "Are these your friends?"

"Yes, this is Walt—and Joe."

Joe stepped forward and held out his hand. "It's a pleasure to meet you, Mr. McGrory." Her father took Joe's hand warily.

"I've made other friends, too, Da. They could help you—"

"We don't need no one's charity, Meg." He got to his feet shakily, his legs unsteady. Walt got to his feet at the same time and steadied her father with his arm around his shoulder.

"There's no weakness in accepting help from someone," Joe said in a surprisingly deep voice.

Madge smiled at him and then looked back at her father, who had completely changed in the two seconds she had looked away. He had straightened his back and pulled back his shoulders. His eyes had sharpened and cleared. He looked at Joe and Walt as if he had just awoken from a dream. Then he looked back at Madge.

"You're right about that, son," he told Joe. And then to him and Walt, "You two keep an eye on my Meggie. And take care of yourselves, too." He started walking away, but then he turned back and looked at Walt. "And stay away from that man, son. He's no good."

"Da!" Madge cried, getting to her feet. But her father

broke into a trot that she wouldn't have thought him capable of a moment ago and vanished into the fog. Madge started to go after him, but Joe stopped her.

"He's not ready," he said, leading Madge back to the bench. "But it made him better to see you."

"You two made him better," Madge said. "You said just the right thing to him, Joe, and you gave him your strength, Walt . . . but what did he mean about staying away from that man? Did he mean Mr. January? What happened, Walt?"

"Nothing," Walt said in an oddly flat voice. "I caught up to him . . . and I hit him but it didn't matter to him. He just laughed."

"Still," Joe said, "you showed him we mean business."

"Yeah, and not all this blood is yours, so now we know he's just a normal guy like the rest—"

"He's not!" Walt cried, suddenly alert. "He's not normal and he's nothing like the rest of us. When I hit him, his face felt spongy and he didn't even flinch. I coulda beat his face to a pulp and it wouldn't have mattered . . . because it's not his face. He wears someone else's because he doesn't have one of his own."

"What do you mean, he doesn't have a face?" Madge asked uneasily. "Everyone's got a face."

"Not him. Don't you see—he's the two-faced knight from the story. We should have realized it right away from the name January; it comes from the Roman god with two faces."

Walt got up and started walking back toward the museum.

"But that would make him hundreds of years old," Madge said, catching up to him. Joe jogged up on the other side of Walt, but he had to duck to keep away from Walt's flailing hands.

"He *is* old," Walt said. "He's somehow kept himself alive. It's like he feeds on evil. . . ." Walt shuddered, and Madge tried to reach out to touch his shoulder, but he threw out his arms again, nearly striking her in the face. Was he afraid of her touching him?

He's frightened, the pesky voice inside her head said. *You have to reassure him—*

"Put a sock in it!" Madge shouted out loud.

Joe stopped and stared at her, but Walt just shook his head and kept walking, muttering, "Okay, I will, that's exactly what I'll do. I'll put a sock in it."

"Good going," Joe said to Madge as he followed Walt.

"I didn't mean . . ." Madge began, but realized that telling the boys she'd been talking to a voice inside her head wasn't going to inspire confidence in her judgment. So she took her own advice and followed the boys into the museum without another word.

19

THE HOUR OF THE FISH

"WHAT TOOK YOU so long?" Kiku asked when they came through the workroom door. She had arranged the pages in a neat pile and sat with her hands clasped over them. If she squeezed them tightly enough, she could keep them from shaking.

"Walt saw Mr. January outside the museum and took off after him," Madge said. "Joe and I went after him."

Kiku saw Madge exchange a look with Joe. Walt wasn't looking at anyone. His hands were jammed in his pockets and he was staring at the table. *They're not telling me something*, Kiku thought.

They don't trust you, a voice said inside her head. It was Morgaine's voice. It had been there since she'd read the chapter alone, which she had done as soon as she had left Miss Fitzbane and come back to the workshop. If the others knew that she had read it alone then they wouldn't trust her anymore.

I should tell them about what happened with Miss Fitzbane, Kiku thought.

If you tell them, they'll really never trust you again. Can't you see—

"So what happened," Kiku asked, "when you caught up with Mr. January?"

"Nothing," Walt said, not meeting Kiku's eyes. "I-I hit him, but it didn't do any good. He just laughed at me and got away."

"And what about you two?" Kiku turned to Madge and Joe. "What were you doing? Couldn't you stop him?"

"He was gone by the time we got there," Joe said.

You see, they're lying to you. What were Madge and Joe doing all that time alone in the forest?

"Did you get lost?" Kiku asked.

"Sort of," Madge answered, blushing. "Hey, is that the third chapter?"

Kiku looked down at the pages under her clasped hands. "Yes," she said, "I figured out the third clue and went to get it."

"All by yourself?" Madge asked.

"I *do* know the museum better than the rest of you."

"That's not what I meant," Madge said. "It's just that we're not supposed to do it alone."

"We're not supposed to read the chapter alone. I didn't read it." The lie came out of her mouth before she could stop it. *They* obviously had their own secrets; why shouldn't she? "I just *found* it."

"Yeah, but . . ." Madge began.

"It doesn't matter now," Joe said. "The important thing is we have the chapter. We can read it and then decode the next clue. What's this one called?"

"I can't make out the writing. Here—" Kiku passed the chapter to Joe, hoping no one would notice that her hands were shaking. Then she got up and walked toward the alcove. "I'll make us some tea while you read it."

"Don't you want to hear it?" Madge asked, getting up to follow her.

She was always bossy, Morgaine whispered in her head.

"Can't you just be quiet for two minutes!" Kiku said to the voice. But Madge must have thought she was talking to her. Her face turned as red as her hair.

"I-I thought you wouldn't want to miss the chapter," Madge said.

"I have a headache," Kiku said. "And I'm sure I'll be able to hear it from here."

"Sure," Madge said, "Sister Veronica was always telling me my voice gave her a headache. I'll just sit down and be quiet while Joe reads it."

Madge went back to the table and sat down with her hands folded tightly in front of her as if she were trying to stop her thoughts from flying out of her fingertips. Kiku felt terrible. Madge had been nice to her, taking her back to her home, doing her hair—

Trying to make you into something you're not.

—but how could she explain that Morgaine's voice was in her head because she'd read the chapter by herself? And how would she sit at the table with them pretending she hadn't read the chapter already? She busied herself making tea while Joe read the chapter.

IN WHICH MORGAINE MAKES A JOURNEY OF HER OWN IN THE HEWAN WOOD.

Morgaine was glad at first to be on her own in the forest. She had grown up an only child in Tintagel Castle and was unused to spending so much time in the company of others. Now she enjoyed the company of trees and ferns and the birds that flitted in the treetops. A flash of gold in the upper boughs caught her attention and she followed it deeper into the woods, straying off the path into a field of bluebells. When she looked up to find her bearings she couldn't find the sun anywhere. The forest was full of a soft golden light that didn't seem to be coming from anywhere at all. She turned in a circle looking for the path back to her friends and found herself facing a small pointy-eared person dressed in a gray-green tunic stitched from leaves and ferns. He wore a wreath of leaves around his head and a mischievous smile on his face.

"Well met, Morgaine le Fay," the person said. "Welcome to Avalon."

"I thought I was in the Hewan Woods," she said, not liking that the person knew her name.

"You crossed over to Avalon as you wandered."

"Have my friends . . . crossed over too?"

The person laughed, a tinkling sound that made the leaves in the trees dance and the bluebells chime. "They are ordinary humans who cannot cross from world to world as you can, Morgaine of the Fairies. You have far more power than them. If you wished, you could rule the kingdom instead of Arthur."

"I am content to be Arthur's sister and friend and to counsel him."

"Are you?" the fairy—for fairy he certainly was— asked, laughing again. This time his laughter made the very trees sway and shake and the air darken to murky green. Morgaine smelled copper and remembered all her grievances: the way Arthur always thought he knew best and Guinevere was always fussing with her hair and Lancelot couldn't keep his eyes off Guinevere.

"Could you show me how to be more powerful?" Morgaine asked.

The fairy smiled. His teeth were pointed and sharp looking. "Yes," he said. And so he did. When Morgaine rejoined the others she had gained powers beyond imagining—nor could she imagine yet how she would use them.

Everyone was quiet when Joe finished reading. Kiku stood in the alcove waiting for someone to say something. Would they know that Kiku had also wandered into Avalon as Morgaine had? Would they guess she had also met someone who had tempted her to betray the others? Why weren't they talking?

Finally, when she couldn't stand the suspense anymore, she brought the tea tray into the room and laid it down on the table. Everyone looked up at her.

They've guessed, Morgaine whispered in her head. *They will never trust you again.*

But then Joe smiled at her. "Is your headache better? We were trying to be quiet while Walt decoded the message until you felt better."

She smiled back at him. "I feel better now." She poured Madge a cup of tea. "You don't have to be quiet on my account."

"Good," Walt said, "Because I've got it. But it's not good. It says: 'You will be given further instructions and the means to carry out your part in the attack on the Day of the Archer at the Hour of the Fish under the Sign of the Bull. Bring a Gladstone.'"

"What the heck does that mean?" Madge asked.

"A Gladstone is a kind of small suitcase," Kiku said. "I think Dr. Bean's got one in his closet here."

"Not *that*," Madge said, rolling her eyes. "I mean the other stuff about the Archer and the Bull and the Fish! I've heard the toughs in our neighborhood talking about sleeping with the fishes, but that's not a good thing."

"They're signs of the zodiac," Walt said. "My aunt Sadie reads her horoscope in the paper. The Archer is

Sagittarius—that's the ninth sign of the zodiac, so that must mean the ninth day—

"Which is tomorrow!" Kiku said, and then looking down at her watch. "Or actually today! What about the Fish?"

"The Fish are Pisces," Walt said. "They're the twelfth sign, so it must mean 12:00 noon."

"Good," Joe said, "that gives us some time to get there."

"What do you mean?" Kiku asked. "You don't want to go to this place!"

"We have to," Joe said. "He says there will be further instructions. If we don't go, we won't be able to figure out where the attack will take place. But what does he mean 'under the Sign of the Bull'?"

"The sign of the Bull is the constellation of Taurus," Walt said. "But I don't understand what he means either. Are we supposed to figure out where Taurus is in the sky and go there?"

"But it's getting light out," Kiku said, looking with alarm at the pale gray light filtering down from the high windows. "And you can't even see the stars well in the city."

"Not in the sky, maybe," Madge said, grinning, "but I know one place in the city where the stars shine all day long."

Know-it-all! the voice inside her head said, but she was no longer sure whose voice it was—hers or Morgaine's.

20

THE WHISPERING GALLERY

LIKE ANY TRUE New Yorker, Madge had passed through Grand Central Terminal more times than she could count, but she almost never paused to look up. *Who has time?* she would have replied if anyone asked. But today, even though she had less time than ever, she stopped right in the middle of the main concourse and tilted her head back, gawking like any tourist.

The ceiling far, far above her was the blue-green shade of tarnished copper and robin's eggs mixed together. The lights twinkled like stars on a summer night, and gold figures of animals and men in togas sprawled across it. She'd never thought much about what they were doing up there while she and thousands of New Yorkers hurried down below. *What does it have to do with me?* she would have said if you'd asked her. But in the last two days she'd realized that the big world around her *did* have a lot to do with her. A man giving an order to drop bombs thousands of miles away had plunged her country into war. A book written hundreds of years ago was changing the way she thought. So maybe she wasn't so distant from these flying animals and robed gods after all (*Only, sheesh! Could that fella with the big vase put some pants on?*). The one thing she did know was that if the great wide world could come busting into *her* life, then she could darn well bust into the world.

The first thing she was going to do was find Mr. January and give him a piece of her mind. The message said he'd be waiting under the Sign of the Bull at noon. But everyone and his uncle knew the place to meet at Grand Central was at the big clock. When they had split up earlier ("In case Mr. January tries to follow us," Walt had suggested) they agreed to enter the main concourse from four separate directions.

Were the others here yet? She looked around the station and saw a girl and a soldier locked in a clinch. *Jeez Louise! They aren't shy at all!* There were two more couples near the big clock and, Madge noticed as she scanned the floor of the vast main concourse, dozens more just like them—gals saying good-bye to their fellows before they shipped out. In fact, the whole station was full of soldiers carrying duffel bags. One rushed by her now, bumping into her. "Hey, watch where—" she began, but when she met the boy's eyes, she swallowed her complaint. Golly, he looked hardly older than Frankie!

"Watch yourself over there, soldier," she said instead.

"Sure thing, doll face. How about a good-bye kiss?"

"In your dreams, buddy! Keep on marching!"

The boy grinned and saluted Madge. Then he ran across the concourse toward the train tracks, joining up with a dozen soldiers in khaki uniforms all slapping one another on the back and laughing in that loud way boys had when they were trying not to show how scared they were. She could hear the sound of that laughter echoing all around the concourse along with the strains of "Chattanooga Choo Choo." That would be Mary Read playing her organ up in the north balcony. Madge had read in the paper that when Mary had played "The Star-Spangled Banner" on Sunday after the attack, everyone in the whole station had stopped where they were and stood with hand over heart singing just as loud as they could. The station managers had asked Mary please not to play the national anthem anymore. After all, they had a train station to run, and it was busier than ever with all the soldiers on the move.

In the middle of all that rushing stood Joe in her father's coat and knit cap, carrying a brown Gladstone bag. They'd decided that one of them would have to pretend to be the dead spy to make the trade off, and since Joe looked the oldest, he would stand under the sign of the Bull and wait for Mr. January. He was looking up at the clock. He could have been any one of the dozens of guys waiting for his girl to say good-bye to. No one would know that he was waiting for a spy with a weapon that could kill everyone in the station.

But Madge knew and it made Joe seem vulnerable to her—like he was pretending to be tough to hide how scared he was.

She looked around for the others—yes, there was Kiku in the east balcony, looking mysterious in the veiled hat Madge had given her, leaning on the ledge just above a sign for US war bonds. She was reading a piece of paper which Madge guessed was the clue that told where the next chapter of the Kelmsbury was. They hadn't been able to figure it out before they left— something about a coffin of bone—and Kiku had brought it along. Madge could tell she didn't like not being able to figure it out.

She looked around next for Walt. He was supposed to be on the south side, but Madge didn't see him. Maybe he was out in the waiting room. She'd just have a quick look to be sure. Freckles had been acting a little funny since his run-in with Mr. January last night in the park.

Madge turned and walked back over the bridge that led to the waiting room. As she passed over the bridge, she saw a flash of red hair on the ramp below that led to the lower level. She looked over the ledge and saw Walt walking down the ramp toward the Oyster Bar. What was he doing down there? Had he gotten lost? Or maybe he had seen something—or *someone*. It would be just like Walt to go after Mr. January all by himself again. She'd better go down and see if he needed help getting out of a jam.

She went around the corner to the entrance to the downstairs ramp and headed down toward the Oyster Bar, where she stopped for a moment gazing longingly inside the fancy restaurant. Once when they'd been taking the train to New Haven to see Aunt Jean in a show, she'd begged her mother and father to take her inside and her father had relented. They'd sat at the counter and eaten clam chowder with little round crackers. It was still the best meal she'd ever had.

She turned back to look for Walt. The area in front of the Oyster Bar was covered by vaulted ceilings that were paved in shiny tiles. Her father had explained that because of how the arches were shaped, sound traveled differently under them so a person whispering on one side could be heard by someone all the way on the other. The vaulted space was called the whispering gallery. She and Frankie had tested it out, sending secret messages like "The coast is clear" and "Beware the man in black" across the crowded space. It was just the kind of thing Walt would love—and there he was! Standing on the other side of the gallery, leaning against a pillar, eating a Nedick's hot dog. No wonder he wasn't at his post—he'd gotten hungry! Madge would give him a scare. He was in just the right place to hear a whisper from where she stood. She was debating between "Back to your post, soldier!" and "Crime does not pay . . . The Shadow knows!" when a man approached Walt. A man in a trench coat with a wide-brimmed hat pulled low over his face and collar turned up.

Mr. January.

Walt turned pale when he saw him, but he didn't run. He stood stock-still while Mr. January leaned toward him and whispered in his ear. A whisper that Madge, positioned in just the right place across the whispering gallery, heard perfectly well.

"Everything is set up as we arranged," Mr. January said. "It's time to play your part."

21

UNDER THE BIG CLOCK

BEFORE MADGE HAD a chance to react, Walt had tossed the rest of his hot dog into the trash and was walking up the ramp to the upper level, leaving Mr. January behind. Madge hesitated, torn between following Mr. January or Walt. *Follow Walt*, the voice said, *he's more important*. For once she agreed.

She took off up the ramp to catch him, wondering what Mr. January had meant by *as we arranged*. Walt wouldn't enter into an arrangement with their enemy. There had to be a mistake. Maybe Mr. January had said that because he knew Madge was listening and he wanted to make her suspicious of Walt—the last person anyone would suspect of being a traitor. Walt was probably headed right now to find her and Joe and Kiku and warn them that Mr. January was in the building.

And yes, Walt was walking across the main concourse straight toward Joe—only Madge noticed now that he was carrying a brown Gladstone bag.

Was *he* planning to make the switch with the spy? But why? If Mr. January knew all about them, why still have his spy make the drop? Madge couldn't figure it out—and neither could Joe, who was staring at Walt as he approached him, or Kiku, who was staring at Walt from the east balcony. But neither of them saw what Madge saw: a man in grimy overalls and a cap pulled low over his eyes walking from the north side of the concourse toward the clock. He was carrying a brown Gladstone bag. Jeepers! If they didn't stop Walt, *he* was going to make the switch.

Madge hurried toward Walt, but a stout lady in a fur coat, carrying half a dozen shopping bags, cut in front of her. "Watch out, lady!" Madge cried swatting aside a violet-bestrewn Bonwit bag. She dodged around a soldier and his sweetheart and a nanny pushing a pram, all the time keeping her eyes fixed on Walt as he shouldered past Joe and kept on marching toward the man in overalls. Joe looked around confusedly. He must have thought it was a change of plan. He caught Madge's eye and shrugged.

"Go after him!" Madge cried. "Stop Walt!"

As Joe turned to follow Walt, the clock struck noon, and Mary Read started playing "The Star-Spangled Banner" in defiance of the stationmaster's request. Everyone in the Great Hall stopped in their tracks, turned to the American flag hanging over the entrance to the waiting room, and, with hand over heart, started singing along. For a moment, time seemed to stop. Madge could see Walt. He had reached the man in overalls and already had his hand out to take the bag from him, but at the sound of the anthem, Walt froze.

He won't be able to do it, Madge thought. Not with the rockets' red glare and the bombs bursting in air being belted out around him by soldiers and their sweethearts, and porters and little old grannies, and a whole troop of Boy Scouts. Madge found herself singing along as loud as she could as if by doing so, she could keep Walt from taking that bag. And it was almost as if Walt heard her. He turned and their eyes met across the crowded station.

Then he turned away and took the bag from the man in the overalls. Madge felt the song die in her throat.

As soon as Walt had the new bag in his hands, he broke into a run, tucking the bag under his arm like a football and sprinting for the tracks like Red Grange the Galloping Ghost going for the goal line. The man in overalls, looking momentarily startled at this turn of events, also turned and ran toward the tracks. Where was Walt going with the bag? Was he getting on a train? It didn't make any sense! All Madge knew was that she had to catch up with Walt before he did something he would regret forever.

As she ran by Joe, he turned and followed her, dropping his Gladstone bag. They ran toward Track 24, shouldering past commuters boarding the train. Had Walt gotten on the train already? There was a train idling on either side of the platform—one for Greenwich, Connecticut, and the other for Poughkeepsie. Walt could have gotten on either one.

"You take Greenwich, I'll take Poughkeepsie," Madge shouted. "Check every car!"

Joe disappeared into the Greenwich train, and Madge hopped on the Poughkeepsie one, dodging past a ticket collector and that same darned fur-coated woman with all the shopping bags. She checked each car, slapping down newspapers held in front of faces and tossing up a beaver coat lying over a sleeping girl in a Vassar sweater, but she didn't see any sign of Freckles. She hopped out of the last car seconds before the train pulled out—and saw Walt getting out of the last car of the Greenwich train, which was already pulling out of the station. Joe sprang out of the moving train right behind Walt. Walt turned to run back toward the concourse, but then he saw Madge.

"It's okay," Madge said, although she really didn't think anything was okay. "The important thing is you got the bag. We can stop Mr. January now."

"No," Walt said. "That's the problem, Madge. We *can't* stop him like this. He's too powerful, he—"

"What did he offer you?" Joe asked. "Did he say he'd help your family?"

Walt turned to look at Joe, then his eyes flicked back to Madge. "Anyone would understand if you made a deal with him," she said. "Anyone would do the same."

Something changed in Walt's face. It was as if all the light went out of it. "Would *you*?" Walt asked. "If Mr. January offered to help get your brothers out of St. Vincent's, would *you* betray your city and country?"

How did Walt even know her brothers were in St. Vincent's? She hadn't told the others. Mr. January must have told him, which made Madge go cold all over. What *would* she do if Mr. January offered to get them out? She opened her mouth to answer. She had every intention of saying, "Yeah, sure," but she couldn't, because she knew it wasn't true. And Walt, looking into her eyes, would know it wasn't true.

"I didn't think so," Walt said. He was about to say something else, but the shrill whistle of a train pulling into the next track cut him off. He looked back at Madge and said something to her quietly, as if they were in the whispering gallery and not on a crowded, loud platform.

"I'm sorry," he said.

Then he leapt in front of the approaching train.

22

COFFIN OF BONE

"WALT!" MADGE SCREAMED, bolting toward the track. But Joe caught her before she could jump after Walt and held on to her as the train thundered into the station. He had seen what happened and needed to make Madge hear him.

"Walt's okay," he screamed into her ear. "He made it to the other side."

But Madge wouldn't take his word for it. She got loose from his hold and ran toward the end of the platform so she could cross over to the other track. Joe followed her, fighting through the mayhem of hysterical travelers who had seen a boy jump in front of a train. When they reached the next track, policemen and conductors were trying to clear the track of civilians, but Madge bulldozed through, screaming that her friend was on the track. A burly policeman tried to hold her back, but Madge kicked him in the shins and ducked around him, and Joe followed in her wake. When they got onto the platform Joe saw Kiku but no Walt. Had he been wrong about what he'd seen? It had seemed incredible that Walt could leap over the width of a train track, but then, Walt wasn't the same anymore.

And neither are you. It was the voice he'd been hearing since last night. He was pretty sure now that it was the voice of Lancelot and he had begun to trust in that voice. But there was another voice in his head that he'd heard when he had touched Mr. January's note last night.

"Where's Walt?" Madge demanded of Kiku. "Did you see him clear the track? Is he all right?"

Kiku nodded, her eyes wide. "He flew across the track like he was Superman and then leapt across the next track and went through that service door." She pointed to a low door beneath the platform. "I called to him to stop, but he wouldn't. I'm afraid he's gone over to Mr. January's side."

"No," Madge said, shaking her head, tears filling her eyes. Joe hadn't seen Madge cry before. It was almost as incredible as Walt clearing that track.

"I'm afraid she's right," Joe said, touching Madge's arm. "Mr. January must have offered Walt a deal when he caught up to him in the park last night."

"He'd just found out that the Nazis were rounding up Jews in France," Kiku said. "If Mr. January offered to help get his family out of France, he might have been tempted."

"I'm sure Mr. January can be very convincing," Joe

said, remembering the voice he'd heard last night, urging him to betray his friends and join his side and offering in return to get Jeanette out of the Mush Hole. Joe had had to scream to make the voice stop, but since then he'd heard it lurking in his thoughts, tempting him.

"Who could blame him if he agreed to take part in the sabotage plot, to save them," Joe said.

"I still can't believe it," Madge said. "Walt wouldn't hurt anyone."

"Maybe not the Walt who we met two days ago," Joe said, "but let's face it: we've all changed in these last two days. The book's changed us. The old Walt wouldn't have hit me last night, and he couldn't have leaped across a train track in front of a moving train."

"So?" Madge challenged him. "The book's given him superstrength just like it's given you the ability to understand languages and Kiku an invisibility cloak."

"It's doing more than that," Kiku said. "I hear voices inside my head."

"Me too," Joe said. "And those voices aren't all *good*. Last night when I touched Mr. January's letter I heard his voice. He tried to make me betray you all, and he offered to make me strong enough to get my sister out of the Mush Hole."

"So you think Walt's got some evil voice inside his head telling him to do bad things?" Madge demanded.

"Maybe," Kiku said. "Last night I heard Morgaine's voice."

Both Joe and Madge stared at her. "And what did Morgaine tell you to do?" Madge asked.

"She wanted me to read the third chapter. I-I . . . sort of did."

"Sort of?" Madge asked. "But we're not supposed to—"

"Do you always do what you're *supposed to*?" Kiku challenged.

"No, but I think I'd stay away from reading a book that's supposed to make you crazy. . . ."

"I read the second chapter on my own," Joe said, inserting himself between the two bickering girls. "The voice told me to. I-I think the voices want us to read it on our own so we're in the book's power and *they* have more power over us."

"Well, *my* voice hasn't told me to read the book on my own," Madge said.

"Your voice?" Kiku echoed. "What *has* it told you to do?"

"Mostly it's told me to pay more attention to you guys."

"Oh," Kiku said, looking a little disappointed. "I guess you got the good voice. I suppose Guinevere always does the right thing."

"I don't think it's Guinevere," Madge said, "but look, we don't have time to argue about who's who. We have to find Walt and find out what's in that bag."

"Walt might have gotten the bag," Joe said, "but we've still got the rest of the spy's message. It might tell us enough about the attack for us to stop it—and Walt."

"But we still need the fourth chapter of the Kelmsbury to decode it," Madge said, "and even Kiku hasn't been able to figure it out."

Kiku took the folded page out of her pocket. "Madge is right. I don't understand it. Maybe you'll have better luck, Joe." She handed the page to him.

Joe unfolded the paper and read the lines aloud:

The last adventure is buried in a coffin of bone
Protected by knights brave and ladies fair.
But first you must cross a bridge of stone
And enter the lion's lair.

"Coffin of bone," Madge repeated with a shudder. "What the heck does that mean? Sir Peanut Brittle must have really lost his marbles."

I know what it means, the voice inside Joe's head said. It wasn't Mr. January's voice, it was the other voice that had come when he read the second chapter by himself. Lancelot's voice. *It's a box. I've seen it.* Joe closed his eyes, and a crowd of images flooded his brain—soldiers, a castle, a hunter spearing a unicorn, a knight battling a lion . . . and then he wasn't just looking at the pictures, he was part of them. He was the knight battling the lion *and* he was the lion; he was the unicorn pierced by the spear, he was the knight storming the castle *and* the knight standing on the battlements. . . .

"Joe!" He came to with Madge holding him by the

arms and shaking him. "Are you all right?"

"I-I think so," he stammered. "Wh-what happened?"

"You were saying all these words in some foreign language and then you passed out."

"I saw this box. . . ." He described the scenes on the box as if he'd only seen them, not lived them.

"I think I know the box you're talking about," Kiku said. "It's an ivory casket in the medieval collection. It has scenes from Arthurian romances carved on it. That must be why Sir Bricklebank hid the last chapter in it."

"Then what are we waiting for?" Madge said. "Let's get back to the museum and find this box."

"It's not in the Metropolitan anymore," Kiku said. "It was moved last year."

"Don't tell me it's on loan to some place in Detroit!" Madge cried.

"Not as bad as that. It was moved to the Metropolitan's medieval museum, the Cloisters."

"I don't suppose you have keys to that museum," Joe said.

"No, and the Cloisters closes at three today." Kiku looked at the slim watch on her wrist. "Which only gives us a few hours to get up there and find it, and I'm afraid it's way uptown."

"Then we'd better get a move on," Madge said. "Where is this place, the Bronx?"

"Almost," Kiku said. "It's at the northern tip of Manhattan, in Washington Heights."

"No problem," Madge said. "We can take the shuttle to Times Square and transfer to the uptown IRT."

"Thank goodness for Madge," Kiku said to Joe as they followed her to the subway entrance. "If I'd told her the Cloisters were in Camelot, I think she'd have gone and found us a train there."

"Yeah, thank goodness for Madge," Joe said, not meeting Kiku's eyes because if he did, he might be tempted to tell her that he'd just been to Camelot. He'd been one of the knights standing on the battlements defending the castle against an invading horde. Morgaine had been there, and Arthur and Guinevere.

He couldn't tell her because then he'd have to tell her that he'd watched them all die.

23

THE CLOISTERS

MADGE FOUND THEM all seats on the shuttle, but when Kiku sat down, the woman sitting next to her got up and moved. Kiku put down the veil of her hat and looked miserable. When they got on the IRT she vanished altogether.

"What the Sam Hill—" Madge began, but Joe put his finger to his lips and motioned at a couple of tough-looking guys jostling each other and talking about "killing Japs."

"Oh," Madge said. "But where do you think she went?"

Joe shrugged. "Let's hope she sticks close and gets off when we do."

They found two seats together that were, unfortunately, directly across from where the loudmouths had sat down.

"I say we toss the lot o' them in jail," one said. "The ones down in Chinatown, too."

"Charlie, we're not at war with China," his friend said.

"Yeah, but you can't tell those gooks apart, and the Japs could be hiding out—hey!" Charlie's cap flew off his head. "Why'dya do that, Fred?"

"Whaddaya talking about?" Fred complained. "I ain't done nothin'."

"Ya knocked my hat off!" Charlie leaned over to pick up his hat, but it rolled out of reach. Madge clapped her hand over her mouth to keep from giggling. Charlie followed his hat down the aisle, stooped over, but every time he almost had it, the hat rolled out of reach. Then it flew up and landed on the head of a nun.

"What the—"

The nun glared at Charlie. "Do you think this is an appropriate time for hijinks and shenanigans, young man?" she asked, removing the cap from her head.

"No, Sister, I—"

"Then keep your hat and your opinions to yourself. The last thing we need at a time like this is to sow hate and suspicion."

"Yes, Sister," Charlie said, taking his hat and returning meekly to his seat, where he sat mutely clutching his errant hat in his meaty fists until he and his friend got off at 175th Street.

Joe and Madge got off at 190th Street. As they came out of the station, Kiku appeared at their side. "You sure showed those fellas," Madge said, clapping Kiku on the shoulder.

"I have to admit I enjoyed it," she said with a smile

that evaporated too quickly. *Poor Kiku*, Madge thought. *It must be awful to hear everyone bad-mouthing the place your family came from.* Madge hated it when she heard people saying all Irish people were drunks. "Here, we can cut through Fort Tryon Park to get to the Cloisters."

Kiku led the way through tall gates and past a garden of low shrubbery, explaining that she'd often visited the park with her parents. "My mother loves when the heather blooms in the spring," she said, "but I guess she won't be here this spring."

Now there were only dead bushes covered in frost, and a man in ragged clothing huddled on a bench.

Give alms before a battle, the voice in her head said.

"Wait," Madge said. She walked over to the tramp, who was eyeing her suspiciously. "Here—" She handed him the buffalo nickel she'd been saving for Frankie. "I'm sorry I don't have more, but maybe it will bring you luck."

The tramp looked up at her with surprisingly clear eyes. "Thank you, my lord. I will hope to be of service to you someday when you are in need."

"Sure, fella, whatever you say." Madge walked away shaking her head.

"Why'd you do that?" Kiku asked.

"I don't know," Madge said. "It just felt right . . . like what Walt would do. At least what the old Walt would do."

"Yeah," Joe and Kiku said at the same time. Kiku led them through the gardens to a stone bridge.

"Just like in Sir Peanut Brittle's clue," Madge said. As they came to the end of the bridge, Madge stopped and gasped. In front of them, a castle rose above the trees.

"Gosh, a real castle! Frankie would flip over this. It looks like something out of a picture book. Or like someone plucked it out of England or France and dropped it here in New York City."

"That's pretty much what Mr. Rockefeller did," Kiku said. "Except he brought a half a dozen different pieces of old abbeys and reassembled them here."

They walked across a lawn to an arched entranceway. It looked like the entrance to the Maiden Castle in the book. They stood in front of the castle, looking up at the tower, the stones golden in the afternoon sunlight.

"It doesn't feel right being here without Walt," Madge said at last.

"No," Joe agreed. "But Walt—the old Walt—would want us to keep going."

Madge nodded. "We have to do this for Walt," she said. "If Mr. January forces him to hurt anyone, he'll never be the same."

"No," Kiku said, "how could he live with himself?" And then, blinking in the sun, she held out her hand. "For Walt." Joe laid his hand on top of hers, and Madge placed hers on top of Joe's. She felt a pulse of energy, a warmth that spread up her arm and through her whole body. She could tell the others felt it too by the way Kiku's eyes widened and Joe's face glowed.

"Let's go," Joe said, starting for the entrance. Kiku followed him. Madge stood for a moment on the threshold, waiting for the feeling to pass.

They were afraid, she heard the voice say in her head, *and you took the fear away. That's what a leader does.* Which should have made her feel glad. Only the fear she had taken from her friends had lodged in her own stomach like a heavy cold stone dropped into a well.

✶　✶　✶

"The museum closes in one hour," the guard told them.

"Oh, I just wanted to give my friends from out of town a quick look," Madge said.

"Yes," Kiku said, "do you know where—"

Madge elbowed Kiku in the ribs. "Where the little girls' room is?" Madge asked. "I had so much tea at lunch, my teeth are floating."

The guard told them where the restrooms were, and they continued on up the steeply sloping ramp. "I was going to ask him where the Arthurian casket was," Kiku whispered.

"I know, but if we have to break a glass case getting it, do you want him to remember us asking for it?"

"I guess not. But now we only have an hour to find the casket. We'd better split up."

"So you can read the chapter on your own again?" Madge snipped in spite of herself. It was the lump of fear lodged in her stomach talking. It was making her impatient and irritable. She didn't like being afraid.

"The museum doesn't look very big," Joe said, looking at a map he'd taken from the information desk. "We won't be very far from each other. I'll look up here in the chapels on the north side, and Kiku can look in the rooms on the south side. Madge can look in the Gothic Chapel and the galleries on the ground floor. We'll meet back here in an hour. There won't be time for anyone to read anything. All right?"

"I guess," Madge said, swallowing the sense of dread inside of her. She took a copy of the map and set out to find the Gothic Chapel. It figured that she would end up in a chapel after all the time she'd spent in the last year avoiding church.

She walked through a gloomy hallway with tapestries on the wall and statues of lean-looking saints. It was cold and drafty. *Sheesh, no wonder they all wore those long, heavy dresses back then and were always dancing and jousting. A body could freeze to death in these old castles.*

She turned from the gloomy hall into what looked like a square room on the map that was called the Cuxa Cloister and felt as if she'd stepped from winter into spring. Sunlight poured into the open well of the courtyard and turned the pink stone of the carved columns enclosing it a warm burnished rose. There were pots of poinsettias and Christmas lilies lining the colonnaded walkway and the paths that crossed the open space. She turned and looked back and saw that the door she'd come through was topped by an arch with strange creatures carved into the stone. There was a lion with a man's head, and a chicken with a snake's tail—she'd never seen anything like this at Our Lady of Perpetual Help in Brooklyn! But one of the creatures did look familiar. It was some kind of dragon with a tail that had a head at the end of it. She wasn't sure where she'd seen it before, but it sure gave her the creeps.

She turned away from the arch and walked into the open garden, tilting her face up to the sun, hoping it would melt the cold dread inside. She knew she should be hurrying downstairs to find the casket, but she couldn't stand the idea of going back inside the cold, gloomy building. It felt like a tomb. She closed her eyes and breathed in the lily-scented air—

And heard bells ringing.

It couldn't be three o'clock yet. And the bells weren't ringing the hour. They were clanging as if signaling an alarm. Had Joe or Kiku gotten in trouble?

She opened her eyes. She was still standing in the open courtyard, but instead of the spindly pots of lilies and poinsettias, the garden was at its full summer height, lush roses basking in the sun. A woman in a long heavy dress made of coarse brown cloth was crossing the courtyard, coming toward her. She had an aged but regal face framed by a white wimple—a nun. She looked, in fact, like Madge's seventh-grade English teacher, Sister Agatha Dorothy (Sister Aggie Dot the girls all called her, but never to her face), who had told Madge she had a real flair for writing.

What was Sister Aggie Dot doing here?

"My lord," she said when she was close enough to be heard over the clanging of the bells, "what news?"

Madge, who was thinking the words *Have you lost your marbles, Sister?* said instead, "We are besieged. The Northmen are invading. I have come for the book."

"What good has come of the book, my lord? All the sacrifices we made and still the land is besieged and slipping into darkness."

Madge wanted to cry out and ask what they were both doing here and who the heck were the Northmen, and why did she keep calling her *my lord* like that tramp in the park had, but instead she found herself saying, "Perchance we held back the dark long enough that others in our names will take up the fight after us—and that is all any of us can do."

Sister Aggie Dot replied, "You'll find the book in the chamber at the foot of the stairs, buried in my trunk. I will fend off the invaders while you secure it." She drew a dagger from beneath her heavy dress and held it up. The sun struck it and seemed to set it on fire. "For

Arthur," she said. "*Rex quondam, Rexque futurus.* And for England!"

The fire seemed to spark in her eyes and then she was rushing away. Madge heard shouts and the clang of steel from behind her, but she was hurrying across the cloister and running down stone steps and into a tiny room tucked beneath the stairs. The room was very plain—whitewashed walls, a low bench with a straw mattress, a wooden chest above which hung a silver dagger with a beautifully carved gold hilt adorned with a green stone.

The dagger was so beautiful, Madge wanted to stare at it, but instead she found herself kneeling in front of a chest and opening it. She buried her hands in cloth—beautiful silk dresses embroidered with flowers and encrusted with jewels—throwing the precious cloth aside until her hands grazed something hard and smooth, something that felt like bone. She drew it out. The part inside of her that was still Madge thought it might be a skull, but the other part that wasn't Madge was not surprised to pull out a box made of carved ivory. Both parts wanted to run her hands over the carved figures on the lid—two knights jousting, ladies on a castle rampart defending themselves from an army of knights who catapulted roses over the castle wall.

The part that wasn't her laughed and murmured, "If only the invaders at our walls were planning to bombard us with roses instead of flaming arrows."

Then she rose and took the dagger off the wall, fitted it into the belt around her waist—which she noticed now was thick and covered with a heavy leather tunic—and carried the box into a narrow stone chapel. Women in long plain dresses were kneeling on the floor, clasping their hands together, wailing, and looking up at the stained-glass window in the curved apse of the chapel. Madge walked past them to a raised platform in the apse on which stood a stone coffin. The carved figure of a knight in armor lay on top, his feet resting on a little crouched dog. She knelt in front of the tomb.

Get up! Madge wanted to cry. *There's no time for praying! Run!*

She could hear shouts from above. Something struck the window, and it shattered into a million shards of jeweled light. A flaming arrow followed and struck one of the women. Madge could hear her screams and smell burning flesh. But instead of rising, Madge was scrabbling with her nails on the stone floor as if she was trying to bury herself. She managed finally to loosen one of the stones and push it aside. There was a small space underneath. She placed the ivory box inside and spoke—

For God's sake, no prayers. Get on your feet and fight! Madge screamed inside her head.

"May the ones who take up our fight have better luck."

Then she stood up and turned, dagger drawn, to face the invaders.

✕   ✕   ✕

Madge found herself standing in the stone chapel, facing not a horde of Viking invaders but an elderly couple in matching plaid raincoats and umbrellas.

"Dearie, do you know where the restrooms are?" the woman said in a thick Brooklyn accent. "Irving and I have lost our way."

Madge shook her head, speechless, but pointed to the stairs. As she raised her arm, she saw she was holding the jeweled dagger from her dream. *Where the heck did I get that?* she wondered. She quickly stashed it in her coat pocket, hoping the old lady didn't report her to the guards. But the old dame must've been blind as a bat, because she only thanked her and turned to help her husband up the stairs. Kiku and Joe came running down the stairs, edging past the old couple.

"Have you found it?" Kiku asked. "We've looked everywhere upstairs. We've only got a few minutes left!"

Madge opened her mouth to speak but found she couldn't. She looked around the chapel. There were a number of stone tombs like the one she'd seen, but they weren't the same. There were stained-glass windows in the apse, but they were all intact. There were no bells ringing, no fire, no invading hordes storming the walls. So why was her heart still racing? She turned away from Kiku and Joe and walked past them into the next room and directly to a glass case. There was the ivory box. It was the same one she'd held in her hands moments ago. She could still remember the feel of the cool ivory as she had placed it in the ground, and the sadness she'd felt at the sureness that she would never see it again. *A foolish expensive trifle—but it was the only thing remaining of our old lives together.*

"That's it," Kiku said, "but the case is locked. What—"

Madge reached in her pocket and drew out the gold dagger. Without thinking, she struck it against the case and shattered the glass. Kiku gasped. Someone shouted from the next gallery. Madge reached inside and grabbed the box, the feel of cool bone making her shiver all over. Joe was pulling her and Kiku out a door, into another cloister. There was a colonnaded walk around two sides of the square, but on the south and west sides, there was only a low stone wall. Madge could see the river over the west wall and trees on the other side of the south wall.

"Not the river side," she said running toward the south wall. "The longships will be coming from there."

"The wha—?" she heard Joe and Kiku saying. But she was already scaling the south wall, tucking the box under her coat for safety, and leaping into the bright clean air.

24

THE FLAGPOLE

BY THE TIME Kiku and Joe reached the top of the wall, Madge was already running across the lawn and vanishing in a patch of trees.

"We'd better follow her," Joe said.

"This is crazy," Kiku answered, her heart racing as she looked down at the steep drop below them. "We'll all be arrested."

"Not if they don't catch us." Joe grabbed her hand. The feel of his hand on hers made her forget the guards behind them and the steep drop in front of them. They had been here before, standing on a wall with danger behind them and danger in front of them. She glanced at Joe and saw, superimposed over the boy, the face and figure of the gallant Sir Lancelot. She knew he would do all in his power to protect her as she would do all in hers to protect him. She trusted him with her life. And so, gripping his hand, she jumped.

As soon as they hit the grass, they ran for the trees.

They went over the stone bridge, climbed a steep hill, and came out in a stone-enclosed circle. For a moment the stones seemed to tower over them, and Kiku thought to herself, *We've crossed over—we're back in Avalon.* Kiku remembered how she had wandered into Faerie last night in the museum just as Morgaine had crossed over into the magical land in the third chapter. Had she unwittingly led Joe into the land of Faerie? But then the stones shrank to a low stone wall and instead of a tall standing stone in the center, there was a flagpole with an eagle carved into its base and the red, white, and blue American flag snapping in the wind. *It stands for the same thing*, Kiku thought, her eyes stinging. *It's what you're supposed to fight for now.*

Madge was sitting on a bench, the ivory box in her lap. The sun turned her hair gold and her plain threadbare coat into a richly embroidered cloak. Then the red-gold head looked up, and she was just Madge again, biting her lip and looking embarrassed.

"I thought you guys had ditched me," she said. "I wouldn't half blame you. I don't know what came over me. Breaking that glass, stealing the box! What if the police catch us?"

"That doesn't matter," Kiku said, sitting next to Madge. She knew they should keep moving, but Madge clearly needed a minute. "You only did what you had to, although I suppose you *could* have just taken the chapter out of the box. Do we even know it's in there?"

"I think it's where she kept the book," Madge said, her hands moving over the surface of the box. She was tracing the figure of a knight on horseback carrying a woman in his arms away from a besieged city.

"She?" Joe asked.

Kiku looked up at him. The features of Lancelot had fallen away, but she could still see the shadow of the man he would become. A man who would always protect those who were defenseless. Then she looked back at Madge. "Do you mean Guinevere?"

Madge shook her head, her brow creased. Kiku had rarely seen her look confused about anything. She was always so sure of herself. "I think it was Guinevere who hid the book in the chapel, but then there was someone else who came for it when the castle was under siege. . . ."

"I've seen that too," Joe said. "I was on a castle rampart with Morgaine."

"I was there too," Kiku said. "With you, Joe, only you were Lancelot. We jumped from the wall." She shivered. "But I don't know what happened to us after we jumped." She remembered that fleeting image of the standing stones when they entered the flagpole circle. Had Lancelot and Morgaine gone to Avalon after Camelot fell?

"In my vision I knew we were going to die," Joe said. "And I knew . . ." He hesitated, looking from Kiku to Madge.

"Go ahead," Madge said, "tell us what you knew."

"I knew that's what would happen to all the knights who heeded the call of the book."

"That's why Dr. Bean didn't want us to read the book," Kiku said. "He knew the knights who heed the call of the book die. He didn't want that to happen to a bunch of kids."

"Well, it's too late for that," Madge said, gripping the box with both hands.

"Unless," Kiku said, laying her hand on top of the box, "we stop here."

"What?" Joe asked, staring at her. "What do you mean?"

"We haven't read the last chapter yet. I-I think that the spell's not complete until we do." She thought back to what Moth had told her last night. "If we don't read the last chapter, we may be able to evade the fate that has befallen all the others who've read the book. We won't have to die."

"But," Joe said, "then we won't know where the attack is. Others will die."

"Yes," Kiku said. "But *we* won't. We could run away, leave the city. That's our choice." She looked from Joe to Madge. "Or you two could go and I could stay. I don't mind doing it. I've already read the third chapter alone. I can read this one and decode the last message. Then you and Joe may be all right."

"No!" Joe cried. "That's not fair. It has to be all of us."

"It's already not all of us," Kiku said. "Walt's not here."

"We're not going to lose anyone else!" Madge cried, then she opened the box and gasped. For a moment Kiku was afraid that the box was empty, but when she leaned over, she saw that the pages lay flat in the casket. The one on the top was covered by an illustration of a courtyard much like one of the cloisters they'd just seen at the museum. A woman in long, plain robes stood at the center of the garden. She faced a man in a leather tunic with a crown on his head.

"It's too late," Madge said. "We're all a part of this now. We have to read it."

"We don't have time right now," Joe said. "Let's skip to the last page and decode the message."

Joe shuffled the pages until he came to the last one and then took out the encoded message from his pocket. It was awkward for him to hold both on his lap, so he passed the chapter to Madge. Kiku handed him a pencil. She wished Walt were here. He always carried a notebook that Joe could have leaned on. That wasn't the only reason she wished he were there. It felt wrong doing this with just the three of them.

That didn't stop you when you read the third chapter alone.

"I've got it," Joe said. "I've got the message."

"Read it," Madge said.

"It says . . ." The blood drained from Joe's face.

The bag contains all that you will need to commence the attack. Once you have introduced the poison into the system, millions will die, the prisoners in the tower first of all. All will know it is useless to fight us.

Joe crumpled up the paper and threw it angrily on the ground.

"But that doesn't tell us where the attack is going to take place," Kiku wailed. "What does it mean by *system*? And what prisoners in the tower? Dr. Bean and Miss Lake? My father? Where is this tower?"

"Maybe we'd know more if we'd gotten the bag," Madge said. She got up and paced to the edge of the stone circle and looked out over the rampart at the view of the city.

Kiku got up and paced to her side. "What kind of systems are there?" she asked.

"Transit systems?" Madge suggested. She'd left the box on the bench, but she was still holding the chapter pages. "Trains, subways . . ."

"But how would you poison those?" Kiku asked. "No, it has to be something that would affect everyone." She stared over the parapet at the city. Hundreds of apartment and office buildings, with round water towers on their roofs, punctuated the skyline like medieval towers. . . .

"Water," Kiku said. "It's got to be the water system. But how would they get the poison into it? They'd have to go to the one place where all the water came from. . . ." And then she knew.

"We're looking at it," Kiku said. She pointed to the southeast. Across a stretch of buildings was a tall tower standing on the edge of the Harlem River. Her father had pointed it out to her once on a trip to Fort Tryon Park. *A marvel of American engineering*, he had called it. "The High Bridge Water Tower. Water passes through it into the city. It would be one of the places where they could poison the water system."

"The poison must be what was in the bag, and now Walt has it," Joe said.

"Walt would never do that!" Madge cried. "Not even to save his family."

"We have to get to the tower and find out," Kiku said. "It could be where they're hiding Dr. Bean and Miss Lake and my father, too."

"Yeah," Joe said, getting to his feet. "We have to get out of here anyway."

He pointed to the path beneath the rampart, where two police officers had just come into view. One of them looked up and then shouted, "There they are!"

"We gotta scram!" Madge cried. She looked back at the box, but Kiku grabbed her hand. "You can't carry it," she said.

"That's all right," Madge said, rolling up the pages and sticking them into her coat pocket. "This is what's important. Come on. Let's get your dad." She grinned, and Kiku felt herself grinning back. This was their fight; this was what they always did, the only thing they could do, even if what Moth told her was true and the price of victory was their lives.

25

THE KNIGHTS OF THE ROAD

IT WAS HIS worst nightmare: being chased by the police. As they left the flagpole circle and ran south, Joe saw there were two more policemen waiting at the exit.

"Quick, I know another way out!" Kiku cried.

Joe followed Kiku into a terraced rock garden, down narrow paths between stunted shrubs, Madge right behind him. They came out at a little cottage. The tramp whom Madge had given the nickel to was squatting on the ground, warming his hands over a fire inside a small tin can. He looked up as they came crashing down the path.

"You're back, my lord," he said to Madge. *Why is he calling Madge "my lord"? The guy must be cracked.* A lot of the tramps he'd met were—done in by drink and loss and the loneliness of the road. Joe hated looking in their eyes because he was afraid he'd see his own future there. But when he looked into this man's eyes, he was surprised to see that they were clear and sharp.

"Behind the eight ball, eh, brother?" he asked Joe.

"What the heck does that mean?" Madge asked.

Joe knew because he'd listened to the hoboes in the park. "He's asking if I'm in a tight spot," he explained to Madge.

"We sure are!" Madge replied. "We've got the coppers on our tail."

"John Law," the tramp said, nodding. Then to Joe he said, "Follow the signs. They'll take you all the way to Big Rock Candy Mountain."

"What signs?" Madge asked.

"The ones shared by the knights of the road," the man said, bowing to Madge. "Your knight here knows."

Joe did know, only he didn't see how hobo signs were going to do them any good. "Thanks, brother," he said, giving the term of address he'd heard the tramps use for one another. Then he was running out of the park. He saw the subway station at 190th Street and wondered if they should head for it, but there would be police on the platforms and in the trains. Ahead of them stretched a wide avenue where it would be easy for the cops to see them. They should get onto the side streets, but Joe didn't know this neighborhood and he might lead them into a dead end. They were on a high ridge above a valley, and they had to cross that valley to get to the tower, but the land was too steep for the streets to run in grids like downtown. How would they ever find their way?

Then, halfway down the block, Joe saw a sign scrawled

on the trunk of a tree. It was a circle with an arrow pointing east. Joe had seen other signs like it when he made his way down from Canada and knew it showed a good route that was free of policemen and bullies. But would it help them now? The tramp had said to follow the signs. What else could they do?

"This way," he told Kiku and Madge with more confidence than he felt. When they reached the tree, Joe saw that the arrow pointed to a flight of steps that descended between two buildings. With the sun setting behind him, it was like he was staring down into a black cavern. If he led his friends here and it was the wrong way, they'd be trapped.

He wiped the sweat from his face and something got in his eye—a piece of grit. He tried to blink it away—he couldn't cry in front of Kiku and Madge!—and when he opened his eyes, the stairs in front of him were sparkling as if the speck of grit was a prism refracting light, only instead of a rainbow, what he saw was a path outlined in gold. All along it he saw signs painted in gold: a curve with a dot above it that Joe knew meant "no cops here" and a circle with a diagonal line through it that meant "good road to follow."

Suddenly Joe heard shouts behind them. "This way!" he shouted. "Follow me!"

They ran down the steps. He could hear the policeman shouting behind them. "Where'd they go? I could swear I saw those kids duck down these stairs."

"Aw, you're seeing things again, Harvey. Better lay off the sauce."

The gold dust had never made him or Madge invisible before without Kiku's help. It must have something to do with being on this path—a path laid out by the knights of the road. They had to stay on it. He only hoped it went as far as the tower. He could see the gold trail stretching out in front of him, but it grew faint at times. He had to concentrate to find where it picked up again. He was so focused on the trail that the rest of the world fell away. He wasn't aware of the buildings anymore, or the cars—

"Watch it, fella!" A yellow taxi nearly ran into him. Joe dodged around it and noticed that there was another sign on the corner: a circle with a little tail pointing south onto an avenue called St. Nicholas.

"This way!" Joe called to the others. He followed the signs through the city streets. Twice he saw policemen, but they didn't seem to see them. He saw other people following the signs—men and women in tattered clothing, wrapped against the cold in shawls and scarves. *The lost*, Joe heard the voice inside his head say, *men and women who have lost everything but who have found kinship with one another.* The Brethren of the Road, the old hoboes called it, or the knights of the road. That's what he and Kiku and Madge were; they had all lost something, but they had found one another.

He saw another sign, pointing toward 171st Street. As they turned the corner, Joe saw the High Bridge

Tower in front of them. The last light from the west hit it and it seemed to glow like it was made of rock sugar, like the Big Rock Candy Mountains the hoboes sang about, where *the farmers' trees are full of fruit and the barns are full of hay, where there ain't no snow, where the rain don't fall, and the wind don't blow.*

As they got closer, Joe felt his eyes stinging. He realized he was tired of running. He just wanted to go home. If only he knew where that was.

"We made it!" Madge cried when they reached the base of the tower. She ran through the door, holding her dagger up. "For Arthur! *Rex quondam, Rexque futurus!*" she shouted. "And for the good old US of A!"

"She's fearless," Kiku said. "I wish I were more like her."

Joe looked at her, surprised. "You're every bit as brave. You jumped right off that wall! You're just a little . . . *quieter.*"

Kiku smiled back at him as they went through the door and then up an iron spiral staircase that wound around massive steel pipes. They could see the glow of Madge's dagger as she ran up the steps in front of them.

"Hey!" Madge's voice came from above. "There's a locked door but the key's in the lock. I'm going in."

"We'd better hurry," Kiku said, "in case it's a trap."

Joe raced up the stairs after her, impressed with how nimbly and quickly she was taking the steps, and only caught up with her on the top landing, where Madge was still fidgeting with the key. "Maybe it's a trick," she said. "I can't seem to . . ."

But then the key clicked in the lock, and the door swung open onto an octagonal room with narrow slit windows, in the center of which were two men tied together back to back.

"Otousan!" Kiku cried, running toward her father. She knelt down and threw her arms around him. The other man was Dashwood Bean. The old guy's hair was standing up, and his spectacles sat crookedly on his face, but otherwise he and Mr. Akiyama looked unharmed. Madge used her dagger to cut the ropes while Joe helped take their gags off. Kiku and her father were talking rapidly in Japanese. Dashwood Bean was blinking as if he couldn't quite make out who they were. Joe noticed an oil lamp and matches and bent to light it. Then he looked around the octagonal room.

"Where's Miss Lake?" he asked.

"Vivian?" Dr. Bean asked, blinking in the flare of the lamp. "Didn't she send you here?"

"No," Madge said, "we've been all on our own."

"Oh my goodness," Dr. Bean said. "I should have had more faith in you. But where's young Walt?"

"I'm afraid Walt's gone over to the other side, sir," Joe said. He knew Madge wouldn't want to be the one to say it.

"Walt? I cannot believe it!"

"I didn't want to either," Madge said, "but we think

Mr. January got to him and offered him a deal."

"Oh my!" Dr. Bean said, his usually benevolent face furrowing and turning purple. "Mr. January must have threatened Walt's family. That . . . that *fiend*! Taking advantage of a young boy's loyalty! I'll have a thing or two to say to him if he has the nerve to show himself here!"

"Will you?"

The voice came from the doorway, where Mr. January stood. "So you want me to show myself, do you? How's this?" He dug his fingers into his scalp and under his jaw and then pulled, peeling away his face, revealing the bloody skull beneath. "How's that for *showing myself*?"

Then he stepped back out of the room, drew the door shut, and locked them inside.

26

THE HIGH TOWER

"HOLY MOLY!" MADGE cried. "Did you all see that? Mr. January—"

"Just took his face off," Kiku said, still staring at the door as if she could rearrange what she had just seen there. It was like the horrible nightmare they had all had, only worse because there was no waking up from this.

"And locked us in," Joe said.

"We gotta find a way outta here," Madge said. Kiku watched as she rattled the door and then followed her to a narrow slit window. There weren't any buildings nearby. No one would hear them if they called out. "We could drop a note, I suppose," she suggested. "But who would see it or believe it? Who's even out there to help us?"

"Vivian is still out there," Dr. Bean said. "And Walt."

Madge looked at Kiku with tears in her eyes, clearly thinking the same thing she was. Dr. Bean couldn't face the thought that Walt was a traitor.

"Miss Lake would have gotten in touch with us if she was still out there," Kiku said. "I think we're on our own."

As you've always been, the voice in her head said.

She sighed—and then heard an echoing sigh from the window, as if the city was commiserating with her . . . or . . .

"Boris!" Madge cried.

Hearing his name, the pigeon flew through the window and landed on Madge's shoulder.

"Is that the thirteenth-century Eucharistic dove from the medieval collection?" Dr. Bean asked. "How did it come to life?"

"We're not sure," Kiku said. "I think it has to do with Madge—"

"But I haven't been able to make anything else come to life," she said, stroking Boris's long neck.

"Hm . . ." Mr. Akiyama said. "He found you, though. He must have navigational abilities. Perhaps we could use that."

"You mean to send a message?" Kiku asked.

"But to whom?" Joe asked. "Who's out there to help us? We don't know where Miss Lake is, and Walt's gone over to the other side."

"Vivian's apartment is in Castle Village in Washington Heights, not far from here," Dr. Bean said. "Do you think Boris can follow a map if I draw one for him?"

"I don't see why not," Madge said. "He's one smart bird, aren't you, Boris?"

The pigeon cooed and bobbed his head up and down as if in agreement.

"See?" Madge said.

"Good bird," Dr. Bean said. "We need some paper— and something to use as a carrier."

"I know," Madge said. "I've got a lipstick case."

"And we can use the netting from my hat to make a carrier," Kiku said, taking off her hat, although it gave her a pang to dismantle it.

"And we can tear off a bit of paper from the end of the chapter," Joe suggested.

"And that way Miss Lake will know it's really from us." Madge took the chapter from her pocket and spread out the pages on the floor while Kiku fashioned a minia- ture vest from the veil on her hat, using the little sewing kit her mother had given her and which she always car- ried with her.

"Here," Joe said, leafing through the chapter, "this last page is almost blank." He tore off a bit of paper. "Does anyone have a pen?"

"That man took our pens from us," Mr. Akiyama complained. "He was afraid we'd fashion a weapon from them."

In the end, they used Madge's lipstick—Coty's Mag- net Red, which Madge informed them had cost a whole dollar but "Heck," she said, "we're gonna have to take it out of the tube anyway to send the message."

SOS, Madge wrote in bright red lipstick. *TRAPPED IN HIGH BRIDGE TOWER.*

Dr. Bean used the rest of the lipstick to draw a map on the floor showing Boris how to get to apartment 9B in Castle Village, which Boris pecked at in a way that seemed to indicate that he understood. They rolled the message up, slipped it into the lipstick tube, and slid it into the little net vest Kiku had made and put on Boris.

"Aw," Madge said when Boris was all outfitted and ready to go. "He looks very handsome. Like a soldier going off to war."

"Well," Dr. Bean said, "a homing pigeon *was* awarded the Croix de Guerre in the last war. We will all have our part to play in this one."

"I wish Walt were here," Madge said. "He'd know the right thing to say to send him off."

It hurts her the worst that Walt has abandoned us, Kiku thought, putting her arm around Madge's shoulder. "I think he'd say what you said when you charged up the stairs."

Madge grinned and took out the dagger she'd taken from the Cloisters.

"For Arthur. *Rex quondam, Rexque futurus*," they all said together. And then Madge added: "And for the good old US of A."

Boris seemed to understand. He bowed his head once, trilled a long rousing note that sounded like a call to battle, and then spread his wings. They gleamed in the light of the oil lamp, like the bronze and enamel he'd been made of, and then he took to the sky. As he sailed west, he seemed to carry that glow with him, and Kiku realized that some of the gold dust from the pages had gotten onto his wings. He looked like a meteor trailing a fiery tail as he flew, like the rockets' red glare and the twilight's last gleaming from the song they'd all sung today in Grand Central Terminal. She felt Madge and Joe standing beside her and realized that she *wasn't* on her own. And she never would be, as long as she had something this important to fight for.

"He'll be okay," Madge said, handing Kiku her handkerchief.

"I know," she said, wiping her eyes, "it's just going to be hard waiting. . . ."

"Well," Joe said, "there is something we can do while we wait." Kiku turned and saw that Joe had gathered the pages off the floor. "We can read the last chapter."

✶　✶　✶

They sat in a circle on the floor with the lamp in the center, and Joe read aloud by its light.

THE MAIDEN CASTLE

**Our heroes met once more in front of the Maiden
Castle, but they were not the same as when they had set
out on the edge of the forest. The journey had changed
them, as journeys will, but they came together, for no
one is ever truly alone when united in a quest.**

Joe paused and looked up at Kiku and Madge, his
eyes gleaming. Dr. Bean nodded at Mr. Akiyama, who
bowed back to him, and Joe continued.

**The sorcerer Merlin met them at the drawbridge
that went over a deep moat and said to them: "You
have all done well to have come so far, but there is one
quest left for you to accomplish. The Lady of the Lake
is held prisoner in the high tower, guarded by a horrible beast. You must slay the beast and free her. Then
she will tell you how you can save your land, and give
you the power to do so."**

"Why couldn't Merlin just tell them?" Madge asked.

"Maybe he didn't know," Kiku suggested.

"Or maybe," Mr. Akiyama said, "they would not have
been prepared to hear what he had to tell them until after they had gone through the castle."

"Or," Dr. Bean said, "perhaps the poor woman had
been imprisoned in the tower by an evil witch and she
needed rescuing. Go on, Joe."

The four crossed the bridge to the tower, but halfway across a knight charged them on horseback. He wore the same boar helmet as the two-headed knight whom Lancelot had beheaded.

"I will take care of this one while you go on," spoke the brave Sir Lancelot.

The others went on, passing safely over the bridge into the courtyard, but there they encountered a host of ghostly soldiers standing guard. "They are illusions," Morgaine said. "I will enspell them while you two go on."

Arthur and Guinevere were loath to go on without her, but they knew they must reach the lady in the tower, and so they ran into the keep. They started up a spiral staircase, but a great fog rose around them so that they could not see their way. Guinevere drew forth her dagger from her girdle—

"Her girdle!" Madge exclaimed.
"A kind of belt," Dr. Bean explained.

—and held it up to part the fog. What she saw made her almost wish that she had not. A dragon crouched at the top of the stairs. It opened wide its horrible jaws and belched fire. They would have been burned to cinders, but Arthur held up a shield to protect them.

"How will we get past it?" Guinevere asked.

"While I divert it, you must go on," Arthur answered.

But Guinevere had already engaged the dragon in battle and shouted for him to go on. Arthur hesitated, not liking his lady to battle the dragon, but seeing that she had the matter well in hand he continued on. He had to squeeze past its scaly body until he reached the top of the stairs. There he found an eight-sided room in which the Lady of the Lake sat at a tilted table with pen and ink and paint and brush at hand. She didn't look up as he came in, only lifted her brush to finish a detail of the drawing on the page in front of her. Another painting lay on the floor. He knelt to retrieve it and saw with amazement that it showed himself entering the tower room, and that behind him was the tail of the monster, and at the end of the tail was a monstrous head with three rows of teeth ready to devour him.

He spun on his heel and raised his sword just in time to sever the monster's head from its tail. The monster shrieked and tried to back up the stairs to face him, but Guinevere drove her dagger into its throat and, with a great roar, the monster vanished. The others came running up the stairs to join Arthur in the tower room and together they faced the Lady.

"There," she said, dipping her brush back into a dish of gold paint. "And here you are." She lifted her face to the four and gazed at them with eyes the deep blue of a mountain lake. "I have been expecting you. You have done well to come through so many perils and dangers to save your people and their land. Only those joined in true bonds of friendship could have come so far."

"We have not always been together," Morgaine replied.

"Nor free of jealousy and doubt," said Lancelot.

"And of thought of turning back," spoke Guinevere.

"And of mistrust in our quest," Arthur said, bowing to the Lady on bended knee. Then he asked how the Lady knew what they had endured.

She showed them all the pages on her desk and they were amazed to see that their own adventures were shown therein—their meeting with the two-faced knight and the lion in the forest, their wanderings through the Hewan Wood, their meeting with Merlin on the bridge, the attack of the knight in the keep, the ghostly horde, and the two-headed dragon on the stairs. The last page showed them standing in the tower with the Lady. It was that picture she had finished as they came through the door.

"How wondrous strange that you know all we have seen and done while you sit up here in your tower," Guinevere said.

"It is the curse our half sister Belisent put me under," the Lady said to Arthur. "I was compelled to stay in this tower until four knights rescued me, but while I waited, I could see all that was happening in the land and beyond. What I see now are invaders coming to our shores, plunging us into darkness."

"We will raise an army and fight them," Arthur said.

"Yes," the Lady replied, "and you will hold them back for a while. You will rule over a golden age of fairness and plenty wherein love and beauty will flourish. It will be such a time that bards will sing of your exploits and poets will write of your deeds.

"You each have your part to play. You, Lancelot, so keen of eye and quick of tongue, will travel wide, avenging the wronged and protecting the innocent. To you I give the gift of language to pass down the accounts of all you see.

"And you, Morgaine, so clever and brave, you will become a great sorceress, weaving spells to protect the kingdom. Some will call you witch and accuse you of betrayal, but the ones who love you will know your true heart. To you I give the gift of invisibility so you may ply your magic in secret.

"And you, Guinevere, well I know how you chafe against the restraints of your gender. Where others see only beauty, I see strength and resolve. You will fight to keep the kingdom whole until your last breath, even when you lose your true love. To you I give the gift of bodily strength so you may never feel weak again.

"And you, Arthur, have already united the warring chieftains of this island. It is your love that draws your people together. To you I give the ability to bring out the best in all who love you. You will rule well even after the kingdom you build begins to fall.

"To all of you I give the greatest gift—the gift of your friendship for each other. Although you may wander far from each other and even hurt one another, when it is time for the last battle, you will fight together unto your last breath."

"But why?" Guinevere asked. "Why mayn't we stay together always? Why must we ever hurt one another?"

"It is the sacrifice you must make, the sadness that makes your story complete, the ink that binds the word to the page, the grit that makes the pearl. It is your grief that will make your story eternal and keep the flame alight. Others will come in your wake to kindle the light—they will come in your names, inspired by your deeds, chastened by your flaws. For how else to raise a hero from the page if we do not see ourselves in their mistakes?"

"And that is our quest?" Lancelot inquired with a tart tongue. "To go and make mistakes? To wander far from home—"

"To lose the one I love?" spoke Guinevere.

"To hide my true face?" asked Morgaine.

"To build a kingdom only to see it fall?" demanded Arthur.

"Just so," spoke the Lady of the Lake. "Your legacy will give hope to the people of Britain and to all who

strive to live an honorable life." She stood and lifted a dish of the gold powder she had used to make the gold paint for the book. She flung what remained of it into the air, and it settled on the heads and shoulders of the four as she spoke. "The gold paint I have used in the book is no ordinary gold. It was given to me by a fairy, one of the oldest of the old things, and it will give you the power to save your land. I warn you, though, that every power comes with a price. Be careful how you use what has been given to you."

Joe lifted his head from the page. "The chapter ends there," he said.

"No!" Kiku said. "There must be a page missing."

"Well, there's the page we read before, at the beginning," Joe said. "But that just said they all went back to Camelot."

"That's it?" Madge cried. "The Lady told them to go forth and . . . what? Hurt each other? Well, I'm not buying it. That's a terrible ending. And it certainly isn't *our* ending. It doesn't mean that what happened to them is going to happen to us. It's not the same. For one thing, Walt's not here."

"But I am."

The voice came from the doorway. They'd all been so engrossed in the story that they hadn't seen it open. Walt stood there beside a man in a trench coat. *It's true, then,*

Kiku thought, feeling something sink inside her. Walt had come back with Mr. January.

The man in the trench coat came forward and took off his hat—it was Miss Lake! Boris was perched on her shoulder.

"There you are, Dash," she said, sweeping into the room and patting her hair smooth. "Walt and I have been looking all over for you. I should have known Mordred would stash you up here. It's positively medieval."

27

ZYKLON B

MADGE LOOKED FROM Miss Lake to Walt. Walt looked back at her sheepishly.

"I'm sorry I couldn't tell you what was going on. Miss Lake said it would only work if you all thought I'd gone over to the other side."

"Then you're not . . ." Madge began, but then her throat closed up so tight, she couldn't finish her sentence.

"A traitor?" Miss Lake said. "Heavens, no. Walt's done more for America in the last twenty-four hours than most patriots do in a lifetime."

"But you acted so strangely when we found you in the park," Joe said. "I thought that Mr. January must have turned you then."

"He tried to," Walt admitted. "When I caught up to him, he told me that he could get my parents out of France. I-I was tempted. But I said no. He laughed at me and then he said, 'Come see me in Belvedere Castle when you change your mind. And you *will* change your mind.'

Then he left. I sat there, unable to move because I was afraid that if I got up, I'd go find him. Then Miss Lake showed up."

"I'd been keeping an eye on Mr. January," she said, "but I saw an opportunity when he tried to enlist Walt."

"She told me that if I pretended to give in to Mr. January, I could find out what he was really up to. I hated pretending around you, and I hated when you thought I'd betrayed you."

"It must have been awful," Kiku said, laying a hand on Walt's arm. "I'm sorry I ever doubted you."

"Well, that was the plan," Walt said, blushing. Then he looked toward Madge. But Madge only stared at Walt dumbfounded, for once in her life unable to speak.

"Gee, Madge, are you sore at me for fooling you? I tried to tell you I was sorry, but I guess you couldn't hear me over that train whistle."

"I heard you, only . . ." How could she tell Walt that she had thought he was saying he was sorry because he had betrayed them? How could she tell him that she'd finally believed he was a traitor and it had felt like her last bit of trust in the world was dying? How could she tell him that she felt guilty now that she'd ever doubted him? She couldn't. So instead she threw her arms around his neck and hugged him so tight he yelped. When she let go, his face was so red, his freckles had vanished and he was the one who couldn't talk. But Madge had regained her voice.

"What are you all standing around gaping at? We'd better get cracking! What's the plan?"

*   *   *

Joe watched Miss Lake bring in the Gladstone bag from the landing. "I knew that Mordred would try to get one of you to betray the others," Miss Lake began, putting the bag in the middle of the room.

"Mordred?" Joe asked. "Like from the story?"

"Yes, that's who Mr. January is. That's his real name. He was Arthur's nephew and squire."

"Isn't he supposed to be Arthur's son?" Kiku asked.

Miss Lake shook her head. "That part of the story got mixed up over the years. Mordred was Arthur's nephew, the son of his half sister Belisent. Arthur treated him like a son and made him his squire, and Mordred repaid him by betraying him. On the day of the tournament at Camelot—the one that begins the story you've been reading—Mordred asked if he could take part in the tournament, but Arthur told him he was too young. Then he sent Mordred to retrieve his helmet. Angry because he would not be allowed to fight—as young people sometimes are"—here she looked knowingly at Walt—"he decided he would steal the king's helmet and take part in the tournament in disguise. The helmet he found had a visor carved with a boar's face. His mother, Belisent, knowing her son would claim it, had enchanted it. She cast a spell that anyone who wore it would have eternal life. So when her son challenged Sir Lancelot, he thought he was invincible. And, as you have seen, he lived even after Lancelot cleaved his head from his body, and he lives even today."

"But how'd he lose his face?" Madge asked.

"That was an unfortunate side effect of Belisent's spell. In addition to eternal life, she enchanted the helmet so that any who wore it *would always bear the face of victory*. And so when Mordred lost to Lancelot, and Lancelot tore the helmet from his head, the helmet tore away the face that was no longer the face of victory."

"Ugh," said Madge.

"It took his face with it," Kiku said, looking pale. "How awful!"

"Yes," Miss Lake said, giving Kiku a grave look. "One must always be cautious using magic. Our spells often work differently from how we intend. Belisent was devastated at what happened to her son. It turned her into a monster." Miss Lake's voice shook, her usual calm demeanor gone. She took a breath to calm herself and went on. "She cast an enchantment to give him a false face whenever he needed one. He used it to impersonate an envoy from King Arthur and make a pact with the Norse invaders. Because of him, Britain was overrun by invaders and fell into a long period of darkness. But the legacy of King Arthur and his knights lived on, giving hope to the people of Britain and to all people who strive to live an honorable life."

"That's what the Lady of the Lake said. . . ." Joe began, but then his eyes widened. "It's you, isn't it? You're the Lady of the Lake!"

Miss Lake smiled and smoothed her hair. She was seated on the cold stone floor, her stockinged legs tucked beneath her, but she looked suddenly as if she were seated on a throne. Her gleaming hair uncoiled from its neat upsweep and streamed around her shoulders like a waterfall. The stone tower suddenly smelled like cold lake water and pine trees. "Do I really look that old? Heavens, Dash, perhaps I should change my hairstyle."

"You are eternally young, my lady," Dr. Bean said, bowing low to her. When he stood up, he was no longer a squat balding man in a suit but a gray-haired wizard in flowing blue robes.

"And you!" Joe said. "You're Merlin!"

Dashwood Bean bowed to Joe. "That is one of the names I have gone by," he said. "But I've come to rather like Dashwood."

"Gee, Doc," Madge said. "If you and Miss Lake were there when this all began, couldn't you have just cut to the chase and told us the dope straight out? I mean, why'd we have to run around all over the place looking for an old book?"

"Well," Dr. Bean began, looking embarrassed, "I

didn't think you four could possibly be the ones. After all, you're children!"

"Children who have proven themselves worthy of the quest," Miss Lake said, gazing at their faces.

"Yes, they certainly have," Dr. Bean agreed. "But still, I cannot be blamed for my reluctance to place children in such great danger—a danger that still exists. The quest is not yet done. We must still avert this horrendous attack on New York that Mordred has planned."

"Isn't the answer in there?" Madge asked, pointing to the Gladstone bag, which was squatting in the center of the room like a poisonous toad. "What's in it, anyway?"

Walt unzipped the bag, carefully unfolded a piece of blue canvas cloth, and lifted a heavy metal canister out of it. A skull leered up at them from a label on the canister.

"*Giftgas zyklon?*" Madge read the words above the skull and crossbones. "What does that mean? It doesn't *look* like a very nice gift. And who's Zyklon? He sounds like the bad guy in a Flash Gordon comic."

Joe, who was staring at the words, spoke in a trembling voice. "That's the canister I saw in my vision before. It's what the Nazis are going to use . . ." He hesitated, looking warily at Walt.

"To kill people," Walt said. "It's a cyanide-based poison they use to kill bugs—*vermin*. They're going to use it in the Nazi camps. They . . ." Walt braced his hand against the wall of the tower as if a strong wind was blowing. "They'll herd them into rooms they say are showers and release the gas until they are dead." He looked around the room, meeting each of their eyes until he came back to Joe. *He looks five years older than he did before he started talking*, Joe thought.

"What's he going to do with it here?" Madge asked. "It's not as if New Yorkers are going to file into a shower room without armed guards making them do it."

"No," Miss Lake said, "but that's the problem. We don't know how he plans to use the poison. When we got the message from Boris—that was clever, by the way, to send him—and found out you were all up here in the water tower, we thought Mordred's plan might have to do with the water system, but only a fraction of New York's water goes through this tower and this canister wouldn't be enough to poison it."

"Do we know if he has more of this stuff?" Kiku asked.

"We think so," Walt said. He pulled off a tag from the handle of the Gladstone bag. It had a large 3 on it and the initials *B.S.*

"Hm," Madge said, "so we know there must be at least two other bags, but what does *B.S.* stand for?"

While she was speaking, Joe reached for the tag, but Kiku stopped him. "Wait! The last time you touched something that monster wrote, he tried to get in your head, and it hurt you."

"Yes," Joe admitted, "but if I can find out what *B.S.* stands for, maybe we can figure out his plan. It will only be for a second. Maybe it won't be so bad with the rest of you here."

"Hm . . ." Miss Lake said, "Walt told me some of the things you've done when you're together, like bringing Boris to life and becoming invisible. I think the magic is working differently in you four. It has a stronger power when you join forces. Perhaps if you hold Joe's hand when he touches the tag, Mordred won't be able to hurt him."

"You're not sure, though, are you?" Madge asked.

When Miss Lake shook her head, Kiku burst out, "How can you not know? You made the book. Shouldn't you know how it works?"

Joe stared at Kiku. It was so unlike her to challenge an adult! But then he realized she was doing it because she was trying to protect him. Miss Lake sighed, a sound like wind moving over water.

"You're right, Kiku. I *should* know, but when I made the book, I used gold dust given to me by a fairy, and fairy dust is as unstable as the creatures who made it. I'm afraid its effects on certain people are rather unpredictable."

"Then let me try on my own," Joe said, reaching again for the tag. "I don't want anyone else hurt by Mordred."

"No," Kiku said, grabbing his hand. "I won't let you do it alone."

"Me neither," Madge said, taking Kiku's hand. "Like you said, Walt, All for one . . ."

"One for all," Walt finished, taking hold of Madge's hand. "We do this together or not at all."

They stood in a linked chain—like a tug-of-war team, Joe thought—with him at one end. He didn't know, though, if they would be able to hold him back from the yawning gulf that might open up when he touched Mordred's writing—or what would happen to them if he pulled them into that abyss. He didn't want anyone else to get hurt, but he also knew that he wasn't going to talk them out of doing it with him. The truth was he was glad he didn't have to face Mordred alone.

He reached out and touched the tag with two fingers just as Madge was saying, "Hey, maybe it's just some poor sucker's initials. . . ." But then the words stuck in her throat. They all heard the voice at once. At first it was impossible to even tell what it was saying because it was so *horrible.* All the pain and anger Mordred had ever felt was in it, and with that pain and anger came a probing hatred that clawed at each of their minds, looking for a way in like water looking for a crack to flow through. It looked for what it *knew.*

In Madge's mind it found the guilt that her last words to her mother had been unkind, and the anger that she had been taken from her.

In Walt's it found the shame of his cowardice in hiding from the Nazis and his fear that he would always be a coward.

In Kiku's it found the embarrassment of always being stared and pointed at and the resentment of never being seen for who she really was.

But where it found the deepest well of anger was in Joe. Eight years in the Mush Hole, of being treated like an animal, of having his mouth washed out with soap if he spoke his own language, of being beaten for speaking up when another child was hurt, of going to bed hungry because he'd given his portion of gruel to another, and then the final outrage of seeing Jeanette struck by the principal—

Who could blame you for hating the whole world? Mordred whispered. *Join me in destroying it and you will have your revenge.*

This is how he makes people do what he wants, the other voice in his head countered. *He controls them through their worst fears. Don't let him do it to you.*

"But I don't hate the whole world," Joe answered aloud. "I have found friends who care about me in this city. I won't let you destroy it."

And then, squeezing Kiku's hand, who in turn squeezed Madge's, who gripped Walt's so hard he yelped, Joe fisted his hand around the luggage tag and *pushed*. They all felt a resistance as Mordred summoned all his hatred and anger into a fiery barricade. Pushing against that anger felt like letting in all the bad things that had ever happened, like standing under a waterfall of pain.

Joe didn't think he could bear it one second longer, but then he felt Kiku and Madge and Walt standing by him. He saw and felt all the bad things that had happened to them: Kiku's classmates jeering at her and strangers on the street staring at her; Madge's mother falling in the kitchen and her father sitting down in a rocking chair that fell to pieces. Through Walt's eyes he saw a Nazi officer gun down an old man in the street and heard a hundred children crying on a train for their parents. And then he saw the things that had happened to him: the teachers washing his mouth out with soap, the look on his *Tóta's* face when he could not remember his own name, the principal striking Jeanette.

But he wasn't alone. His friends were there now beside him, witnessing all that had happened to him just as he had seen all their sad and terrible moments. The pain and anger were still there, but they didn't tear him apart. Instead they made him—and all of them—stronger. Strong enough to push through the fiery wall until it gave way and crumbled into ashes and dust.

In its wake they all saw a building standing by the river with steam coming out of a smokestack, and they heard the words *Burling Slip*. They saw other buildings like it in other parts of the city, and then they saw men with terribly vacant looks in their eyes slipping metal canisters into satchels and lunch pails.

See what good it does you! Mordred cried, laughing. And then he was gone.

Joe let go of the luggage tag and Kiku's hand at the

same time. "It's meant for a place called Burling Slip," Joe said.

"That's a steam plant," Walt shouted. "My class went there on a—"

"Field trip," Madge finished for her. "Sheesh! I wish I went to your school."

"They're going to put this poison in the steam system," Kiku said. "But will that be enough to poison the steam?"

Mr. Akiyama, who had been staring at the canister, suddenly grabbed it and wrenched the lid open. Kiku screamed and Madge covered her nose and mouth, but they all peered into the can. Amidst the white pellets were flecks of gold.

"The devil!" Miss Lake cried.

"You'd better close that, Kenji," Dr. Bean said, laying his hand on his friend's shoulder.

"What does it mean?" Madge demanded as Mr. Akiyama replaced the lid.

"He's added gold fairy dust to the cyanide pellets," Miss Lake said. "It will make the poison a hundred times more powerful. If that gets into the steam system, then all the steam in New York will become instantly deadly."

"Why, half the buildings in New York are heated by steam!" Kiku said.

"Including Pennsylvania Station and Grand Central Terminal," Dr. Bean said.

"All those soldiers shipping out!" Madge cried.

"There are steam vents on the streets," Mr. Akiyama added.

"It will kill thousands . . . millions, even!" Joe said.

"There are five more plants in the city," Mr. Akiyama said. "He'll be sending operatives to each one. They might be doing it as we speak."

"No," Kiku said, "remember what the message said—the attack will take place on the tenth—that's tomorrow."

"Not really," Miss Lake said, holding up her watch. The time read 3:10. How had it gotten so late in the night? Joe wondered. How long had he been holding the luggage tag, battling Mordred's mind?

"We have time," Dr. Bean said, "but not much. We must alert the FBI and the police right away."

"I don't think we'll have any trouble finding the police," Madge said. She had moved to the window and was looking out. They all crowded around the window beside her.

"What is it?" Joe asked, unable to see past them.

Miss Lake and Dr. Bean stood aside so he could look down. At first he was confused by all the lights, but then he saw a uniformed man get out of one of the cars and hold up a bullhorn. "Come out with your hands up," he boomed. "You're surrounded."

28

SURRENDER

WALT STARED DOWN at the moving searchlights and uniformed officers. There were dogs, too, barking and straining at their leashes. For a moment he was back in Germany, watching from his apartment window as the Nazis patrolled the streets. He heard breaking glass and remembered the night that gangs ran through the street shattering the windows of synagogues and Jewish-owned businesses. *Kristallnacht*, they called it, a pretty name for a nightmare.

"It will be all right," Dr. Bean said, putting his hand on Walt's shoulder. "I'll explain who we are and what we've been doing."

"Sure, Doc," Madge said. "You try explaining to a couple of New York's finest that we stole a box from the Cloisters because it had a magical book inside and I'll be seeing you in the funny papers." Her voice was light and casual, but she'd come to stand close to Walt. Looking around, he saw that Joe and Kiku looked scared too.

Joe was wanted by the police, and Kiku and her father might still be detained at Ellis Island. They had more to lose here than he did. He turned to Miss Lake. She had found him in the park after his run-in with Mordred and given him a chance to turn his fear into a way to be brave. But she wasn't looking at him now.

"We'll have to surrender." She took a white handkerchief from her coat pocket and waved it out the window. Walt caught a scent of perfume and watched as Boris flew out the window. Even he was abandoning them. "We're coming down," Miss Lake called in a fluting voice that carried on the wind. "And we're unarmed."

"It will be all right," Walt told Madge as they made their way down the stairs, trying to reassure himself by reassuring her. "We know where the attack is planned. They'll have to listen to us."

"Will they?" Madge asked. "A dotty old museum curator, his assistant, an 'enemy alien,' and four kids—one of whom stole a priceless medieval box from the Cloisters in broad daylight?"

"Was that you?" Walt asked, impressed, and when she nodded, "Holy smokes! How'd you do it?"

"I just broke the glass and grabbed it," she said, unable to stop herself from grinning. "It felt like it belonged to me. Then I high-tailed it out the door and over the wall. I haven't run so fast since the Sorensen twins were chasing me and Frankie for breaking my team out from jail in ring-a-levio."

"I wish I could've been there to see that," Walt said, shaking his head in admiration.

"Me too," Madge said, turning to look at him at the bottom of the stairs. "But I'm glad you're here now. I-I never wanted to believe—"

"It's okay," Walt said, squeezing her hand. "This whole thing is almost over and then . . ."

Whatever would happen *then* would have to wait. The police were shouting at them to put their hands up and get down on their knees. "Like we're Bonnie and Clyde," Madge muttered. "Hey," she whispered to Walt. "You could deck one of them with your superstrength and get away."

Walt shook his head. "It wouldn't help the rest of you. And I don't want to be on my own anymore." As he said it, he knew it was true. And suddenly he didn't feel so afraid anymore. Whatever happened now, they were all together.

They all got down to their knees except for Dr. Bean, who addressed the police officer who approached them. "My dear man, I am Dr. Dashwood Bean of the Metropolitan Museum of Art. We have information of grave importance to impart to your superiors. Please contact Hilary Chester at the FBI immediately and the mayor as well. Fiorello will want to know about this."

"Sure, Doc, shall I get FDR and Winston Churchill on the horn while I'm at it?"

"Well, I don't know about Winston. . . . I'm sure he's

awfully busy with the Blitz. But, yes, Franklin will want to know," Dr. Bean said, waving his arms in the air. The police officer caught his right hand and wrenched it behind his back.

"Sure, Doc, and then I'll send a wire to the King of Siam and the Queen of Sheba." He cuffed Dr. Bean and pushed him against the squad car. Dr. Bean let out a surprised yelp.

"Hey," Madge cried. "Whatcha doing, bullying an old man?"

"Look, Harvey, we got a real spitfire. Better watch out before—"

But Madge had already landed a kick on the shin of the officer manhandling Dr. Bean. She was promptly restrained and cuffed. *How dare they handle Madge like that!* Walt ran toward the officer, face red, fists curled, but Madge shouted at him, "Don't do it, Walt, you might really hurt one of them and then you'll be in real trouble."

"Yeah," Officer Harvey said, laughing, "like I'm real scared of the scrawny kid!"

"Those are children you're mistreating," Miss Lake said authoritatively while putting a restraining hand on Walt's shoulder.

"Thieves and runaways," Officer Harvey said, sneering at Joe. "This kid matches a description of an Indian runaway wanted for putting his principal in the hospital." And then, eyeing Kiku and Mr. Akiyama, "And enemy aliens. I'm takin' the lot of youse down to police headquarters."

They were thrown into a paddy wagon. When the van pulled out, they were jostled to and fro against the walls. Miss Lake helped Dr. Bean onto a narrow wooden bench while Kiku brushed Madge's hair out of her eyes and used her handkerchief to wipe her face.

"Thanks," Madge whispered. "I'm just mad at that big goon for treating the doc that way."

"Of course you are," Kiku said. "We all are."

Walt sat stone-faced, clenching his hands. What good was it to have superstrength if he couldn't use it? "They'll be sorry when they learn who the doc is," Walt said.

"If they believe us," Kiku said. "You heard that officer. He said he had orders to take us all down to police headquarters. Who do you think gave those orders? And how do they know about Joe?"

"I'm afraid it means that Mordred has infiltrated the city government. He was always very good at insinuating himself into the halls of power," Miss Lake said. "He's able to control weak-minded people using the book. Remember when he sweet-talked that Viking chieftain into siding against us, Dash?"

"Have you really been fighting him all these years?" Walt asked.

"Yes," Miss Lake answered. "Sometimes he vanishes

for a century or two, but he always resurfaces. Dash and I knew he was back when we saw Hitler rise to power."

"But can't you ever defeat him for good?" Walt asked. "After all, the two of you are . . . well . . . *legendary.*"

"All our power went into making the Kelmsbury books," said Dr. Bean, who, with his glasses askew and hair standing on end, looked small and flustered rather than legendary. "We saw that our day—the day of dragons and unicorns, wizards and sorceresses—was coming to an end. Our magic was no longer able to change the world of men and women. So we poured the last of it into the books so that they would call the best of you forward to take up the fight when needed."

"But then why does Mr. January—Mordred—use the Kelmsbury as a cipher with his spies?" Joe asked.

Dr. Bean looked at Miss Lake, and she nodded. "Tell them, Dash."

"We made the books so that only the true of heart could use them, and only when they were united. We wove a spell into each one that made it dangerous to any who tried to use it for evil purposes or who tried to use it alone. It drives that person insane. We thought we were only safeguarding its power, but it had an unintended consequence."

"Mordred found one of the books and learned how to use it to corrupt men. You may have noticed how you started hearing voices when you read the book."

They all nodded.

"I think it's Morgaine's voice I hear," Kiku said.

"And I hear Lancelot's," Joe said.

"I'm not sure who I'm hearing," Madge said. "I guess it must be Guinevere."

"I started hearing Mordred's voice after I met him in the park," Walt said. "And then Miss Lake showed me how to turn off all the voices. But you never explained how the book makes us hear those voices."

"As I told you, when I painted the pictures in the book, I used fairy gold. When Arthur, Guinevere, Lancelot, and Morgaine found their way to the Maiden Castle, I had each of them touch the books so their spirits would be infused into the paint and carried through time to the new knights. But what I didn't realize was that Mordred had already found his way into the mind of one of them, and in that way he found his way into the book too. That's why he gives it to his spies. Over the years he's collected four of the books and used them to recruit spies. When his spies use the book as a cipher, they become malleable to his power and eventually go insane."

"What if he's got the whole city under his sway?" Madge asked.

"He can only influence a handful using the book," Dr. Bean said. "Which is why he goes for weak-minded men he can use as tools or for men in powerful positions.

We'll have to find a way to get in touch with my friend at the FBI to intervene."

"I'm afraid we haven't ingratiated ourselves with these officers," Miss Lake said.

"I have an idea," Mr. Akiyama said. He'd been quiet for most of the trip, but now he sat up straight and addressed the rest of them. "I know how to get your friend at the FBI down to the station."

⋆　⋆　⋆

Mr. Akiyama told them his idea as the paddy wagon sped downtown. It was a long way from the High Bridge Water Tower to police headquarters—practically the whole length of Manhattan—and Walt, looking down at his watch, was nervous to see the time passing. It was after four a.m. by the time they reached police headquarters, and they were still arguing when the wagon drove down the ramp into the bowels of the building.

"You can't tell them that," Kiku cried "They'll execute you for treason!"

"Dashwood's friend Agent Chester will make everything right afterward," he told his daughter.

"But what if it doesn't work?"

Mr. Akiyama turned to his daughter and took both her hands in his. "Then what will it matter what happens to me? I will have died trying to help my friends and my country just as you have fought valiantly beside your friends. I was wrong before when I scolded you for trying to help. I didn't really see you. You have become a strong, brave young woman. I am proud to have you as my daughter. And now I hope to make you proud to have me as your father."

Kiku burst into tears and tried to hold her father back as the doors were opened, but Mr. Akiyama removed himself from her arms and walked to the back of the van so he would be the first out. Kiku cried out, but Joe put his arm around her to hold her back.

"I wish to make a statement," Mr. Akiyama announced in a loud voice. "I am an agent of the imperial government of Japan, and I have knowledge of a plot to destroy New York City. But I will only divulge it to Agent Hilary Chester of the FBI."

29

THE FLEA FLICKER

NONE OF THE two dozen policemen in the basement of police headquarters could get Mr. Akiyama to budge or say a word. He closed his eyes and sat perfectly still. Madge was impressed. She didn't think she could stay still and quiet for so long.

"Take the rest of them into a cell and call the chief inspector," Officer Harvey barked. "And call that guy at the FBI he mentioned—"

"Chester," Dr. Bean said. "Hilary Chester."

"I'm not leaving my father," Kiku said when a policeman tried to lead her into a cell.

"That's fine, missy," Officer Harvey said. "Pete, Hank . . ." He called over two burly policemen and gestured at Mr. Akiyama. "Haul this fellow into holding cell B and throw the lot of them in there with him. Might as well have all the crazies together when the G-men come to visit."

Mr. Akiyama allowed himself to be led into the cell

only on the condition that Dr. Bean and Madge were un-
cuffed. He still refused to talk, and once he was inside
the cell, he sat back down on the floor in the same cross-
legged position with his eyes closed.

They all sat on narrow benches along the wall, except for Kiku, who sat on the floor next to her father.
Madge stared at a tiny window high up on the wall. She
could just make out a square of pavement that turned
from black to gray as they waited.

"What's taking so long?" she complained. "It's morning already and no one's come to see us. Do you think
your fellow Chester could be on the take, too, Doc?"

"Not Hil Chester," Dr. Bean said. "They might have
had trouble tracking him down, though. He's been awfully busy since Sunday."

The reference to the day just made Madge more nervous. It was Wednesday now, the tenth of December.
January's spies—the men they'd seen in their vision—
would be getting ready to go to their jobs at the steam
factories, cyanide canisters hidden away in lunch pails
or satchels. Madge shifted nervously on the hard bench
and then got up to pace back and forth. She had counted
the number of paces in the little cell ten times when she
heard the sound of footsteps coming down the stairs.

"Hey, someone's coming," she called to the others,
pressing her face to the bars to see who was walking down
the stairs. She could make out two pairs of dark pant legs
followed by a pair of stockinged legs and alligator shoes.

"Two fellows and some dame . . ." Her voice curdled in her throat when the two men reached the bottom of the stairs. It was Mr. January, his face reassembled beneath his fedora, but Madge thought she could see now the seams where it attached to the skull. It looked rubbery and wrong, like the face of Frankenstein's monster after he was all sewn up.

"Good job catching them, Morris," Mr. January said to the chief inspector.

"It was your tip what cinched it, Tony. Who'd've thunk a fellow as respectable as Dashwood Bean would be behind an operation like this! And corrupting minors—"

"You've got it all wrong!" Madge cried, clutching the bars. "Dr. Bean's trying to save the city. This fellow isn't who he says he is. That's not even his real face. Pull it off and you'll see!"

Mr. January smiled at Madge, his lips stretched so far over his teeth, Madge thought she could see a bit of the bloody skull beneath. "What an imagination! Want to have a tug at my face, Morris?"

The chief inspector laughed nervously. "Kid's been watching too many horror films."

"*Chill*-drun ought to mind their own business."

Madge tore her eyes away from Mr. January to look at the woman standing next to him. "Hey, it's Miss Fitzbane from the museum. Can't you vouch for Dr. Bean? You know he wouldn't do anything to hurt the city."

But Miss Fitzbane only glared at Madge, light flashing off her round glasses, and held up a printed map. "We found this map of the city's water system in Dr. Bean's workroom, evidence of his plot to sabotage the city's water supply."

"And we have the poison canister you had at the High Bridge Water Tower." Mr. January held up the Gladstone bag they'd left in the tower room. "I'll be taking that with me to FBI headquarters."

"Since I came to work at the museum, I've suspected Dr. Bean and Miss Lake of un-American sympathies," Miss Fitzbane said, glaring at Miss Lake.

Miss Lake, who had come to stand beside Madge, stared back at her. "It's you, isn't it? I thought you were dead."

Miss Fitzbane parted her lips and smiled, revealing her crowded, awful teeth.

Where have I seen those teeth before? Madge wondered.

"As you see," Miss Fitzbane snarled, "you were mistaken."

"I know a way to release you both from the curse," Miss Lake said. "You could find peace at last."

"Peace!" Miss Fitzbane sneered. "Your peace would leave us powerless, *sister*."

Sister? Madge stared at the two women and saw for the first time a similarity in their features. Only in Miss Lake, kindness and serenity had smoothed her features into beauty, while envy and greed had turned Miss Fitzbane's face into a stern mask—just as much a mask as Mordred's. She controlled it now into a smirk. "You see, Chief Inspector, they're subversive pacifists. They'll be executed for treason."

Then she turned her gaze on Kiku. "As for the Akiyamas, clearly they are enemy aliens. Now . . ." She looked at her watch. "Hadn't we better go, Mr. January? I believe you want to deliver that canister to its proper destination."

"Yes, Miss Fitzbane," January said quickly. "Thank you again for all your help. We'll leave them here"—he glanced down at a steam radiator across from the cell—"where they'll be nice and cozy when the twelve o'clock whistle blows."

He smiled at Miss Fitzbane, and for a moment, the mask seemed to slip, and Madge saw something surprising. *Why, he's scared of her*, she thought as he turned to leave.

"Who is she?" Madge asked when they had gone.

"Belisent," Miss Lake answered. "My half sister, and Mordred's mother. It was she who gave her son the enchanted helmet that gave him eternal life and tore his face away."

"What kind of mother does that to her own son?" Walt cried.

"In her zeal to use him as a weapon against Arthur she was careless of how her magic might harm her son," Dr. Bean answered. "And now she uses him as a weapon against any who wish to live in peace and happiness. She's been spying on us at the museum."

"Miss Fitzbane found me there last night," Kiku blurted out. "She told me that if I helped her find incriminating evidence against Dr. Bean and Miss Lake, she would make sure my father and I would go free." She looked at her father, her eyes filled with tears. "She told me I'd be able to save you if I helped her. I'm sorry, Otousan, perhaps I should have! Now you'll be executed for treason. But I couldn't betray my friends."

Mr. Akiyama rose stiffly to his feet and stood facing his daughter, his face grave. "Of course you couldn't, Kiku-chan. I am proud of you." Then he bowed his head to her. Kiku let out a cry and threw herself into his arms. He held her tight, patting her back.

When he let her go, Miss Lake offered Kiku her handkerchief. "You did the right thing, Kiku. Belisent is not trustworthy. And her magic never works exactly as she thinks it will. Most magic doesn't, as I imagine you four are finding out."

"I accidentally hit Joe," Walt admitted.

"And I almost got lost in a tapestry," Kiku said.

"And when I tried to break the code without the Kelmsbury, I could hear Mr. January's voice in my head," Joe said.

"No wonder you had a headache," Madge said. "At least you all have magic. I don't have any."

"That's not true," Kiku said. "We were able to bring

Boris alive only when you were there and we were all working together."

"But we couldn't do it again," Madge said.

"If the three of you hadn't been with me, I wouldn't have been able to read the luggage tag without falling under Mordred's power," Joe said.

"That's true," Madge said. "Hm, that does give me an idea. What if . . ." She pulled Joe and Kiku and Walt into a huddle and whispered in their ears. The three of them listened to her as if she were Coach Bob Zuppke giving them the moves of his famous flea-flicker play. When they all nodded their agreement, they broke apart, and Madge said in a carrying voice, "Well, at least one of us has gotten out. Agent Chrysanthemum will carry word to the rendezvous point."

One of the guards perked up his ears. "What are they yakking about, Harvey?"

Harvey looked up from his racing form and glanced into the cell—then did a double take. "Hey! Where's the Japanese girl?"

"Who?" Madge asked, all wide-eyed innocence. "I don't know what you're talking about." She looked around the cell at Walt and Joe, Dr. Bean and Miss Lake, and stared especially hard at Mr. Akiyama, who looked upset to realize his daughter was gone.

"Where's your kid, Pops?" Harvey said, approaching the cell.

"What kid?" Mr. Akiyama replied.

"She was here a minute ago," Harvey said, taking his keys off his belt. "Maybe she's hiding under the bunk."

"Hey, that fella said not to open the door on any account," the other guard said.

"Whatsamatter, Pete? Are you afraid of some eggheads and a pack of kids? You stay outside." As Harvey opened the cell door, he lost his balance and fell against the bars. "Hey, you don't gotta push me. . . ."

But Pete didn't answer. He was staring at the handcuffs that had been attached to his belt a few minutes ago and were now hovering in the air. As Pete turned to catch them, Walt grabbed his arms and pulled them behind his back. "Sorry, Mister, I don't want to hurt you. Just let me put these on you."

Pete struggled but couldn't get free of Walt's grip. Harvey started toward him but tripped again. Joe helped him up and led him over to the bunk. "Maybe you'd better sit down," Joe suggested.

"Yeah, maybe . . . Hey!" he yelled as the three kids and three adults left the cell and locked the door behind them.

"Wait," Madge said, "we'd better make sure Kiku's with us. . . . Oh, here she is." Kiku had materialized, holding the guard's ring of keys.

"Didja see that?" they could hear Pete saying as they ran up the stairs.

"I ain't sayin' I saw nothin'," they heard Harvey reply. "And you better not neither, if you want to see your pension."

They burst out onto the street laughing. But then the clock on top of the police headquarters struck eleven, and they all stopped laughing.

"Mordred said the attack would take place at noon," Dr. Bean said, hailing an approaching taxi. "We've only got an hour. We have to get to FBI headquarters right away!"

"But what if Mordred has gotten to someone there," Joe pointed out, "and you can't get to your friend?"

"We should split up and go straight to the steam plants," Walt said.

"He's right, Dash," Miss Lake said. "You go to FBI headquarters. Kenji and I will go to the Kips Bay station—it's the largest one. The rest of you go to Burling Slip. It's the second-largest and closest to here."

"Shouldn't we split up, too?" Joe asked.

"No, the four of you are more powerful together. Dash will have them send policemen to the other plants. You four try to stop Mordred and Belisent." She pushed the four of them into the taxi and gave the driver the address and a ten-dollar bill. They'd pulled away before they had a chance to even say good-bye.

30

THE SLIP

THE CAB TOOK a right on Kenmare Street and then a right on the Bowery and continued downtown to Water Street. Walt recognized the route from when they'd followed the Packard to Battery Park—and sure enough, he could soon smell seawater. Instead of going all the way down to Battery Park, though, they took a left on John Street. Ahead of them loomed a tall building with several smokestacks.

"That's it!" Walt cried, thumping the driver on the shoulder. "You can let us out here."

"Sure, kid, whatever you say. Do you want your change?"

"You can keep it," Walt said, getting out.

"Big spender," Madge said, following Walt out.

"It's not like we're going to need it."

They stood in front of the building, looking up at the towering smokestacks. Walt felt as if they had all stood like this before, only instead of smokestacks, they had been looking up at the towers of a castle.

Camelot, he heard a voice say in his head. It made him glad the voice was back, even though the word was spoken so wistfully that he was pretty sure that they hadn't come out of that castle. Madge must have felt it too, because she said, "If only I knew that Frankie and the twins were going to be all right."

"Dr. Bean and Miss Lake will make sure they are," Joe said. "They'll take care of Walt's folks and Kiku's father and . . ."

"Your sister Jeanette," Kiku said, taking Joe's hand. "I feel sure of it. That's what they do . . . after."

The word seemed to echo in Walt's head as if it was the last word of a story. *And they all lived happily ever after.* Only Walt didn't think their story ended that way. Still, if his folks were okay . . .

He heard a soft sigh and turned, wondering who had made that mournful sound. It came from Boris, who had landed on Madge's shoulder. Madge turned her head and grinned at Walt. "It looks like we're all here," she said. "Let's go stop Mordred from wrecking our city."

As they walked toward the door, Kiku vanished. She was supposed to slip inside and try to find Mordred, but Walt couldn't let her face him on her own.

"Let me take care of the guard," Walt said, curling his fists.

"Wait," Joe said. "Let's try reasoning with him."

When they reached the guard, Joe stepped forward and addressed him. "We're here to stop an attack on the factory," he said in a deep, calm voice.

"What?" the guard began, eyeing Madge and Walt warily. "With who? The Lollipop Guild?"

"With my friends," Joe answered.

The guard shook his head but then looked again at Joe. "Hey, you're on the level, ain't you?"

"Yes, sir," Joe replied, looking steadily at the guard. "You should call your colleagues at the other plants and tell them to look out for saboteurs."

The guard held Joe's gaze for another long minute and then nodded. "All right, son, I'll do that."

He turned to a red phone on the wall, and Madge and Walt and Joe walked into the steam plant.

"How did you do that?" Walt asked. "Is that part of your power?"

"I don't think so," Joe said, looking Walt square in the eye. "I just told him the truth. I didn't want you to have to hit him because . . . When I hit the principal it didn't feel good even though he really deserved it. I was hoping you wouldn't have to do that."

"You talked to him like an adult," Madge said, "and so he listened to you like you were one. I don't know if it'll work with this guy, though. He looks kinda sore."

A burly man in overalls with a hat that said FORE-
MAN across it was approaching them, a wrench in one
hand. Before Joe could say anything, Madge spoke up.
"Hey, Mister, where would a fella go if he wanted to
poison the steam?"

The man stopped in his tracks, looking confused.
"Why would anyone want to do that?" the man asked,
wiping his face with a red bandana. "The steam comes
from pure drinking water heated in the *berler*."

"The *berler*?" Joe asked.

"I think he means the boiler," Madge said.

"That's what I said, the *berler*," the foreman said,
pointing to a huge machine that rose ten stories from
the plant floor. "You'd have to pour it into the valve on
top—Hey, what's that?"

The foreman stared up at the towering boiler furnace,
where a narrow catwalk ran between a complicated
network of pipes. "That fellow shouldn't be up there."

They all looked up and saw Mr. January on the catwalk. Walt saw a gust of steam leak out of one of the
pipes and form into the shape of a slight girl with a
wrench in her hand, sneaking up behind Mr. January.
It was Kiku, her invisible shape revealed by the steam—
and by the creak of the metal catwalk. Mordred whirled
around and grinned when he saw the steam shape.

"You should have taken the deal with Mother," he

said, and then he lunged at Kiku and pushed her off the catwalk.

She landed on the platform just below the catwalk, where her body, fully visible now, lay twisted and limp.

Joe cursed and Madge screamed.

"Go help her," Walt shouted at Joe and Madge. "I'll take care of him."

Walt ran up the steps, Joe and Madge behind him, keeping his eye on Mordred. He was kneeling in front of the huge boiler, turning a bright red metal wheel. The Zyklon B canister sat on the metal grid beside him. It was already open. Walt could see the glint of gold dust mixed in with the cyanide pellets. When Mordred poured the mixture into the boiler the steam would become poisonous. Families sitting down for lunch, kids in schools, soldiers saying good-bye to their sweethearts in Penn Station and Grand Central—all those lives snuffed out in a breath of air, just as thousands would be killed in Europe.

The thought of it made Walt angry. His heart pumped blood to his legs and arms, filling his body with so much power, he could feel his muscles swelling, straining the seams of his jacket. He ripped it off and, holding it like a cape, strode across the shaking catwalk toward Mordred. Mordred looked up with a new face, this one like some horrible giant insect. He was wearing a gas mask. He quickly grabbed the canister of Zyklon

B and held it over the open valve on the boiler.

"Ah," he said, his voice deep and echoing under the mask, "I see the book has given you brute strength, but that won't be enough to save everyone. What shall it be, Walt? Should I pour this one in the boiler?" He shook the open canister in his right hand. "Or should I pour out this one . . ." he reached into the satchel and took out a second canister with his left hand. ". . . and kill you and your friends right now? The decision is yours. Save yourself and your friends and know that thousands died because of your selfishness, or sacrifice your friends to save the many and die with them."

Walt stared from one hand to the other. Mordred's arms seemed to have grown longer, as if he had willed his bones to stretch like rubber tentacles, his fingers splayed out around the two canisters like giant spiders. Could Walt stop both arms at once? And if he couldn't, which should he choose?

For a moment Walt didn't feel strong at all. He felt like he had when he had hidden in the wardrobe while the soldiers came to take Jacob Goldblatt's father away. He had wanted to call out—to do *something*—but he had known he would endanger his own family. It hadn't been fair having to make a choice like that when he was only a kid. And it wasn't fair now. How could he ever live with either choice?

You won't be able to, the voice inside his head said. *No matter how you choose, you will suffer with that choice for the rest of your life. Believe me, I know.*

And then he knew what he had to do. He launched himself at Mordred, flying through the air like a rocket aimed right at the middle of Mordred's chest. When he hit, he snatched the open canister out of Mordred's hand and rolled it up in his jacket in one swift move, while grabbing hold of Mordred. Mordred dropped the closed canister and reached for the one in Walt's jacket, but Walt couldn't let him get it.

"Madge!" he cried, spying her on the platform below. "Catch!"

He yanked the sleeves tight on the bundle, said a prayer that it would hold, and lobbed it to Madge. Then, without waiting to see if she caught it, he tightened his hold on Mordred and rolled them both off the edge of the catwalk. *I should've wished for flying powers*, Walt had just time enough to think before they both plummeted to the floor ten stories below.

31

THE END OF THE TAIL

MADGE SAW THE bundle flying at her and put up her hands the way Frankie had taught to catch a fly ball when they were playing sandlot baseball. She pretended it was a baseball she was catching, not a canister of poison. The bundle rattled in her hands when she caught it, but Walt's jacket kept all the pellets in.

"I got it!" she cried, looking up to see Walt's expression. Instead she watched in horror as Walt and Mordred plummeted to the steam-plant floor. There was an awful *thud* as they landed. She could see Walt's back. At least he had landed on top. Maybe Mordred had broken his fall. She wanted to run to him, but she was still clutching the canister of poison, and Kiku had only regained consciousness in time to see Walt fall.

"Is she okay?" Joe asked anxiously.

"I'm fine!" Kiku shouted at him. "Go help Walt. Madge will help me!"

"Golly, Kiku," Madge said as she helped her up, "I

didn't know you had such a set of lungs on you!" Kiku leaned heavily on her as they made their way down the stairs with Madge keeping the bundle tucked under her arm, and saying a Hail Mary in her head and promising God that she would go back to church if Walt was alive. *Just let him be alive!* she said over and over again in her head for what felt like an endless descent. When they reached the ground, Kiku took the bundle from her and gave her a little push.

"I'll take care of this," Kiku said. "Go to him."

Madge ran on ahead. Joe was leaning over Walt, his hand on Walt's neck.

"Is he . . . ?" She was unable to say the words *alive* or *dead*.

"I don't know!" Joe cried. He rolled Walt over. His face was a ghastly white and splattered with blood. But was it his blood or Mordred's, a pool of which was spreading out from his broken body? At least *he* was dead, but would he stay dead? And what did that matter if Walt was gone, too?

"Why did he have to do it?" Madge wailed.

"It was the only way to stop Mordred," Joe said, easing Walt's body off the broken, bloody mess that had been Mordred. Only the horrible gas mask was whole. "He couldn't choose between us and the city. So he sacrificed himself."

"No!" Madge cried, taking out her handkerchief and wiping the blood off Walt's face. "That's not fair! It's not supposed to be like that. We're in this together! Do you hear that, Walter Rosenberg?" She put her hands on his shoulders and shook him until his head fell limply to one side. "You don't get to play the hero and leave us behind."

Then tears were streaming down her face, dripping onto Walt's. She bowed her head and rested her forehead on Walt's chest and sobbed for the first time since her mother had died. She didn't care who saw her; she cried into Walt's chest even as she heard footsteps hurrying across the plant floor and men's voices shouting "FBI!" and "Stand down!" She didn't care even when she heard them telling Joe and Kiku that they were heroes. That they'd stopped the mastermind behind the sabotage plot and that the FBI had rounded up the other saboteurs before they were able to hurt anyone. What did any of that matter if Walt wasn't here to see it?

It didn't matter to Joe or Kiku either. They sat on either side of Madge, their arms around her shoulders. She could feel the warmth from their arms coursing through her back, into her chest, and down into her hands, which still gripped Walt's shoulders, pooling at a point in her forehead which still rested on Walt's chest—

Where she felt something go *thump*. She sat up and stared at Walt's face. Had it been? It had felt like his heart beating—

Then Walt's eyes flickered open, and he was looking up into Madge's face.

"Madge, why are you crying? Did we fail?"

"No, sport," Joe answered, because Madge couldn't speak. "You did it. You stopped Mordred before he could put the poison in the boiler. The FBI caught the other saboteurs. You saved the city!"

Walt sat up and blinked at them. He looked at Mordred's mangled body and then at the FBI men who were spread out, scouring the plant for evidence. They had retrieved the two poison canisters and were talking to the foreman and the guard. "The last thing I remember was flying through the air—" He stared back at Mordred's body. "Why aren't I dead?"

"Because—" Kiku began, but before she could answer, a horrible shriek cut her off.

"Let me in! Let me in!" someone was shouting. "He's my son!"

"It's Miss Fishbone," Madge said as the woman came running across the steam plant.

"My son! My son!" she cried, kneeling beside Mordred and clasping his limp head to her chest. Then, looking up, the light flashing off her glasses, she spat, "What have you done to him?"

Madge stared at her, not sure what surprised her more, that Miss Fishbone had feelings or that anyone had loved Mordred. But then she remembered something her mother used to say: *Everybody was somebody's beloved child once.*

"He was going to kill innocent people, Miss Fish—Fitzbane. We had to save the city."

"Innocent people?" Miss Fitzbane hissed, spit flying out of her mouth. "No one's innocent here, little girl. And we'll see about your precious city!"

She got up and stalked across the floor, hips twitching, heading toward the back of the plant.

"Hey, what do you think she means?" Walt asked.

"Maybe we should tell the FBI men that she made a threat against the city," Kiku said.

"There's no time," Joe said. "She's heading for the loading docks. I think we'd better follow her—that is, if you're feeling up to it." Joe slapped Walt on the back.

"Never felt better," Walt said, springing to his feet. "Let's go see what she's up to."

"Yeah," Madge said, getting to her feet. "Although I can't imagine an old dame like Miss Fishbone doing much harm."

"She's not just an old woman," Kiku said as they followed her out onto the loading docks. "Remember she's Belisent, a—"

"Witch?" Miss Fitzbane turned from the edge of the loading dock. The wind off the East River was tugging at her skirt. "Yes," she hissed, baring her yellow teeth. "A more powerful witch than dear sweet Vivian or little Morgaine." She took off her glasses and tossed them into the river. Her eyes bulged and shone like yellow lamps.

"And neither Vivian nor Morgaine can do *this*." She touched the brooch on her lapel. *Does she mean to jab us to death with that ugly brooch?* Madge wondered. But then she noticed that Miss Fishbone's long skinny body was getting taller, like a piece of saltwater taffy being pulled out on a taffy hook, and her skirt was shaking like Minnie the Moocher doing the hootchy-kootchy.

"What the heck!" Walt said.

"There's something under there!" Madge said, taking a step closer.

"It looks like a—"

"Tail!" Madge shrieked. A long scaled tail whipped out from under Fishbone's skirt and reared up in front of Madge's face.

At the end of the tail was a human head with a woman's face on it—Miss Fitzbane's face, but with a mouth yawning open with three sets of teeth and a long forked tongue. "What's the matter, Miss McGrorrr-ry?" The awful head rolled the *r*s around her long forked tongue like they were appetizers. "Cat got your tongue?" Then the head lunged at Madge, mouth gaping wide, teeth gnashing. Walt pulled Madge back just as the teeth grazed Madge's scalp. She could smell burning hair. The tail lashed back and the two horrible heads laughed in unison. The bigger one was now elongated, with the snout of a serpent and sulfurous burning eyes. Green scales were popping out from her skin. Where Miss Fitzbane's arms had been, leathery wings unfurled and beat the air. The kids had to press themselves back against the loading-dock wall to keep from being flayed by their razor-sharp edges. Miss Fitzbane had grown into a huge monster, into a—

"She's an amphisbaena!" Kiku said. "Like the one on her pin!"

"Always the clever one, little sister," Miss Fitzbane said. It was the head at the end of the tail that spoke. "But you won't be clever enough to stop me from destroying the spirit of this city."

The tail lashed again and the head nipped the beast's side. The amphisbaena let out a horrible roar and sprayed the dock with sulfurous flames. Then it sprang from the dock and launched itself into the air, heading downriver, toward the harbor.

32

THE LADY OF THE HARBOR

"WE HAVE TO stop her!" Walt cried, watching the horrible monster growing smaller and smaller as it flew away from them. It was heading downriver, to the harbor, which gave Walt an uneasy feeling. What was she planning to do *there*?

"But how?" Madge asked. "The last time I checked, none of us could fly."

"No," Kiku said, "but I can steer a boat. There!" She pointed to a small motorboat tied to the dock. She was already jumping into it. Joe followed her and reached out a hand to help Madge, but she leapt in past him, Walt following. As soon as they were all in, Kiku shouted for someone to untie them. Then she started the engine and steered out onto the river.

"How do you know how to drive a boat?" Madge asked, impressed.

"My father likes to go fishing out in Montauk. I've watched him lots of times."

"*Watched* him?" Walt repeated as Kiku narrowly avoided a fishing boat. He wished he knew how to steer a boat, but he had spent the whole voyage over from England seasick.

As they approached the harbor, there were more boats on the water. It was full of merchant ships and naval vessels and cruise ships that had been reoutfitted to carry troops, all preparing to sail to Europe. *That's why New York's so important to the war effort*, Walt's cousin Ralph had said three nights ago. *We've got the best harbor on the Eastern Seaboard. All the boys I know are shipping outta here.*

Kiku had to maneuver around the other boats to keep Belisent in sight. She was so high in the air, she could have been an airplane or a child's kite. Once or twice it looked like she was going to dive-bomb one of the ships, but at the last minute she would swerve out of the way and climb back into the sky.

"It looks like she's trying to choose which one to attack," Walt said. Belisent had boasted she would destroy the spirit of the city. Would scuttling one ship do that? What if it was one of the cruise ships carrying thousands of soldiers to England? Or one of the ferries packed with families and schoolchildren? Walt could see the passengers on one ferry shouting and pointing at the strange creature, the pilot shouting and shaking his fist at it. *What must they think?* Walt wondered as the ferry continued on its way to—

Walt stared ahead, his mouth opening in horror. For a moment he was two years younger, steaming into the harbor for the first time. He was so weak from seasickness and the measles that he could barely stand, but his uncle Sol had helped him out onto the deck so he wouldn't miss his first view of the city.

"Look at her," Uncle Sol had said, "the greatest city in the world. They even put a lady out in the harbor to welcome you."

And Walt, burning with fever and the shame of leaving his parents behind, had looked up into the eyes of the woman rising out of the harbor and had known for the first time that things might be okay. That this was a place where people came to start over. *This* was the spirit of the city.

"I know where she's heading!" Walt shouted, pointing to the towering figure that stood guard at the mouth of the harbor. "She's going to destroy the Statue of Liberty! We have to stop her!"

But as if she knew the game was up, Belisent was already winging straight toward the statue. "But how can she destroy it?" Kiku asked.

"I don't know," Walt admitted, "and I don't want to find out. Look—there's a space next to where the ferry's docking. Can you pull up there?"

Kiku steered the boat toward the dock and threw Walt a rope to tie them up. No one on the ferry noticed them, because they were all looking up at the sky.

"I bet it's a German zeppelin disguised to look like a dragon," a schoolteacher told his class.

"Maybe it's a publicity stunt for a new movie," a pretty girl in a fur coat said.

"Sheesh," Madge said. "Why can't people believe what's right in front of their noses?"

"Yeah," Joe remarked. "It's almost like they think two-headed dragons are malarkey."

Madge stuck out her tongue at Joe. Kiku shook her head and said, "Sometimes we don't see what's in front of us because we're trying too hard to make it fit into what we already know. It's easier to believe in zeppelins and movie stunts than—"

Suddenly the amphisbaena swooped down on the people waiting on line to get inside the statue, spewing flames from its gaping jaws. A woman's hat caught on fire. A troop of schoolgirls screamed and ran for shelter on the ferry, where the passengers were all crowding inside the cabin. The creature followed them and landed on top of the ferry and started rocking it back and forth.

"We have to stop her!" Walt screamed. He jumped onto the ferry and started to climb up to the roof. Joe and Madge and Kiku followed him, shouting for him to come back. But Walt was too angry to listen. When he got to the roof, he grabbed the creature's swishing tail by its hair and yanked hard. The head at the end of the tail looked up at Walt and snarled.

"They never should have sent *chill*-drun to do a

grown-up's job," she spat. "You'll die like the rest of your vermin kin!" Then the tail snapped back and forth fast and knocked Walt off the roof of the ferry and into the water.

✶　✶　✶

Kiku watched Walt fall in the water. She was going to help him, but then she saw Joe and Madge run to the edge of the dock and pull him out of the water. When she turned back, she found herself face-to-face with the horrible head at the end of the amphisbaena's tail.

"Hello, sister," it hissed. "Nice to see you again."

"I'm not your sister," Kiku said, but inside her head, she heard Morgaine's voice. *She is our sister, and that might be our best chance to stop her. Bargain with her.*

But what do I have to offer?

Yourself.

Kiku was about to say she didn't understand, but Belisent was rearing back her head, about to strike. Below them, a group of schoolgirls in navy uniforms huddled together screaming and crying. *Wait*, Kiku thought, *I recognize those uniforms!*

Her school, Spence, had chosen today for a field trip to the Statue of Liberty. One of the girls, Trina van der Hoek, was pointing toward Kiku and shouting something in another girl's ear.

"Ssssee," Belisent hissed, "the common people don't

appreciate us. You don't belong with them. You belong with me."

And then Kiku *did* understand. Belisent was lonely. For all these hundreds of years, she'd plotted her revenge on the descendents of Camelot because she'd been ousted from its gates. She pretended to hate everyone because it was too painful to admit she didn't want to be alone anymore.

"Yes," Kiku said, looking into the monster's yellow eyes. "We do belong together. I'll go with you if you just leave my frien—these people—alone."

Belisent's face hovered above her, swaying with the rocking of the boat and the swish of the monster's tail. "It's a trick," she snarled, baring a mouthful of sharp teeth.

"No," Kiku said, looking down at Trina van der Hoek and Gertrude Pillager clutching each other. "I'm tired of trying to fit in where I don't belong. I'll go with you."

A long forked tongue slid out of her mouth and flicked over her reptilian lips. "Hmmmm . . ." Belisent hummed, looking down at the troop of schoolgirls. "Are these the *chill*-drun who have been taunting you?"

"Yes," Kiku admitted.

"Well, then, prove your loyalty to me by punishing them."

Kiku stared at Belisent and then down at her schoolmates. They stared back at her, goggle-eyed and terrified. *This is what they expect of me*, she thought angrily, *that I really am a monster.*

"How?" Kiku asked.

"You have more power than the others," Belisent said. "You can do more than become invisible. You have all the power of the witch Morgaine."

Is that true? she asked the voice in her head.

Yes, but . . .

Kiku let the anger build inside her. It felt like electricity fizzing through her veins. All she had to do was let it go. She looked down at the girls huddled together. Trina van der Hoek, who had called her a squinty-eyed Jap, and Gertrude Pillager, who had spilled yellow paint all over her. But then she looked past them and saw Madge and Walt and Joe standing together on the dock, Walt dripping from his dunk in the harbor, Madge's red hair flying wild in the wind, Joe staring at her with his steady eyes.

Those girls may see you as a monster, but your friends don't.

And then she knew what she had to do.

She let all the anger bubble to the surface—and turned it on Belisent. A wave of pure energy poured out of her and hit the monster. She saw the surprised look in both sets of eyes and then Belisent was falling back off the ferry. The girls on the boat clapped and cheered. Kiku felt something lift in her chest. But then Belisent righted herself in the air and lashed her tail at Kiku.

"You'll be sorry, girl," she spat, and then she launched herself into the air and began flying toward Kiku's friends.

*   *   *

Joe saw Belisent coming and pushed Madge and Walt to the ground. He felt the heat of the flames singe his hair and his back. When he looked up, he saw Belisent raking the ground with flames. Tourists jumped into the harbor to quench their burning clothes. *She'll kill them all,* Joe thought, but then she was flying up, climbing toward the top of the statue. She could kill more people by destroying the statue.

"We have to stop her!" Madge yelled, scrambling out from under Joe and getting to her feet.

Walt grabbed Madge's hand and ran toward the entrance to the statue.

Joe got to his feet and looked around for Kiku. She had climbed down from the ferry and a couple of schoolgirls were clambering around her, hugging her and slapping her on the back, but she broke free and ran toward Joe.

"Where are Madge and Walt?" she shouted.

"They've gone into the statue," he said. "to stop Belisent from destroying it."

Kiku looked up, shading her eyes to follow Belisent's

progress. The monster was winging past Liberty's face, belching flames into the windows of the crown. Joe heard the screams of the tourists who had been caught in there. Men and women were leaping from the windows to get away from the flames.

"No!" Kiku screamed as a man fell burning into the harbor. "We have to get up there and stop her." Kiku began running toward the statue, but Joe stood staring at the harbor, where the man had plunged to his death. He was staring at all the ships and remembering something Billie had told him about the city. *The great city at the mouth of the Hudson*, he had called it, and then explained what made New York City so important.

It has the best harbor. Ships come from all over the world and then all the goods they bring go up the Hudson River and then travel west on the Erie Canal to the rest of the country, and all the things made in the whole country are shipped back down to the harbor and out to the rest of the world.

Joe could see it in his head: a great network of men and women and the things they would make—food and uniforms and guns and tanks—all traveling through New York Harbor and out to Europe where the war was being waged.

But what if nothing moved through the harbor? What if it was plugged up like a bottle with a cork in it?

Joe looked up at the statue of the proud woman. She reminded him of the powerful clanswomen who led his people, who appointed the chiefs and held the names of all the children in their baskets.

She reminded him of his own *Tóta*, who had given him his name—

But now the proud woman was shaking. Belisent was gripping the lady's torch and was rocking her back and forth, loosening the statue from its base. She was trying to topple her into the harbor, where she would crash into the big ships that surrounded her. Who knew how much destruction it would cause, how many lives would be lost, and what damage it might do to the harbor itself? It would take years to clean up the mess, and in the meantime the war would rage on in Europe. Joe remembered the visions he'd had when he'd touched the gas canister—the millions who would be herded into gas chambers to die, the millions more who would die if the war went on.

He looked back at Kiku. "Yes," he said, "we have to stop her even if it's the last thing we do."

*   *   *

The last time Madge had visited the statue, it had taken an hour to climb the crowded stairs, but now they were racing up the stairs, taking two at a time. As she ran, Madge found herself picturing the green-robed woman they were inside. She remembered what her mother had said the day she'd brought her to Battery Park to see the statue: *Always remember you come from women who know their own minds, and that you're just as strong.*

But then her mother had died, and she'd wondered how strong she, or any of them, could be if a little thing like a blood clot could strike them down. And suddenly she didn't feel very strong anymore. She slowed, slumped against the wall.

"What's wrong?" Walt asked.

"I-I need to rest a moment."

Walt stared at her and then looked up as Joe and Kiku came running up the stairs.

"She's headed to the torch," Joe shouted. "She's going to topple the statue and take out the whole harbor."

"That will cripple the US's war effort," Walt said, his face pale as he looked down at Madge. "We have to go back down and then up the stairs to the torch."

"Go on without me," she said.

Walt looked aghast at her but then turned to follow Joe and Kiku. Madge couldn't look at him anymore, so she turned to look out one of the crown's windows. She could see the harbor spreading out far below. It would be very, very far to fall if Belisent was able to topple the statue. She leaned for a moment against the cool curved metal wall, her forehead pressed against the inside of the statue's forehead.

Please let me be strong, she said to herself. And then

aloud, "Please let me be the girl my mother thought I was."

The coolness of the metal felt good, like her mother's hand on her brow when she had a fever. And then she did feel a hand on her brow. She opened her eyes and saw Miss Lake, only she was wearing a long gown and her hair was longer. "You are strongest when you're together," she told Madge. "When you lead the others, they give you their strength and you give them yours." Then she vanished.

Madge lifted her head and looked up at the torch. Belisent was perched on it, rocking it back and forth. The whole statue was trembling. She could feel it beginning to rock on its foundation. If she let her friends face Belisent alone, they would all die.

"No," she said aloud, "I won't let that happen."

She raced back down and then up the stairs to the torch, feeling strong now, feeling like herself. The Amazing Magical Madge, ring-a-levio leader and jacks champion of Our Lady of Perpetual Help. When she reached the top, she saw that Walt and Joe and Kiku were standing at the door leading out onto the balcony that encircled the torch. There was a sign that said CLOSED TO THE PUBLIC on the door and heavy chains. Walt was trying to pull the chains apart. Madge laid her hand on his and took Kiku's hand and Kiku grabbed Joe's hand. Instantly, Walt was able to pull the chains apart. They burst out onto the narrow walkway. Belisent was hanging on to the torch, her claws sunk into its base, her tail wrapped twice around the balcony to steady her grip. When she saw them in the doorway, her tail-head laughed while the beast-head hissed fire. Madge smelled burning hair and heard Kiku yelp.

Madge edged past her friends. She tried not to look down at the harbor where the tiny boats looked like the toys the twins played with in their bath. Each of those ships carried thousands of men, men who were ready to fight for their country. How much damage would the statue do as it fell in the crowded harbor? How many ships would it take out? How many lives would it end? All of that was unfathomable to Madge, but she knew that watching the Lady fall would be like watching her mother fall all over again. Tears stung her eyes and were whipped by the cold biting wind.

"What can we do?" Kiku shouted over the roar of the wind.

"Let's rush her!" Walt cried.

"If we all do it together, maybe we can unbalance her long enough to take her down to the water," Joe said.

And take us all down with her, Madge thought. She looked at her friends and saw that they were ready to do it. They would give up their own lives to save the spirit of the city. That's what they had always done—sacrificed themselves. And suddenly it made her angry. *Not this time! There has to be another way—*

"Hey," Madge said, "remember when we all brought Boris to life?"

"What?" Kiku said, looking at her as if she were crazy. "You did that."

"No, I didn't. I couldn't do it alone. We were all holding hands." She reached out and grabbed Kiku's hand.

"But it didn't work when we held hands before," Kiku said as she took Joe's hand.

"We have to remember what we were thinking about in the Great Hall," Madge said. "Remember? You asked us all to picture ourselves floating, so I thought about walking into the ocean holding my parents' hands. What did you think about, Walt?" She took Walt's hand as she asked.

"I was riding the carousel before the war," Walt said.

"I was in my favorite painting, floating in the clouds," Kiku said.

"I was remembering how alone I'd felt when I first came to the city," Joe said as he grabbed Walt's hand, "and then how good it felt that I wasn't anymore." The second their circle was complete, Madge felt a pulse of power. "Keep thinking all that," she said. Then she looked down into the face of Lady Liberty. "Please," she whispered. "Help us."

Through her tear-blurred eyes, she thought she saw those grave, serious eyes stir.

They *were* stirring. They blinked and then looked up at Madge.

The eyes were no longer the blank metal of tarnished copper; they were the blue of the Lady of the Lake's eyes, of her mother's eyes. They regarded Madge first with studied calm, but then the giant brow creased with anger. Suddenly the balcony shuddered violently and plunged downward. Had Belisent finally toppled the statue? Kiku and Joe screamed and clung to the railing. Joe was shouting something in Madge's ear, urging her to go back inside the torch, but Madge couldn't take her eyes off the Lady's. She was no longer standing on the top of the Statue of Liberty; she was in the kitchen of the tenement apartment on Fifth Avenue and Seventy-Third Street in Bay Ridge, Brooklyn. She could smell the oatmeal cooking and see the back of her mother's head as she leaned over the pot to stir it. It was the moment before her mother fell to the floor. The moment she always came back to, wishing she could make it different—

And now she could.

Her mother turned and said, her blue eyes locked on Madge's, "I know."

Madge blinked, and she was back on the torch, clinging to the frail balcony. Liberty had lowered her arm so that the torch was level with her eyes. She looked at Madge, those eyes full of the same knowing as her mother's eyes, then she switched her gaze to Belisent, who was trying to get her claws unhooked from the base and her tail unwrapped from the balcony. The tail-head got stuck, though, between the railings, where it began to scream piteously.

"Please don't hurt me! I was only trying to protect

my son. You're a mother—surely you can understand!" But even as the tail-head was pleading, Madge saw that the beast-head was opening its mouth wide to devour them.

The Lady saw it, too. She pursed her lips, as if about to shush her, and blew. The stream of air, smelling of copper and saltwater, rushed past Madge, hit Belisent full on, and ignited the torch. Belisent, unable to free herself from the torch, went up in flames. She struggled to get free, claws skittering against metal, both heads shrieking. When she finally got herself free, her wings were too damaged to fly.

She began to fall.

Madge saw the terror in the monster's eyes and, before she could think about it, reached out her hand. "Grab on!" she shouted. She was leaning over the railing, but the others held on to her so she wouldn't fall. She could feel the power they had together. Enough power to save a monster from itself. For a moment she thought Belisent would grab her hand. The beast-head's eyes locked on hers imploringly. It stretched out a claw, but then the tail-head lashed forward and bit its own claw, hissing, "We don't need anyone else!"

And that's how it fell, twisted in a knot of its own making.

Kiku, Walt, and Joe watched to see if she would come back up, but Madge turned back to the Lady. A tear had fallen from her wide somber eye, streaking her pale-green cheek. Madge dug a handkerchief out of her pocket and reached up to wipe it away.

"I'm sorry," she said, repeating the words she'd told her mother.

The Lady didn't speak, but in her eyes Madge saw all the love she had seen in her mother's eyes, and knew it had always been there, and that the piece of herself that had broken that day had finally healed.

33

AULD LANG SYNE

AFTERWARD, A FEW dozen sightseers claimed to
have seen the Statue of Liberty swat a fire-breathing,
two-headed dragon into the harbor, but these reports
were dismissed by the newspapers as hysterics caused
by a county fair stunt pilot who had gotten lost. Private
First Class Tony DeAngelo, on board a ship bound for
Europe, though, always maintained that he had seen the
Statue of Liberty move her arm.

"Look, boys!" he cried to his fellow crewmates on
deck. "The Lady's waving us good-bye!" He wrote to his
new wife, Jean, about it, but the censor removed the line
as he had been ordered to by his superior in the Military
Intelligence Division. Jean McGuckin DeAngelo would
have dismissed the idea of a moving statue as so much
malarkey anyway, as she did all of her niece's attempts
to explain why she'd missed three days of school. As she
told that sweet old fellow Dr. Bean on Christmas Day at
his swank mansion up in Riverdale, "I guess I'd better

take a firmer hand with Madge from here on out."

"Oh," Dr. Bean replied, "I don't think Madge will give you any more trouble." He pointed to where Madge sat with Frankie and the twins under the Christmas tree. She was helping set up a toy castle that Frankie had found under the tree "from Santa." Walt, that nice boy from Brooklyn whom Madge had struck up a friendship with, was helping the twins line up a bunch of toy knights and explaining how a catapult worked. Madge looked happier than she had since before her mother died. And why not? Things were finally looking up for the poor girl. A week ago, Madge's father had shown up at the apartment. His clothes were old and worn and smelly, but they didn't smell of liquor, and his eyes were clear. He told Madge and Jean he hadn't had a drink since the night he'd met Madge in Central Park (she'd have to talk to Madge about wandering around the park at night!). He said he'd found a job as a night security guard at the Metropolitan Museum and rented a little apartment up in Washington Heights. He'd applied to get back custody of Frankie and the twins. Would Madge want to come live with them?

"Boy would I!" Madge had cried. Then she had looked sheepishly at Jean. "Not that it hasn't been swell staying here, Aunt Jean."

Her niece had looked so much like her sister in that moment that she'd had to pretend she spotted a crumb on the counter until she was able to tell her that it was all right by her if she went to live with her father and brothers. Now she turned to Dr. Bean and said, "You know, I think you're right. Madge has done a lot of growing up in the last few weeks."

✣　✣　✣

Joe also felt happier than he had since . . . well, since he'd left his home to go to the Mush Hole.

"I went home to talk to my parents and grandmother about it and they said they wanted us to go to Fieldston," he told Madge. "Miss Lake says the school is very different from the Mush Hole. We can speak our own language— in fact, there's a teacher there who wants us to help with a class on Mohawk culture—we can go home for holidays, our parents can visit, and . . ." Joe looked over Madge's head to where Kiku and Jeanette were seated at the piano, paging through sheet music.

"You'll be near your new friends," Madge said, grinning. "I hear Kiku's father has been cleared of any suspicion." Mr. Akiyama was sitting on the couch, arguing with her father about the Dodgers' chances to win the World Series.

"Yeah," Joe said. "They'll be allowed to stay in their home, but her mother's still stuck in Japan. It's not going to be easy for her while the country's at war."

"No," Madge said, "I don't suppose it's going to be easy for anyone for the next few years. . . ." She paused and pointed to the doorway where Dr. Bean and Miss Lake were standing, waving at them. "I think they want us to come with them. I bet they're going to give us our presents! I'll let Walt know. Why don't you go tell Kiku?" As Joe watched Madge leave, he looked around the room—at Madge's aunt Jean, whose eyes were rimmed with red, at Walt's cousin Ralph in a new army uniform, and finally at Walt, who was supervising an attack on the toy castle walls. He was just a boy playing with toy soldiers, but suddenly Joe felt cold, as if a draft had blown through the cheery firelit room. If the war went on five more years, he and Walt would be old enough to enlist! And somehow he didn't imagine Walt would wait that long. His folks were still in France. That was the one trick Dr. Bean hadn't been able to pull off. The new Walt—the one who'd faced down Mordred and Belisent and risked his life to save the city—wouldn't be content to wait around to save them. Joe knew he himself wouldn't.

✫ ✫ ✫

When Joe came over to tell Kiku that Dr. Bean and Miss Lake wanted them to follow them, his sister Jeanette looked up and said, "Okay, Sose Tehsakóhnhes, but you'd better get back before dinner. I'm not waiting for you to start."

When they were in the hallway, Kiku repeated the

words, sounding out the syllables. "Zohseh DEH-saw-GÓHN-hes? What does that mean?"

"Sose means Joseph, and the rest is my Mohawk name," he told her. "The name my *Tóta* gave me."

"Uh huh," Kiku said. "I guessed *that*. But what does it mean? Jeanette was explaining that your grandmother gave you your names based on what you were like, so . . ." Kiku arched her eyebrow.

Joe looked embarrassed. "I guess I was always trying to take care of Jeanette when she was born. It means: 'he protects them.'"

"Oh!" Kiku said, her eyes widening. "That . . . that suits you. Say it for me again."

Joe repeated the name three times while Kiku said it after him, both of them standing in the hall, looking into each other's eyes. For some reason that Kiku couldn't identify, they both suddenly blushed and looked away from each other. "Um . . . I just have to powder my nose," Kiku said, "you go on."

She took out the new compact Madge had given her for Christmas and applied powder until the pink in her cheeks subsided. *What was that about?* she wondered. They'd only been repeating Joe's name . . . *Tehsakóhnhes*, she said softly to herself now . . . but suddenly it had seemed as if they had been saying something else, as if they were telling each other a secret. Or as if they were really seeing each other for the first time. But that was silly. It was just Joe and they were old friends by now.

When she snapped shut the compact, she saw she was standing in front of a pretty watercolor of fairies dancing in a circle. Why, it looked like an original William Blake! She recognized it from her art history class. It was William Blake's illustration for *A Midsummer Night's Dream*. The man and woman on the left-hand side were Oberon and Titania, king and queen of the fairies, and the pointy-eared man dancing in the middle, with hands flung up and a wreath on his head and a mischievous smile, was Puck.

Only now that she looked at it more closely, she thought Puck looked sort of familiar.

"What's wrong?" asked Walt, who'd come up next to her.

"Does this look like . . ." But then she realized Walt had never met Sir Peter Bricklebank, and anyway, the idea was absurd. Just because she'd met the real Merlin and the real Lady of the Lake didn't mean she'd met the real Puck.

It was true that, to his knowledge, Walt had never met Sir Peter Bricklebank, but he had met a man who looked an awful lot like the dancing man in the painting. It had been two years ago on his first visit to the Metropolitan Museum. He had come on a school field trip, but because he didn't know enough English to trust himself talking to his classmates, he had wandered away from his class. He'd been standing in front of a landscape painting that reminded him of home when he heard someone sigh.

He turned to find a strange, spindly man in a tweed suit and lavender cravat, leaning on a goat's-head walking stick. "I miss my home, too," the strange man said. "We are fellow exiles."

Walt had been too surprised to ask how the strange man knew he'd lost his home. Instead he had blurted out, "It's not my home I miss, it's my parents."

"Oh!" The man had turned his elfin face to study Walt. "That *is* bad. We must see what can be done about that. . . ." And then he had wandered off, swinging his walking stick and talking to himself.

Crazy, Walt had concluded, but he'd come to the museum every Sunday after that in the faint hope that the man would reappear with some plan to bring his parents over from Europe. Eventually he had forgotten about the strange man and found other distractions and comforts in the museum—in its ancient artifacts that had outlasted plagues and wars, in paintings that captured lost places and faces of long-gone people, in every creation that shouted or whispered "I was here! Remember me!"

And eventually coming to the museum had led to meeting Joe and Kiku and Madge and Miss Lake . . . and Dr. Bean, who had drawn him aside earlier to tell him he knew where his parents were and he had a plan for getting them out.

So in a way, he had the funny old man to thank.

"Thank you," he said to the dancing man in the picture.

As he turned to find the others, he thought he heard the echo of laughter.

⋆　⋆　⋆

Miss Lake ushered Madge and the others into an octagonal room at the base of a tower that overlooked the river. Madge thought she'd had enough of towers to last a lifetime, but this one looked pretty cozy, with a cheery fire burning in a grate, comfy chairs, books lining the walls, and a big desk covered with papers and teacups and quill pens. She really should get the doc to hire her as an assistant; she'd have this mess sorted in a trice. There was also a big cardboard folder covered with swirly lines and tied together with a ribbon on top of the desk.

"That's my Christmas present to Dash," Miss Lake said when she saw Madge looking at it. "Just some boring old drawings. I think you'll like your presents better."

She handed each of them a little cardboard box, covered with those same swirly lines and tied with ribbon. Madge opened hers, tucking the ribbon in her pocket to save for later. Inside was a little enamel pin shaped like a shield, quartered, with four symbols inside it: a cup, a sword, a crown, and a wave.

"You are truly Knights of the Kelmsbury," Dr. Bean said while Miss Lake pinned the shield on each of them.

"Does this mean we get to keep the powers we got?" Walt asked, his face glowing in the firelight.

"You'll always have some of the power you've been given," Miss Lake said. "Joe will understand languages, Kiku will be able to move unnoticed wherever she wants to go, Walt will be exceptionally strong, and Madge . . . Madge will always be able to bring out the best in all of you. You'll have to watch to make sure you are always using your gifts to good purpose, or they will prey on you. But they will fade into exceptional talents, not supernatural ones, unless . . ."

"Unless what?" Kiku had asked.

"Unless we—or the people we love—are threatened again," Joe said. "Right?"

"Belisent might not be dead," Kiku said. "I saw a ripple in the water after she went down, like a snake slithering beneath the water—"

"And when the FBI agents took off Mordred's gas mask, they found an empty set of clothes," Walt said. "Isn't that right, Doc? They might both be alive, licking their wounds, planning their next move."

"Yes," Dr. Bean said, looking suddenly old and very tired. "But let us hope that it takes them a very long time to recover and that we can undo the harm they did. And that the war will be over and all our loved ones and families"—he looked meaningfully at Kiku and Walt—"are reunited and safe by then. In the meantime, I believe we've got a Christmas dinner to eat, which I can tell by the smells emanating from the kitchen is almost done. Shall we?"

Miss Lake held out her arm to steady Dr. Bean as he got up. *Gosh*, Madge thought, *he* is *old*. She followed the rest of them out but trailed behind them, and halfway down the hall, she doubled back to the study. She was just going to do a little tidying up so the doc would come back and find a neat desk, but when she entered the room, she went straight toward the big cardboard folder. *Boring old pictures, my foot*, Madge thought. *Sheesh, adults really are dim sometimes.*

As she opened the folder, the pages inside came sliding out, as if they had been waiting for Madge to free them. "Eep!" Madge cried, kneeling down on the floor to pick them up. "Why'd you have to go and do that? Now I'll never get them in order."

The pages looked a little like the ones from the Kelmsbury, with the same brightly colored figures and fancy borders and gold swirly lines all over. Only the paper wasn't old and the paint looked fresh. It all looked new, she thought as she shuffled the loose pages together, so Miss Lake *had* been fibbing. There must be something she didn't want them to see—but what? She looked at the page on top of the pile she'd made—and gasped when she recognized herself in her old wool coat, tam-o'-shanter, and saddle shoes standing in the Arms and Armor gallery with Walt and Joe. Why, it was a picture of when they had met for the first time. There was Mr. January—Mordred—sneaking up to the display case to steal the Kelmsbury page! Madge shuffled to the next page and saw a picture of the four of them sticking their hands in the mouth of the lion statue, and there was Walt hiding in that big sarcophagus, and Kiku walking through a forest filled with flowers, and one of Joe talking to some Egyptian guy, and one—Madge was pawing through all the pages now—of Madge walking through the Cloisters and vaulting over the wall (*Sheesh! Did I really do that?*) and a big scary picture of Belisent turning into the amphisbaena. All their adventures were here—even a picture from that vision she'd had in the Cloisters of herself and the nun—

Only in the picture it wasn't Madge talking to the nun in the cloister, but a man in a leather tunic with a crown on his head. Because that's who she'd been in the vision—Arthur. Only she hadn't told anyone that because . . . well, because that was the biggest piece of malarkey yet.

She looked down at the bottom corner of the page and saw a tiny gold monogram: **VdL**. Miss Lake had drawn the pictures, just as she had drawn the original Kelmsbury, only this time it was about the adventures of Madge and her friends. It felt funny to be part of a book (*Is my hair really that red?*) and to think of kids reading it one day. They'd think it was all made up, of course, *a bunch of malarkey*, but maybe they'd still feel a little bit of the magic.

She opened the big portfolio to put back the pages and saw that there were more pages inside. The first page showed Madge and Walt and Kiku and Joe on a big ship. That was funny; they hadn't gone on a big ship. She turned the page and saw a picture of the four of them climbing a mountain in the middle of a blizzard—

"They may not come true."

Madge turned and saw Miss Lake standing in the doorway. "They're visions of a possible future if you choose to answer the next call. I'm not sure if these things will happen, but I think you'll have a choice."

"You *think*? Don't you know?"

Miss Lake tilted her head so that the wave of silvery hair hid one eye, and she smiled. "How could I know for sure? None of the knights have ever made it this far."

"Then why have we?"

"I'm not entirely sure," Miss Lake said, "but I think it may have to do with you being children. The rivalries and jealousy that broke up Arthur, Guinevere, Lancelot, and Morgaine just weren't important to you four. Perhaps it's because the bonds we make as children are the most important ones."

"Oh," Madge said, "I can see that, but you said that was only part of the reason."

"The other part is who you are. You each had lost something so important that you needed each other very much. And so the bonds you formed with each other are stronger than any that the others have made."

"I guess that makes sense," Madge said. She looked down at the page she had turned to. It showed Walt and Kiku jumping out of a burning plane while Madge and Joe leaned out the plane door yelling, bombs exploding all around them.

"The next call will be to get Walt's parents," Madge said.

"That doesn't mean you have to—" Miss Lake began, but Madge didn't hear the rest of what she said. She was looking down at the page. Her hand was trembling. She could turn to the next page to see if Walt and Kiku had landed all right—to see what happened next—or she could toss all the pages in the fire. Part of her just wanted to be a kid again. To go to school, and be a big sister to Frankie and the twins, and goof around with her new friends.

But she knew that when the call came, she would answer it. In the meantime, though, she could smell something good coming from the living room. She closed the portfolio and walked back with Miss Lake. They found everyone gathered around the piano. Kiku was playing that song everyone sang on New Year's Eve that Madge never did really understand (just what the heck was an

"Auld Lang Syne," anyway?), but when they came to the verse—

> We two have paddled in the stream
> From noon until dinnertime,
> But seas between us broad have roared
> Since times gone by.

—Madge sang louder than anyone.

Let the seas roar as loud as they liked. Nothing was going to get between her and her friends from now on.

ACKNOWLEDGMENTS

THANK YOU TO my knight-in-shining armor agent Robin Rue and her ever-helpful squire Beth Miller of Writers House for championing this book. Thank you to my wizard of an editor Kendra Levin for shepherding it through its many shifting shapes until it reached the right one. Thank you to Janet Pascal and Laura Stiers for your careful fact-checking of many, many details, and to a whole Round Table of brave knights at Viking who brought this book to light: Nancy Brennan, Maggie Rosenthal, and especially Ken Wright.

Thanks to my ever-faithful friends Wendy Gold Rossi, Scott Silverman, and Ethel Wesdorp, for plowing through early drafts, and thanks to my family, Lee and Nora and Maggie, for listening to all my versions of this tale. Thank you to Peter Bricklebank for lending his magical name. Thanks to Sarah Alpert and Leon Husock for contributing their love of Arthurian lore, and a big special thanks to Haruko Hashimoto for reading and consulting on Japanese details.

There were many research squires involved: Matthew J. Boylan, Senior Reference Librarian of the New York Public Library, gave me a very thorough answer to my query on library hours in 1941. Valerie Phillips took me through the exhibit on Indian boarding schools at the Heard Museum in Phoenix, Arizona, that first inspired the character Joe. Elizabeth Graham's book *The Mush Hole: Life at Two Indian Residential Schools* (Waterloo, Ontario: Heffle Publishing, 1997) was an invaluable and heartbreaking guide to the history of the Mohawk Institute.

I owe a special thanks to Arnold Printup, Tribal Historian of the Saint Regis Mohawk tribe, for listening to me patiently as I described the quest I was on, sharing with me his own knowledge of the Mohawk tribe, and then referring me to Carole Marie Katsi´tsienhá:wi La France Ross (aka *Tóta*), tribal elder and Mohawk language teacher. Carole, your knowledge and generosity brought Joe to life. Your dedication to keeping your own language alive has been an inspiration. *Niáwenhkó:wa.*